F. Graham Peebles

THE
POWER
OF WATER

VOLUME ONE
Of
THE WEB BETWEEN
THE WORLDS

©**F. Graham Peebles** June 2006

All characters in this story are fictitious
and any resemblance to people
living or dead is coincidental.

Fonts
Arial, Georgia,
Lucida Handwriting
and Jokerman

Maps, Layout and
Cover Photo
River in Spate
by H. J. Peebles

This book is dedicated to those

who help to redress the balance

between too much and too little.

ABOUT THE AUTHOR

F. Graham Peebles was born in England,
moved to the northeast of Scotland
in the early 1990s,
and now lives and works
in the Scottish Borders.

For more information, please go to
www.ShapeyBeings.com

ACKNOWLEDGEMENTS

The Web between the Worlds has filled my head for a quarter of my life. Over these years, many people have listened to ideas or read different versions. I am hugely grateful to the following who are listed more or less in the order in which they started to influence the course of my life and the book's:

William and Andrew

Cilla Conway
who word processed the earliest drafts and showed me through her *Intuitive Tarot* why one of the central relationships is the way it is

Carrie, Veronica, Luci, Kenny, Jo, Max, Mo, Elaine, Margaret, Stephen, Jenny, David, Carolan, Susan, both Sues (one of whom is largely responsible for the appearance of Inika Smith) and Ruth

Hugh
who in addition to everything else has done a lot of wonderful techie stuff

CONTENTS

Part One	The Travels of Inika Smith	1
Part Two	Tenja's First Love	45
Part Three	Shadow Heart	79
Part Four	The Power of Water	153

Maps

The Western Empire	facing page 1
The Railways of the Don Basin	78
The Land between Two Rivers	152

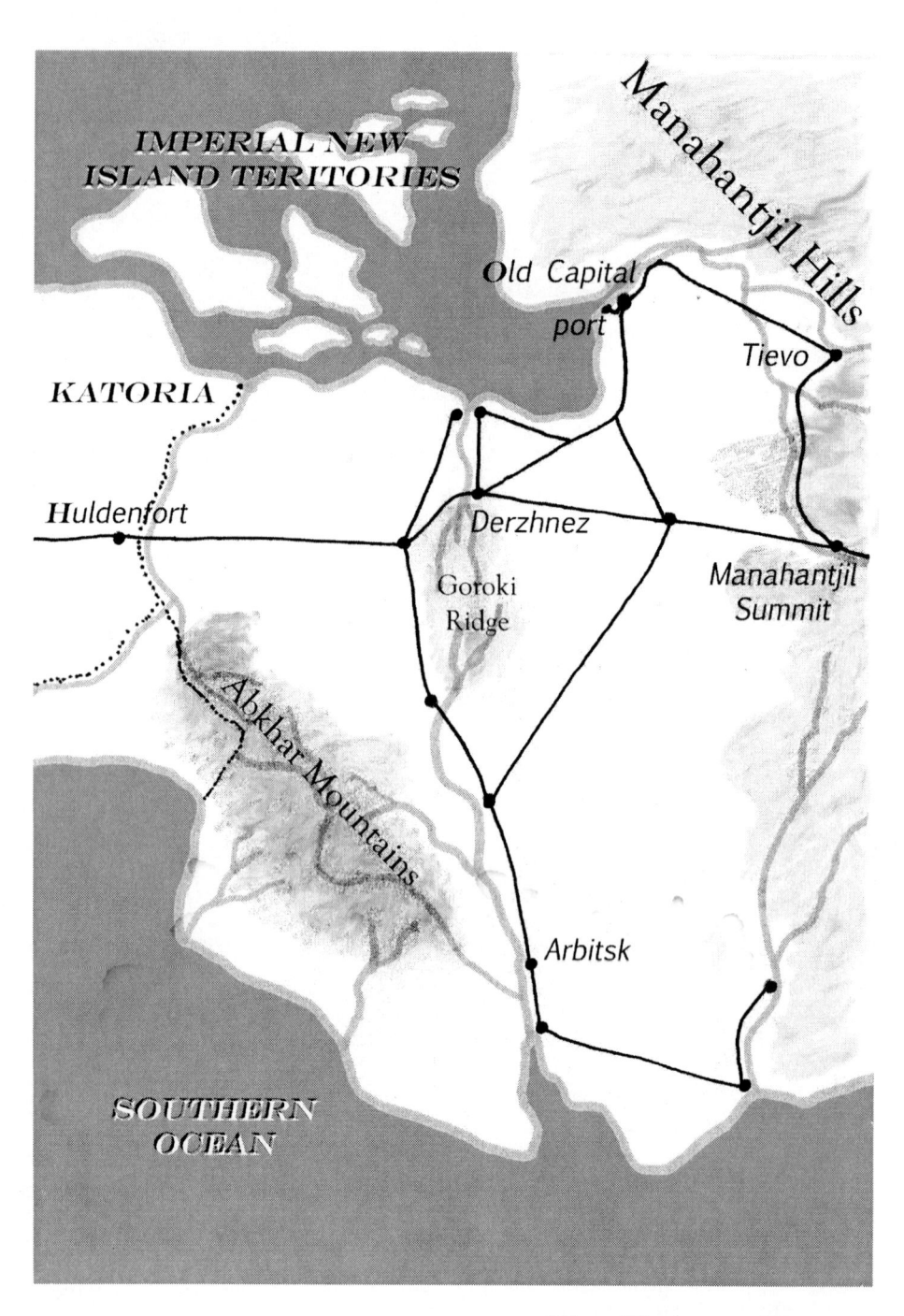

The Western Empire

PART ONE
THE TRAVELS OF INIKA SMITH
Spring 2005

1.

When Inika Smith announced her intention to visit the land of her father's birth, her family and friends were scornful.

Her mother said, "Your father started a new life when he came to this country. If he managed to forget his past, you should too."

Her husband said, "I'm not wasting my precious holiday going to a godforsaken place like that!"

Her friends said, "Why bother to go there when you can find everything on the internet?"

"You think I haven't tried? Google has over twenty-one thousand references to Alfin Pater and I've been through most of the ones in English. Not that I understood them. So far as I can make out his ideas were very controversial. Critics used to dismiss his version of physics as metaphysics but recent discoveries are proving he was right all along. I'd no idea he was so important in his field. He was just my dear old dad who happened to work in a lab rather than an office or a factory. But about his origins, nix, nada, nothing, and not knowing is driving me crazy."

"Your mother must know something," her husband said. "Ask her again."

Over the phone her mother sounded irritable, "Stop dwelling in the past and get on with the present."

"It's like the present has a huge hole where my father's half of the family should be and I wish I could fill it."

"All the wishes in the world don't change anything. I wish your father hadn't tried to mend the roof at his age, but he did. He fell off the ladder and died. The end. I had to get on with life. You must too."

"There has to be something you can tell me about him."

"No there doesn't."

"Are you ashamed or something? Ashamed you married a black man?"

"Of course not," her mother said, too fast to be convincing.

Shocked by how angry she felt, Inika dared not reply.

"The truth is," her mother began, then faltered. "No, I won't say anything about your father's family. Go and find out for yourself what they're like."

The travel agent apologised for calling Inika at work. "For some reason they won't explain, they want you to collect your visa in person."

Inika's line manager grumbled when she asked for a Thursday off because Thursday was the only day when the visa section was open.

"Do you think I want to waste a whole day going to and from London?" Inika said, "I'm beginning to wonder if the whole journey's worth the hassle."

To enter the imperial embassy in Kensington was to step back into an elegant past. The hall floor was marble, the reception desk was polished wood, the telephone was a black Bakelite monstrosity. The uniformed official's greeting was formal, and his manner was dignified as he conducted Inika to a small waiting room on the first floor.

"Her Excellency the Ambassador will join you shortly," he said. He left the room before Inika could ask why the ambassador should be concerned with a matter as minor as her visa. Suddenly nervous, she could not sit on either of the settees. She went to the window that looked out on to a small garden of gravelled paths and raised beds arranged around a fountain. She examined the pictures on the walls.

Above the fireplace hung the life-sized portrait of a moustached man whom Inika presumed to be a nineteenth century Emperor. Something in his expression, the downturn of the thin lips perhaps, or the line of the eyebrows, reminded her of her father, and the sense of loss was suddenly as raw as it had been immediately after his death. The intensity of emotion surprised her and she tried to rationalise it: this was the closest she had yet been to her father's native land. Delving into her handbag for a tissue, she turned her attention to nice safe landscapes which could have been painted in the Cotswolds.

Of more interest was the bronze bust of a woman's head and shoulders which stood on a spindly-legged table opposite the window. She gasped because she saw the same tilt of the head, the same twist of the mouth every day in the bedside photograph that her husband loved and she loathed.

The door opened to admit a tall woman with silver frosted hair, who had such a headmistressy air of authority that Inika moved away from the table almost guiltily. The woman introduced herself as Shira Marmasye. Flustered, Inika said, "I'm only here to get a visa."

Smiling, Shira Marmasye said, "Your application is hardly an ordinary one."

"Isn't it?"

"Haven't you seen the reflections of yourself in here? The man in the portrait was Count Mikel Sillin, usually called Mishka, the longest serving Minister of the Interior and as much of a reformer as a minister was allowed to be in the service of an autocrat. He was cousin to your great-grandfather. Your father was said to take after the Sillin side of his family. The bronze head is of the Countess Tenja Sillin-Vrekov, cast when she was much the age you are, and no wonder you resemble her. She was your grandmother."

"I had no idea," Inika said faintly.

"So I see. Perhaps we should sit down."

Perched politely on the edge of a settee, Shira began, "We like to keep in touch with those of our citizens who choose to live here, particularly those who were distinguished or notorious at home. Your father was born distinguished and in his early fifties he became notorious by falling passionately in love with a younger woman, a younger foreign woman, for whose sake he left everything, family, work, homeland."

The suggestion that her father and mother had been passionately in love did not fit with Inika's experience. Her energetic practical teacherish mother had always seemed exasperated by her father, who had always been rather sad.

"They never told me," Inika said.

"I'm not surprised. Your father, from the little I knew of him, was not the man to dwell on past glories, and your mother... well, she's raised you as a good solid middle class Brit. In her eyes that is what you are, but in our eyes, you are also a peculiarly well-connected subject of His Imperial Majesty's."

"Oh," said Inika. In the several fantasies she had created about her father and his line, the men had been scholars, teachers, while the women had been endowed with the artistic and musical talents that Inika would like to have inherited. Essentially though, she assumed that her father's forebears had been as bourgeois as her mother's. That they might have been aristocratic had not occurred to her and given her mother's strong opposition to the monarchy, the House of Lords and all privileges conferred by birth, she did not find it easy to adjust to her change of status.

Shira Marmasye said gently, "If you wish, I can arrange for you to meet some of your relatives."

Inika gulped before she consented.

"I shall write to your aunt, the Countess Fyedora Nallikino," Shira continued. "At eighty something, she remains a person of consequence, very much the head of the family. I cannot guarantee she will receive you, but I expect she will arrange something special for you." She drew a sheet of paper from the folder that she had brought to the meeting, "Here is your visa for this trip. Perhaps on your return you will consider taking up the dual nationality to which you are entitled." The ambassador rose gracefully to her feet before adding, "From the vantage of knowing more about your family's past and present than you do, I would like to offer a word of caution. Your visit to the Empire will be an adventure. I doubt it will be a holiday."

2.

Three weeks later, Inika left her husband asleep in bed, went by taxi to the station, caught the early train into London, then a second train out to Gatwick, where she waited somewhat fretfully for her flight to Huldenfort in Katoria. She had never travelled outside the UK on her own, and she felt almost naked without her laptop, mobile and MP3 player. For reasons Inika could not comprehend, the Empire chose to stick with the technologies of the nineteenth century and the import of electronic devices, even those intended for personal use, was prohibited. Inika tried to concentrate on her novel rather than speculate about what awaited her at her journey's end. The flight was without incident.

The international terminal at Huldenfort reeked of citrus-based cleaning fluids. The foreignness of the smell was balanced by the familiarity of the style and content of the adverts. Inika's passage through immigration and baggage reclaim was processed with rare efficiency. A taxi whisked her along the motorway to the railway station. The driver did not bother to chat.

She had to wait to board the train. Wishing for someone to talk to, she thought of her husband, but decided that the air over the Atlantic en route to America was a better place for him. Van's fretfulness in supermarkets, at traffic lights, wherever he was held in line, meant that he was not the ideal companion for these circumstances, whereas Sheila, with whom Inika had backpacked across Australia, tolerant, observant Sheila would have been perfect. Inika wondered what Sheila was doing these days.

The line shuffled forward. Inika noticed a little girl who was staring at her, so she smiled. The child's expression remained disdainful.

A group of ten or twelve Katorians, mostly men in suits, seemed to belong to the elite because they walked quickly past the queue and boarded the train.

Twenty minutes later, Inika reached the front of the queue. She held her passport, her visa and her ticket fanlike in her hand. The impassive inspector chose her visa, but as he read it a grin split his face, "My sister also has name Inika. Is usual name in Great Britain?"

"Not at all. My father gave it to me because he was born in the Empire."

"How is he named?"

"Alfin Pater."

"Pater is not our surname."

"Perhaps he changed it when he came to England. His mother's name was Tenja Sillin-Vrekov."

"You joke me!"

"No joke."

"I must tell everyone we have grandchild of Tenja and great-grandchild of Bogan Sillin-Vrekov on train."

The Katorian behind Inika coughed significantly. The guard's eyes narrowed, and his explanation to Inika of where to find her compartment seemed deliberately long-winded. Aware of the impatience behind her, Inika kept thanking him for his assistance, and was glad when he finally hefted her suitcase into the carriage.

She had a compartment to herself. One berth was already made with sheets of starched linen and a thin wool blanket which smelt of lavender. Old-fashioned as everything looked, it was also oddly familiar.

'I have come home,' she thought, sitting down on the bed.

Doors slammed, whistles shrilled, signal lights changed from red to green, the Arbitsk bound train spasmed into motion. Inika's stomach told her that lunch was probably overdue, but her eyes showed the shadows of late afternoon spread across the rows of boxlike houses and neat little gardens that were the suburbs of Huldenfort. Abruptly, the town ended and the countryside began, with rows of trimmed trees pretty with blossom, long green lines of young crops, fields of cows heavy with milk.

After a few miles, Inika was bored by the scenery. Once more, she wished for someone to chat with and thought again of Van on his way to Boston.

She noticed that this train did not go clackety-clack, clackety-clack like British trains did. It went der-der-der-de-er up a tone, then der-der-der-de-er down a tone. The repetition dulled her, until some time later she was roused from reverie or sleep by a knock at the door. "Madame Smith, if you please, tea will be served in ten minutes."

The moment she appeared in the dining car, everyone stood up to applaud her. Although it was not the raucous applause of fans at a rock concert, more the polite clapping awarded to a string quartet, it embarrassed and confused her, because she had done nothing to deserve it.

"Please," she said, looking at the sea of faces like hers and, "Thank you, thank you all very much."

She was ushered to a table set for one where the plates were china, the cutlery silver plate, the napkin monogrammed linen. A middle-aged man in a dark uniform cleared his throat as the signal for the applause to end. His speech involved so many bows in her direction that it was obviously about her, but the language was incomprehensible. She stared at her empty plate, 'I'm not going to cry, I am not going to cry.' She managed not to.

At home she was used to being one of a minority, a substantial minority in metropolitan areas, but a minority nonetheless. A male who fancied himself more than he fancied her had once called her 'dusky maiden,' which had wrecked any chance he might have had. Sometimes she liked being different, exotic, but mostly she felt like a visitor, not quite sure of the rules. Here where she looked similar to everyone else, she was actually a stranger, and ignorant of the rules.

A man wearing the kind of ill-matched clothes worn by the kind of person whose mind is busy elsewhere, patted Inika on the shoulder before sliding into the seat opposite.

"I am Marku Illino, military historian at university in Arbitsk. I will translate. What you want me to say?"

"Tell me why everyone is making so much fuss about me," she said.

Marku's eyebrows rose incredulously, "Do you truly not know?" He rattled something in his own language at which his audience clicked their tongues, and shook their heads. "They find it odd that you do not know," he explained.

"Odd or not, I don't," Inika snapped.

Marku Illino shook the folds from the napkin and showed her the embroidered monogram, "S for Sillin, V for Vrekov, do you see? Railway Company still bears your great-grandfather's name. He was great man and we wish to honour you because you are his descent. If we embarrass you we are apologetic."

"Oh," said Inika. Her cheeks felt hot. "No need to apologise to me, I apologise to you for my ignorance. My mother is English you see."

"So you need English remedy. Tea."

While they waited for the tea to arrive, Marku translated for Inika the greetings and good wishes of the passengers who filed past their table. She smiled until her cheeks ached, touched by the friendliness which was contrary to her expectations. It had not occurred to her to question the accuracy of the British press which portrayed the Empire's people as dour and xenophobic because they did not encourage tourism or otherwise engage with the rest of the world.

"Goody goody," said Marku when he saw the plate of teatime confectionary that the waiters brought for Inika. "My favourites." Helping himself to the most appetising of the cakes, Marku continued with his mouth full, "If you like I give you informations about Count Bogan Sillin-Vrekov."

At a nod from Inika, he launched into a lecture.

To understand Bogan Sillin-Vrekov, it was imperative to realise how unusual his background was. He was born in imperial year 555. (Inika tried to translate this into anno domini and came up with 1860 or thereabouts.) As his parents were nobles, it might be assumed that he was a typical child of his class. That he was not was due to his grandfather, Sev, who was born into the peasant class in the late 490s.

"Sixty per cent of imperial subjects are peasants still today," Marku declaimed. "Not like here," he waved a dismissive hand at the fields beyond the window. "Farming is business here. They kill soil with heavy machines and 'cides for bugs and weeds. Soil needs attention. Soil needs love. In empire we give our soil much attention, and it gives us most all we need. Today to be born peasant is good. When peasant Sev born, it was not so good."

Marku went into a complicated explanation of land ownership, from which Inika understood that all the land except the Heartlands - where the Heartlands were and why they were exceptional remained vague – belonged to the emperors, who rewarded their favourites with titles and the rights to live on and to keep the revenues from designated estates. Usually these estates were passed from father to son as though they were family property, but at any time emperors could, and the most vindictive ones did, reclaim imperial property. With land came the peasants who worked it. Most landowning families regarded the peasants as their property though in law they belonged to the land they worked, therefore to the emperors. When land changed ownership, the peasants did too.

Most nobles treated their peasants on a par with their horses, providing sufficient food and accommodation to keep them fit for work. Some were crueller, some kinder. Sev was fortunate to have been born on the estate of a baron of comparatively modest means but sincere faith. The baron chose to nurture talent where he spotted it among the sons of his workers. The sculptor Brak Senabin whose works can be seen in the Imperial Museum of Fine Art was one of his protégés. Sev was another, and the first of Sev's talents to manifest was boat building. The second was his ability to make money.

Even in an agrarian economy such as the empire's, foods and goods need to be transported from one place to another, and in Sev's day, most were moved via rivers and canals. Sev designed and built barges that carried greater bulk for less cost. In his will, the childless baron bequeathed the whole fleet to Sev, who took his patron's surname as a mark of respect. The Vrekov Barge Company was born.

Nobody knows quite how Sev found his way into the company of Countess Verja Sillin. Sure, by the 520s, he had become wealthy, but according to the social code of the time, a peasant-born trader like him should never have met an unmarried noblewoman, yet meet they did and she determined to wed him. When her father forbade her to have any contact with Sev, she appealed to the emperor.

People born in democracies do not easily understand the arbitrary nature of emperors whose powers are limited only by conscience and the wisdom and tenacity of their advisers. Fyedor the Third was a complex unpredictable man, able to listen to the dictates of his faith, willing to be persuaded by his councillors, equally capable of acts of generosity and of meanness.

Fyedor the Third chose to be generous to Verja, granting her petition on condition that her new husband affix her name to his. Sev Vrekov became Sev Sillin-Vrekov. Some years later Fyedor granted him the title of count.

Marku paused to ask for a fresh pot of tea. Inika realised that she and Marku were the only passengers left in the dining car and that the two waiters were laying the tables for dinner.

"Perhaps we should go," she suggested, but Marku shook his head, "They are our servants. They like us to be happy. I am very happy to tell you history."

Three of Sev and Verja's children survived into adulthood, two daughters, whom Sev adored, and one son, with whom Sev quarrelled on every subject except marriage. Sev more than approved of his son's choice of bride, he loved his daughter-by-marriage as if she had been the child of his body and was devastated when she was killed along with her husband in a coach accident. Sev and Verja took their four-year-old orphaned grandson into their household.

Where the son had been a disappointment, the grandson was a delight. As Bogan was inquisitive, and good with his hands, Sev provided a practical education that gave the lad's inventiveness free rein. Encouraged by Bogan, whose fascination with steam power began at the age of eleven or twelve, Sev hired Katorian engineers to build steam engines for his fleet of barges, which improved the service immeasurably because steam is superior to sail against the current. The next stage was to develop steam power for use on land.

Again with the assistance of foreign experts, Bogan and Sev built a railway to provide a direct route from Verja's estate to the port that Sev had established on the Olnish river. That first line was over two hundred miles long and most of the land it passed through was farmed by members of the Sillin family.

Sev invited the emperor to ride aboard the train. Fyedor enjoyed himself hugely. Every boy wants to be an engine driver! Bogan asked permission to build railways across the empire. Fyedor refused. Bogan insisted. Fyedor lost his temper and ordered Bogan to dismantle the Sillin line. Bogan refused. Fyedor punished him by sending him off on – how do you call it in English? - a wild goose chase.

Not that Bogan had to chase geese. No. He had to chase and kill one specimen of each predator in the empire. Fox, wolf, wolverine, weasel, stoat, sea eagle, bar-tailed eagle, osprey, buzzard, red falcon, wild cat, Aleksandrov's cat, and so on and so forth up to mountain lion and all types of bear - brown, Nanson's, honey and great white. The collection can still be seen in the Imperial Museum of Natural History.

By sending Bogan into the wilds, the emperor killed his friendship with Sev who had been the closest to an intimate that Fyedor had allowed himself. The last years of the emperor's reign, which included the war years, were lonely and bitter.

The train slowed and drew into a floodlit empty station.

"We have reached Katorian side of border. Don't be nervous. Their customs officials will not bother us. They are glad to see our backs," Marku said. Inika was tempted to tell him that she was too experienced a traveller to be nervous. Marku meant to be kind, and maybe only sounded patronising when he spoke English.

A pair of black-uniformed black-capped officers entered the dining car. They were tall young men, and Inika saw them as both handsome and chilling. She looked at Marku for reassurance and was surprised by the change in his expression. While he had been enthusing to her about Sev and Bogan, his face had been open. Now his features were blank and cold.

"Why do you dislike them?" Inika asked. Although she spoke quietly, Marku shushed her, "Later."

The Katorians passed the table without a word, but Inika felt the contempt with which they saw and did not see her. In their wake, the man who had made the speech brought a bottle and three glasses. He sat down next to Marku, pulled the cork, and half-filled the glasses. Much to Inika's puzzlement neither man picked up his glass.

Neither of them said anything. They sat and waited in silence, so she did too.

With a jerk, the train moved forward. Marku grunted. The other man wiped his forehead with a spotted handkerchief. They stared out into the night. The sound of the train changed.

"We are on bridge," Marku muttered, before he grinned, "Now we are home." Grasping Inika's hand, he lifted his glass in a toast. "Welcome to empire."

The older man drank too, while Inika swirled the viscous liquid round in the glass, reluctant to try it because she did not usually drink spirits. She did not usually arrive in her fatherland. The brandy burned.

The train stopped again to allow the imperial customs to board. As soon as they reached the dining car, Marku called to them, "This lady is descended from Count Bogan."

Without reading her passport or visa, the officials smiled, shook her hand, welcomed her to their country and moved on. Gradually, the dining car filled up with imperial subjects eager to celebrate their return home. Marku, and consequently Inika, had to toast each of them. The brandy bottle emptied and the rest of the evening passed in a festive blur.

3.

Der-der-der-de-er (up a tone) der-der-der-de-er (down a tone) der-der-der-de-er (up a tone) der-der-der-de-er (down a tone). Inika's head thumped in time with the rattle of the train. After a while she realised that the room was swaying because it really was in motion. She lifted a corner of the cloth blind. It was still dark outside. Der-der-der-de-er (up a tone) der-der-der-de-er (down a tone) der-der-der-de-er (up a tone) der-der-der-de-er (down a tone). She did not think she could get back to sleep.

She woke again to voices and the rattle of crockery in the corridor. As her door was unlocked and opened, she pulled the sheet up to her chin. A uniformed woman, whom Inika did not remember from the night before, placed a tray on the table by the window and retreated without a word. Inika was grateful for her tact.

When she summoned the energy to sit up, she found a tall glass of red berry juice, presumably high in vitamin C, a glass bottle of water, a pot of tea and a round of plain brown toast. The train crew obviously expected their passengers to be fragile.

Once she started to feel better, Inika raised the blind and, blinking at the brightness, had her first sight of the empire. Its fields, hedges, clumps of trees, and streams looked much the same as rural England's, or perhaps more like John Constable's England, for the roads were rutted tracks, and, charmingly, the transport was horse-drawn. Inika saw the idyll of imperial country life, rather than the hard labour.

The morning passed. The sensible breakfast, the constant rhythm of the wheels over the track and the pleasant landscape eased her hangover. Feeling hungry she decided to see what else was available.

In the dining car, she was served with more of the sharp tasting juice, a fresh pot of green tea, boiled eggs and toast, but no coffee, because it was not grown in the empire. With a cheerful "Good morning my dear," Marku sank into the seat opposite her. Unfairly, for he must have drunk twice as much brandy as she had, he appeared no more dishevelled than he had the night before.

"Last night you asked why we do not like Katorians. Now is time for answer." Before Inika could protest he embarked upon another lecture, "In imperial year 587, on First Summer's Eve…"

"587?" Inika interrupted. "That's over a century ago."

"We have long memories. Besides they have yet to apologise."

The well-dressed woman who was sitting at the opposite table said, "Excuse me, I hear what you say and I have to tell you there is Katorian delegation aboard this very train. They come to discuss how to phrase their apology."

"How difficult is it to say sorry?" Marku scoffed.

"Very," said the woman. "The big question is how they say sorry to Shoshanu people whom they extinguished. Shoshanu are dear to my heart because I come from Abkhar mountains." She peered out of the window. "It is not clear today, but later you will be able to see them on horizon. They are very beautiful. Shoshanu lived there long before my family, family of Marmasye, arrived. They were good friends to us, but for reasons too long to explain, bad enemies of Spears of K'fir. During Western War, Spears exterminated Shoshanu like vermin… It is not easy to forgive genocide." She wiped her mouth with her napkin.

"Spears of K'fir," Inika tested the words, "They sound medieval, like the Knights Templar."

"Spears are older," Marku said.

"And they still exist," Madame Marmasye said. "They grow strong again. They offer young men strength and certainty, and young men who feel weak and unsure in Katoria's changing society gladly accept Spears' discipline and peculiar form of worship."

"Are the Spears of K'fir a kind of warrior sect?"

"Exactly so," Marku agreed. Stroking his moustache he lowered his voice confidentially, "I want to share something with you ladies that I cannot share with my colleagues in university. They are jealous because I am first imperial historian allowed to study records in Katoria Central Library. I cannot tell them that what I have read does not fit our history... Every child of empire is taught at school that Western War started because of argument about coalmines in Imperial New island Territories. Is it not so Madame?"

The woman at the opposite table nodded in confirmation.

Marku said, "I have to say our lessons are wrong. I found evidence in primary sources dated to their equivalent of imperial year 574 which shows that Spears of K'fir already plan capture of Abkhar and destruction of Shoshanu. This is three years before coal was discovered under New Island Territories. In those days coal was important to economy of both countries, so dispute about coal is understandable cause of war. War for possession of Abkhar mountains is not understandable. Abkhar does not hide coal or diamonds or gold or anything of value."

"Nothing of economic value," Madame Marmasye said quietly.

Without noticing her stress on the word economic, Marku continued, "At last we go back to sure fact, invasion on First Summer's Eve 587. First Summer's Eve is big party when we eat and drink and dance and tell traditional stories, like how our people were first brought to this land from the deserts of the south by Third Incarnation of Most Holy Incarnate, how Woldymer Chrezdonow was inspired by Third and Eleventh Incarnations to conquer whole empire, how Emperor Nikolka Second built his city of seven rings. We have not forgotten stories. We are nation of storytellers.

"Familiar with how we celebrate, the Katorians attacked when border guards in Second Army were drunk after First Summer's party. Invasion was complete surprise. Second Army was wiped out in early hours of war. Expecting our peasants to welcome them as liberators from tyrannical masters, Katorians marched east. Peasants did not welcome them - they love their land too much, but resistance with pitchforks was useless against guns. Katorian army marched over western plains hundreds of miles into imperial territory until they reached high bank of Derzhnez river in north and Goroki ridge in midlands.

"Emperor Fyedor Third had ordered defence of river and ridge and his forces managed to hold Katorian armies there for days, then weeks and months. It became war of attrition and very terrible. Total number of dead will never be counted but definitely it reaches three millions, possibly four, with deaths from disease as many as deaths from wounds. Our troops had not proper equipment. At worst time in summer and early autumn 587, five soldiers shared three pairs of boots and two rifles. They fought in shifts and took what weapons they could from dead. By winter that year every family west of Manahantjils had lost one man at least. No good news came from front to capital, just lists of dead and wounded and demands for more - more food, more bullets, more uniforms, more bandages, more anaesthetic. And man in charge of delivering more of everything was Acting Marshal Count Bogan Sillin-Vrekov, because he was expert in distribution of merchandise. What Count Bogan did was not glamorous work, only necessary, and once he was in charge, soldiers at front began to get guns. Part of why we held Goroki and Derzhnez was your great-grandfather, and another part was decision of Spears of K'fir to head south to capture Abkhar in spring 588.

"And this is next discovery I find deep in archives of Huldenfort library. Katorian High Command did not expect Spears to invade Abkhar mountains. There is whole folder of letters of complaint which Spears never answer. They are more loyal to their head priest, so-called Voice of K'fir, than to commander-in-chief or to Katorian government. Eventually Katorian government arrested and tortured Voice of K'fir, so Spears attacked main part of Katorian army."

"Enter my hero," Madame said with a reminiscent smile "Erwan Filowet, at twenty-five youngest imperial colonel, handsome, brave."

"And lucky," Marku interrupted. "Most lucky that he did not get shot by our side. He stole supplies from other units but emperor forgave his crimes because his exploits boosted morale."

She continued as if Marku had not mentioned criminality, "On a raid behind enemy lines, Filowet acquired maps marked where Spears of K'fir intended to attack main Katorian army, and therefore where we needed to attack them both. Early in 589 we launched our counter-offensive and slowly, at cost of many lives on both sides, we pushed Katorians back to their own frontier."

Throughout her account Marku was shaking his head, "That is popular version. Actual truth is very different. I have read in Emperor Fyedor's diary how he had late night meeting with Count Bogan where they discussed four-pronged attack on Katorian armies. They decided to credit Filowet for this plan, because real source was not believable. I suspect something mystical, such as prophetic dream."

Madame Marmasye sniffed, "Prophetic dream indeed!" With a curt farewell she left her table.

Marku said sadly, "See how she treats me because I tell different and truer version of history. My colleagues will be worse. If I have access to Sillin-Vrekov records, maybe I find Count Bogan's account of conversation with Emperor Fyedor."

Inika promised to ask her aunt about the family archive. "If I meet her," she added, "If she likes me."

4.

Twenty-two hours after leaving Huldenfort, the train drew into Arbitsk, the Empire's capital. Despite the length of his lectures, Inika was reluctant to part from Marku. She promised to stay in contact with him and felt apprehensive as he bid her farewell.

"Madame Smith?" someone asked as she stepped on to the platform. "I am your guide and translator for your stay in Arbitsk." She introduced herself as Malinina Ostjena ("Call me Lina. It's easier than Malinina or Madame Ostjena") explained that the band, the soldiers and the red carpet were not on the station forecourt for Inika's benefit ("If you ask me it is better they welcome you than the Katorian delegation") and started to explain the changes that had been made to Inika's itinerary ("You will spend only tonight in Arbitsk. This evening instead of going to the imperial opera, which I think you would have enjoyed very much, I have been told to take you to a special gathering of the tribes, which I do not think is interesting.")

In English complete with the definite and indefinite articles, Lina talked throughout the journey from the station to the hotel about the superiority of the tour that she had organised for Inika over the new one arranged by the Nallikino family. Inika would like to have asked about their vehicle, which appeared to be electrically powered, about the buildings they passed, which were an interesting mixture of wood brick and stone, about the absence of advertising which rendered the streets colourless and drab, but she could not break into Lina's flow.

Once she had registered at the hotel, Inika announced that she wanted a shower. Lina said, "You'll have to be quick or else we'll be late for our appointment at the Imperial Museum of Natural History."

The museum was a short walk from the hotel. Inika wanted to linger on the wide pavements, to window shop, to people watch. Lina hurried her along. Inika was tempted to say, "Whose holiday is this?"

Through the glass of the museum's revolving door, Inika could see the row of staff ready to greet her. Save for Lina behind her, she would have revolved back out into the street. The museum's director, a dumpy harassed woman, gave a speech which Lina translated, to the effect that it was a great privilege to welcome Inika, especially as she was the first member of her family to see the Sillin-Vrekov collection in its new display. Despite her annoyance with her aunt, or whichever of her relatives had rearranged her tour, Inika made a short but fairly graceful reply. Afterwards she was conducted into the exhibition hall where the predators shot by her great-grandfather were shown against reconstructions of their natural habitats.

There was a white bear that was actually yellowish and a silver fox from the northern tundra, a wolf, a wolverine, three types of bear and several members of the weasel family from the forests east of the Manahantjil hills, five different species of cat, six types of eagle, including one almost the size of a condor from the Abkhar mountains, and too many sorts of owl to count. Some of the individual specimens were moth-eaten, and all were rather sad, for Inika could not understand the mentality of the hunter who killed for the pleasure of killing. She did not mention her disapproval, but the director, seeming to sense it, said in careful English, "Count Bogan did not enjoy to kill. He had to obey emperor. He learned to love these animals. See over here the pictures he drew to go with the articles he wrote for *Huntsman's Quarterly* magazine."

The pencil sketches beneath the glass of the display cases gave Inika a new sense of Count Bogan. He became more than the man from Marku's stories who might or might not have had a prophetic dream. The almost cartoon simplicity of his drawings revealed the tenderness with which he had observed these creatures and the regret with which he destroyed them. She was suddenly grateful to whoever had sent her here.

From the museum, she was taken by car to a restaurant in the main square. Lina talked about why this restaurant was not the one she would have chosen, until Inika said, "Please, be quiet!"

Lina's jaw closed with an audible click. She sulked for the rest of the ride.

At the restaurant, they were met by a very suave elderly gentleman attired in black tie and tails, whose pleasure it was to escort two lovely young ladies to dinner. He could well have been a retired diplomat because he talked knowledgably and humorously of Europe and the States without mentioning what he had done there. Treated like a favoured grandchild, Inika soon forgot that her clothes did not match the grandness of her surroundings and began to enjoy herself.

Only water was served with the four courses of dinner, but after the dessert came brandy.

"This is thirty year old Mardestiniak," the former diplomat said. "Infinitely superior to the rotgut you drank yesterday."

"How do you know I drank rotgut?"

"Because everybody does. It is tradition."

Inika sipped and savoured the Mardestiniak. Her world acquired a warm glow, which was fractured only when Lina announced, "It is time to go."

Their host said, "Don't fuss! We are going from imperial time into tribal time, which means that whenever we arrive will be precisely the right time."

Outside the restaurant, a chauffeur opened the doors of a stately Mercedes. Inika thought how easily she could become accustomed to luxury. As the car purred along almost empty streets, her host explained that they were headed for the park, where for the first time in hundreds of years the tribes had gathered. "We must consider ourselves fortunate to witness their dance tonight. It is more than entertainment, it is the first in a series of ceremonies that are intended to bring peace between the spirits of the Shoshanu and their killers."

"Before the conquest," Lina said making Inika think irrelevantly of 1066, "The area around here was home to the Minagwe, who were nomadic cattle herders, and worshippers of a warrior goddess called Mu-Mumis. Maybe their religion provoked them to battle, maybe they were just bad-tempered. Their fights and feuds were vicious, yet every year round midwinter, they laid down their weapons to dance and drink and trade the meat, cheeses, hides, horns of their cattle for the goods made by other tribes. The Shoshanu came down from their mountains with the honey and mead that the Minagwe prized, the Miacharnay came from the north with furs and precious metals and gemstones, the Elantsim came from the Manahantjils with clothes and blankets that they made from the wool of their sheep, and the Descharnay brought the horses that were the ancestors of our Western Reds."

"Don't forget the Fofani," their host added, "They came from what is now Katoria to sell their daughters for whatever small trinkets girls were worth. Who knows how many years the tribes met here until we Settlers arrived and behaved as conquerors usually do? We put an end to the midwinter fair and reduced the tribes to a shadow of their former selves. When the Minagwe and the Descharnay resisted, we killed the men and forced the women, and would have done the same to the Fofani except that the Katorian Knights did it first. The Miacharnay survived because we hated the cold and dark of the tundra too much to bother to trap furry animals. The Shoshanu were another exception, because the Lord Stewards of Abkhar protected them for five hundred years."

"Until the Spears of K'fir murdered them," Inika said. "I travelled from Katoria with Professor Illino. He told me about the Shoshanu."

"And much much more, I'll wager." Her host was obviously acquainted with Marku.

Walking through the park gates Inika was reminded of childhood bonfire nights, for men, women and children in outlandish costumes and half-masks milled around a huge bonfire, chatting, laughing, eating, drinking. Flames licked at the dark sky.

Instead of the sudden explosions of fireworks, the background noise was the constant rhythm of drums. They grew so insistent that the crowd gradually moved away from the bonfire to regroup in a wide circle round the musicians. Nobody, not even Inika's Settler companions, could keep still as the drummers worked their audience higher and higher.

A masked and painted dancer leapt into the centre of the circle, moving with the grace and menace of a tiger. His was not the slightly self-conscious performance of Morris dancers in a pub forecourt; it was the deliberate evocation of such power that a girl screamed in genuine fear when the tiger pretended to pounce on her. Inika shrank into herself in the hope that she would not be noticed, and was relieved when with a last snarl the dancer left the stage.

Smoothly the drummers changed rhythm and were joined by a trio who scraped light quick music out of stringed instruments unlike any Inika had heard or seen. A dozen or so light-skinned women wearing long brown dresses danced into the arena arm in arm. Inika supposed that the series of delicate little runs, back steps and bows to left and right was pretty enough, but the dance lacked the tiger's impact. Just as she wondered how much longer it would last, the dullness was ripped by an animal bellow. The dancing women squealed and scattered to the edges of the crowd while two men adorned with antlers burst into the circle. In stylised steps, they moved around each other probing for weakness before they charged into battle. Their antlers clashed. The loser pulled himself free and slunk away while the victor paid court to one of the women in a ritual dance full of beauty and arrogance. When he too left the arena the women pulled others from the audience to join them.

"Oh no not me," Inika said to the tribal who had chosen her.

"Oh yes you," said her host pushing her forward. "It is an insult to refuse."

Thrusting her handbag at Lina, Inika let herself be drawn into the dance. Eight running steps forward, two slow steps back, sway right, no, left first, then right, sixteen running steps, four steps back, sway left, sway right. 'Shoes are no good. Kick them off. Dance barefoot on the earth. Feels weird.' Eight running steps... 'Feels good. Sway left, sway right.

'Omigod!' In the stags' roars Inika heard the rage of thwarted desire. Along with the other hinds, she shrieked and tried to hide. The crowd would not let her through. As the stags fought, she watched them critically, sensing that one was stronger than the other. She willed him to win, was glad when he did, and was not altogether pleased when he chose to pay court to another. Then she linked hands with two new women and resumed the females' dance around the edge of the arena.

Eight running steps, two small steps back, sway left, sway right, sixteen running steps, four steps back, sway left, sway right, repeat over and over and over.

The stags bellowed for the third time, and alone of the women Inika stood her ground. She wanted the winning stag to come to her. It was her turn, her time, and the stag man, proud in his victory, danced for her, only for her. He danced the fury and lust of the rutting stag, he danced the pride of the man, and the vulnerability of offering his love to the lady. Inika tried to tell herself this was performance, not personal, but she could not deny the eroticism, or the intimacy.

Too soon it was over. She was hand in hand with women, and she wished their touch could have been the stag's, no, Van's, and while her feet performed the steps, she thought of him with longing and disappointment that at no time in their years together had he offered her the gift of his masculinity in a way that made her feel so utterly feminine.

The fourth time the stag fight was real. The contender was taller, his antlers were longer, sharper. He lunged at his opponent, stabbed, drew blood. In the confusion, while some of the women tended to the wounded stag man, the interloper grabbed Inika and rubbed up against her. He smelled of sweat and rotten teeth. He asserted his power over her, the power of men over women. Laughing at the impotence of her anger, he pushed her to the ground as suddenly as he had seized her.

Kind women picked her up, commiserated in languages she did not understand, led her back to Lina, who had the tact to remain silent, to hold her until she stopped shivering, to guide her back to the waiting car.

Alone in her hotel bed, Inika could not sleep. She replayed the dance again and again. Van should have been there tonight to protect her, but if he had been there she would not have joined the dance, would not have received the stag man's gift. It had been so exquisite, so precious, that it was worth the nastiness. Or was it?

5.

In the morning, Lina was already at the breakfast table. "More changes to your itinerary," she announced, dramatically tearing a piece of paper to shreds. "This morning we do not have the tour of the city with a visit to the viewpoint, which is a pity because today the air is so clear the Abkhar mountains look about twenty miles away. Instead, you are summoned to meet the elders of the Miacharnay people."

The solitary woman who waited for them beside the smouldering ashes of the bonfire had the dignity of a queen, though she was no taller than the average eleven-year-old girl. Without so much as a handshake, she subjected both Inika and Lina to inspection, seeming to stare round rather than at them. Reaching up, she clapped her hands over Lina's head and with little brushing motions dusted down the air from her shoulders to feet. Surveying her from head to toe once more, she grunted in satisfaction and turned her attention to Inika, who required far more cleaning and polishing of the air around her. Inika felt nothing except increasingly foolish.

Eventually, the old woman was satisfied. She straightened up and beckoned them to follow her away from the bonfire, away from the earth circle that the dancers had flattened the night before, along the paths of the park to where a man sat on a bench beside a small stream. He stood up when he heard them approach. He was slightly built, fair-haired, pale-eyed, and without the antlered headdress, so insignificant that Inika would not have noticed him in a street, yet his dance had shown her that of all the men of her acquaintance, he was the most certain of what it meant to be a man.

In Canadian accented English he greeted them, commented on the pleasantness of the morning, explained that Hoguya wished them to hear a traditional story. The three women arranged themselves on the bench while he sat cross-legged on the ground opposite them, closed his eyes and spoke.

In the Early Days when the world was new, our Mother and Father were happy to play together all day long and their matings were joyous. The Mother gave birth to the first Miacharnay and to the creatures that live on, over and under the earth and sea.

Those of us who are married know how it is. At the beginning when love is new, we must be with our beloved every moment of the day – and night. Then love grows so much part of us we hardly notice if our beloved is by our side or not, and we may be irritable or argumentative. Perhaps our beloved dares to answer back when we are cross, and we find ourselves in the middle of a row without being quite sure how we got there. If we are fortunate, a wise elder helps us to see we are fighting about nothing, and the kisses and the cuddles of our reconciliation may lead to the making of a child.

Imagine how it must have been for the Great White Bears who were supposed to be the eldest and wisest and were too proud to ask their children to help them back to harmony. Their arguments raged for days, months even, and perhaps during the last of these massive upheavals, the Great White Father forced himself upon the Mother. Afterwards, ashamed, he went to the ends of the sky lest he be tempted to hurt her again, and she hid in her lair deep below the ground, where in due course she gave birth to one brown cub.

We have learned nothing good can be born out of rage, but in those days the Mother was not so wise. She let him suckle. The moment he ventured out of her den, he began to make mischief, so that the other animals complained about him, but to every accusation they brought against him, his Mother replied, 'His behaviour is in the nature of bears.' Even when Otter said, 'He kills fish and does not eat them. He kills for the pleasure of killing,' the Great White Mother stood by her son. 'His behaviour is in the nature of bears.'

'Of foxes maybe, not bears,' said Otter before she dived neatly into the river. The comparison forced the Mother to face the truth about her wayward child.

She found him scrabbling in the earth. Soil flew from his front paws.

'This is Fox's den. Why do you destroy it?' she asked.

'I behave as it is my nature to behave,' he answered.

'That is no excuse,' she said. 'You must change your behaviour.'

'I am what I am. I cannot change.'

'Then you must leave.'

He stopped digging and sat back on his haunches. He was already half-grown. 'Make me leave,' he said.

She launched herself upon him and he fought back. They rolled in the dirt, they bit and scratched, and he was too strong for her, and he meant to kill her, because she had dared to reprove him. At last, hurt and bloodied, she managed to free herself from his hold and she limped away from him.

Slowly, she went in search of the Great White Father who was hunting on the tundra at the end of the sky. When he saw her wounds, he forgot their last quarrel. 'Who did this to you?' he demanded.

'Your son.'

'I'll kill him.'

Full of wrath, the Great White Father Bear pursued his brown son, who was not yet strong enough to fight. The cub ran south and his father followed him, mile after mile after mile, day after day after day, relentless, remorseless.

At last the brown cub reached the edge of the forest and somehow the trees gave him a new strength. He had found a land that was his to defend. He turned to face his father.

Either he had grown on the long hunt south or his father had shrunk, for now they were of a height with each other. The Great White Father looked his son in the eye and for the first time in his long life he saw the possibility of defeat. He backed away, saying, 'I'll leave the forests to you if you'll leave the tundra to your mother and me.'

'The forests suit me better but I'm not one for promises. I'll come back when I want to because I don't think you or my mother can stop me.'

The brown cub flourished in the forests and his family grew and grew. He was too busy to return to the tundra, but from time to time his descendants have come, and unfortunately they have behaved in accord with their forefather's nature.

"Thank you for the story. Thank Hoguya too," Lina said at the end. "The moral is clear."

'Not to me,' Inika thought.

The man said, "In usual interpretations, the brown cub represents Woldymer Chrezdonow and his family the Settler people, but in this case Hoguya means him to be the father of the Kohantsi. Ever have the Kohantsi, the so-called People of the Deer, troubled us and the Nilenish and the Que-Que, and in former times the Settler people too. Last night was the continuation of an old rivalry, and I regret that in honouring you I exposed you to a Kohantsi's mischief."

"Mischief," Inika repeated, "Mischief?"

"From his point of view, mischief. From your point of view, violation, the worst of what men can do to women, whereas I meant the best."

"I know," Inika said, feeling the heat rise up her neck into her cheeks. However uncomfortable this conversation was, she was not prepared to stop it. "Why me? Why honour me?"

"For you, for your ancestry, both," the man smiled up at her. Again she was aware of his ease with his masculinity, which added to her discomfort as a woman and as a wife, yet she persisted, "For Tenja or for Bogan?"

"For Tenja yes, but not for her father, not for the Heedless Hunter. For Tenja, and especially for her mother Fahra who was one of us."

While she had had company forced upon her, Inika had longed to be alone. Now that she had a compartment to herself on the night train to Manahantjil Summit, she wanted someone to talk to, for choice the Miacharnay who was both the stag dancer and an associate professor of anthropology at a Canadian university. He had given her his email, for a future in which she wanted to discuss the rewards and difficulties of life lived between two cultures. She did not think that she would contact him. His dance and the ease with which he had read her mind had been too intimate for comfort.

"You've had too much information too fast, but if you don't hear it from us, you'll hear the Settler version of how Fahra and Bogan met, the one in which she bewitched him," he had said with the tinge of bitterness with which a minority sometimes speaks of the majority. She had asked for the more complex Miacharnay story.

The tale he had told fizzed and crackled with the weirdness of the northern lights, and the weirdest aspect of it was the simultaneous closeness and distance. Two individuals separated her and Fahra. Her father and Tenja gave her the closeness, but three distinct cultures made the divide almost unbridgeable. How could she, raised in the safety of north Oxford, begin to understand the childhood that Fahra had endured in almost constant motion behind the herds of caribou?

As if the cold and dark of deep winter and eight weeks of unbroken daylight and consequent sleep deprivation in summer had not been enough to contend with, Fahra was born with a twin, which in tribal tradition determined that she and her brother Maro had to be trained from infancy to walk the worlds.

"To walk the worlds?" Inika had queried.

"Don't tell me you think this is the only reality!"

"Pretty much yes."

"Please try to suspend your disbelief for the rest of the story, because what she and the tribe believed dictated what happened when Bogan the Heedless Hunter trapped them between two laws.

"On the one hand, the Miacharnay are forbidden to harm the polar bears because they are the original Mother and Father's representatives in this the ordinary world. On the other hand, they are bound to help anyone who asks for help because cooperation is key to survival in the harsh environment of the far north. Knowing this, the Miacharnay are careful what help they ask for, but not so Count Bogan Sillin-Vrekov. By the time he came to the tundra at the start of the summer, the only creatures left on his list of predators were the white bear and the mountain lion, and as ignorant of the habits of the white bear as he was of our culture, he asked Fahra's clan to show him where to find one.

"The elders were aghast, because they could not refuse his request, yet the person who hurt a bear was bound to be expelled from the tribe. Expulsion amounts to a death sentence because nobody can survive alone for long up there. Having just completed their initiation rituals, Fahra and Maro were present at the council of elders in order to listen and learn. They were supposed to be too young to speak, but speak they did. Fahra offered to help the Settler and Maro insisted that he accompany her. When asked why, Fahra confessed that in her dreams and musings she was married to Bogan, and Maro admitted that in his dreams and musings, he lavished the care he was meant to devote to caribou on horses. The elders decided that under their Miacharnay skins, the twins had Settler hearts and that the clan was well rid of them. I have to say that nowadays we Miacharnay have a better understanding of Fahra's purpose and we are ashamed we accused her of disloyalty.

"She and Maro led Bogan to the river. The spring run of red-eyed salmon had already attracted other hunters - eagles and ospreys recently returned from the softer southern winter, wolves and bears newly woken from hibernation, lean, hungry, ready for the feast. From the top of the riverbank, the humans watched the display below them, the deadly efficiency of talons, beaks and teeth and especially the claws of a huge dominant male, known to the Miacharnay as the Old One. The shingle around his huge feet was littered with half-eaten carcasses that the cheekiest of the gulls fought for. At the sight of people, the birds wheeled away, but the great bear ignored them. The fur around his mouth was already stained red, yet he still wanted more food. He snatched a fish, ripped out the tastiest flesh, swallowed and lunged into the river once more, while the hunters prepared to kill him.

"Bogan dropped down the steep bank to land on the shingle upwind of the Old One. Hardly breathing, he sought inside his mind for the alignment between hunter and hunted that made for the perfect kill. When he had reached the place of effortless inevitability, he fired, but what should have been a lethal shot merely grazed the bear. Angry rather than hurt, the Old One turned on his attacker faster than anyone believed possible.

"Scoured by floodwater, the riverbank was concave. Unable to gain a foothold, Bogan could not escape. He could smell the fresh blood and fish on the Old One's breath. Pressed against the dark earth of the bank, he held the barrel of his rifle, to use the stock as a club, the only defence he had against the power and weight of the bear. A poor defence. Expecting to die, he was shocked as much as relieved by the sight of the feathers of a crossbow bolt that stuck out of the Old One's flank. The bear staggered and fell at his feet. Watching the life drain from the bear's eyes, Bogan felt no pleasure, only the certainty he would never hunt again.

"Over the next few months, as Bogan came to understand how his ignorance had forced Fahra and Maro into exile, he was too guilty to be able to hear either of them when they tried to explain how they accepted, in truth wanted, their fate. Maro was very happy to live on Bogan's estates because he was with flesh and blood horses, but Fahra was less content. She believed she was fated to marry Bogan, yet he was distant and she did not know how to draw him closer. She asked the Great White Mother for help, and like an answer to a prayer, the holy man of another faith appeared a few days later.

"On a morning that was cold for Bogan, merely bracing for Fahra, a cart deposited a visitor at the front door of the mansion. The man was a grey-haired elder clad in a blue robe and sandals. His one concession to the frosty weather was the long multi-coloured scarf wound around his neck.

"By chance, or not, depending on your belief system, Fahra was in the hall ready to greet the guest, whom she recognised from the portrait on the altar of the family chapel as the Most Holy Incarnate in His Twenty-Third Incarnation. She tried to behave with appropriate reverence but He was far too jolly to allow for seriousness, and cheerfully ignored her protests when He dragged her by the hand into the one place in the whole house from which she was banned, Bogan's private study.

"Much to her embarrassment, the Most Holy announced, 'I do love a wedding.' Bogan was bemused so the Most Holy had to explain, 'You won't find a more suitable wife you know.' Bogan was obliged to agree.

"Society, of which Count Bogan was an almost acceptable part, did not approve. That the Empire's richest bachelor had thrown himself away on a tribal woman – disgraceful! That the Most Holy Himself had performed the ceremony – well, behind the fans, 'they do say that the old man is become dotty.'"

To Inika, dotty was a mild word for a marriage contracted on the order of a so-called holy man, but she had been assured that Bogan and Fahra's marriage had been a good one, based as much on the recognition of complimentary power as on love and respect.

She lay on her bunk as the train headed north in the familiar rhythm, der-der-der-de-er (up a tone) der-der-der-de-er (down a tone). She thought about marriage and the stag man's inclusion of complimentary power as part of a good one. Her parents had not recognised their powers as complimentary. Nor had she and Van. What kind of power had the stag man meant anyway? She drifted into sleep. The train continued on its journey north.

6.

Mid-morning, she arrived at Manahantjil Summit where she had an hour's wait. She was grateful to the polite phrases that Lina had written out for her to show to the station staff who did not speak a word of English. From which platform does the train to Tievo depart please? At what time? May I have a cup of tea please?

Manahantjil Summit was set amidst long-backed hills that on a cloudy day looked as bleak as Pennines. The station was set above the town and by standing on tiptoes Inika could see over the parapet to the vast bulk of mills and the narrow streets of small houses that reminded her of photographs of northern England in the 1920s or paintings by L.S. Lowry. The wind swirled dust around her feet.

Once again she wondered why the Empire banned air travel. When she had asked the same question in the restaurant, Lina had replied fiercely, "Pollution, " while the retired diplomat had been more urbane, "Our desert cousins have a proverb, 'The mind travels at the speed of a trotting camel.' Perhaps we must be grateful for such speed as the railways allow."

The train to Tievo was Inika's first experience of a local passenger service. She hoped that it would be her last. The seats were hard, the lavatory lacked paper, her fellow travellers, peasants and factory workers at a guess, could not understand why she could not understand them. Once they were satisfied that she was either deaf or stupid because she looked too like them to be foreign, they talked across her. She conceded that the British press might have a point. Through the rain-smeared window, the scenery was the harshness of moorland.

After slow climbs and wild descents, stops and starts in the middle of nowhere, the train dropped from the hills to the plains, and the landscape and the weather both softened. By the time she reached Tievo, the evening was dry, bright and warm.

A man, some years older than her, who was wearing the blue robe and sandals of a monk, met her at the station. Before "Madame Smith I presume" or "Good afternoon" or "Hello," he said in good

English, "You're the living image of Grandmamma!" He enfolded her in a tight hug and when he finally released her, his eyes behind his spectacles were watery. "I'm sorry, I didn't mean to... no-one warned me how like her you've turned out. I loved her very much you see." He sniffed and wiped his nose on his sleeve.

Inika hardly dared to breathe. Distant nods at family occasions were the closest she came to her three English cousins. She supposed that she should have anticipated the existence of imperial cousins, but somehow Shira Marmasye's portrayal of the formidable Countess Fyedora had suggested lifelong virginity, on the basis that no man would have dared touch her. Another possibility crept into her mind. Chill ran down her spine.

"Exactly how are we related?" she asked. Fear made her sound cold.

He stepped back from her. "I apologise. I had meant to be more careful. My name is Pavl. I am your half-brother."

Later, when she and Pavl sat together by the abbey's fishponds under the sunset sky, Inika was ready to hear about her father's other family, and discovered that in addition to Pavl, she had a half-sister Nina and another half-brother Sandro.

"They are unable to meet you this time," Pavl said. "With the Katorian delegation and everything, Sandro's unable to escape from duty." Inika assumed that Sandro was in the army. "Nina is on a fieldtrip in the Okhpati marshes. She does not know you are here, and perhaps that is a good thing. Of all of us, she felt Papa's loss most keenly and your mother's abuse... I'm sorry, it is not respectful of me to speak of your mother in such terms."

"Give me honesty over respectful silence any day," Inika said grimly. Her heart thumped alarmingly at variance with the tranquillity of her surroundings. "I had too much silence at home."

Pavl said, "Do not blame either of your parents. Silence is sometimes better than dwelling on past hurts. Better still is the realisation that hurt can open your heart. What happened opened my heart and brought me to the Church, not as an avoidance of relationship, not as an escape from pain. Escape is impossible when the whole of the ordinary world is here in microcosm within the abbey walls. We monks and nuns must sift through the meanness, the pettiness, all the ugliness in the world... and in ourselves... until we find the beauty... Please sister of mine please keep this in mind as I tell you our past.

"I think Mamma learned to worry in her mother's womb... Grandmamma claimed that my, sorry, *our* father married her to make up to her family for everything they lost during the Years of Turmoil. Be that as it may, my parents loved each other as though love was part of their spiritual practice, which of course it is, but it makes me wonder how important the physical aspects of love were... Obviously they were not absent. They had Sandro Nina and me as proof...

"When Sandro was eighteen, Nina sixteen, and I thirteen, Papa failed to celebrate his fiftieth birthday. I didn't understand why he was morose when I thought he ought to be happy. I was too young to link his sadness with my mother's move to a bedroom of her own.

"A few months later, Nina brought your mother into our family."

Inika jumped in surprise, "You mean my mother has been here?"

"Of course. Three times. The last time she brought you. I remember holding you. I was very happy not to be the baby of the family any more... If this is too difficult, I can stop."

"You've started so you'd better finish... And if the world slips from under my feet like it feels it's slipping, you'll just have to catch me."

"Sit straight, breathe from deep in your belly, imagine you have weights round your ankles to hold you to the ground... There, that's easier isn't it?"

She nodded her thanks. He took her hand in his and said, "You may not value it, I don't mind... I want you to know you are in my prayers, and have been each day since I came to the abbey."

She could not say that his prayers meant nothing to her. They did not, because she had no religion, but the fact that he cared enough to pray for her moved her. She buried her face in the crook of his arm.

Once darkness fell, they moved to benches on either side of the long table in the guesthouse refectory. The light from the candle on the sideboard shone on Pavl's glasses so that Inika could not see the expression in his eyes, but his voice was kind.

"Your mother came into our household as Nina's tutor. Papa had insisted that we study English, the language of Shakespeare. Sandro and I didn't need it for our chosen careers – before the Church called me, I was set to be an engineer – and we learnt it easily, whereas poor Nina who had to pass exams in English language and literature struggled. Hence the need for a tutor, your mother, who stayed with us for the whole of a summer. We noticed how relaxed Papa was when she was near, and Mamma seemed to like her too. The problem was Nina failed the language exam. Your mother came back during the winter and that was when she and Papa decided that they could not live without each other...

"It was a terrible time. Nina failed the exam again and blamed her failure on everyone who had upset her, your mother in particular.

Mamma insisted that Papa did not abandon the family, so he spent every spare moment at the flat he rented for your mother and was like a caged lion when he had to be at home with us. Mamma pretended everything was normal because I think she expected the affair to burn itself out. Sandro distanced himself by going to study in Donsgrat, which left me comforting Mamma and Nina, avoiding Papa's moods, going to school and maturing all at the same time.

"Then Papa spent two months in England. The time he was away was like a truce - the war wasn't over but peace, even temporary peace, was wonderful. When Papa came home without your mother, Nina and I assumed they were finished, but the reality was more complicated. Your mother had sent him back to think seriously where his future lay. At the end of six months he asked Mamma for a divorce.

"Her rage exploded. She had, she screamed, behaved impeccably during the affair, forbearing, forgiving, so how dare he demand a divorce? For the first time she threw things at Papa – I remember a cup and a book - which scared Nina so much that she telephoned Grandma Tenja for advice. Grandma and Grandpa arrived as quickly as they could – they were both octogenarians and arthritic. Grandpa calmed Mamma while Grandma talked to Papa before she talked to Nina and me. Papa loved us, would not stop loving us, she said, daring us to say 'Like he stopped loving Mamma.' Of course Nina said, 'Like he stopped loving Mamma.'

"Grandma gazed up at us. Like you, she was not a tall person. She said, and I have worked to understand her words ever since, 'Perhaps leaving her is the highest expression of your father's love for your mother.'

"For months, years, after Papa left, Mamma alternated between anger and self-pity. Nina married the first man who courted her, which left me to cope with Mamma's moods alone. Just when I was due to start the engineering course at Arbitsk University, Grandpa died. Papa returned for the funeral. The problem was he brought you and your mother with him. You were three or four months old, and I was so delighted to meet you that I couldn't understand why your presence caused such an argument. Nina was the first to object, your mother took offence, Papa defended her and so on and so forth. The sequence is not important, only the result, which was a permanent rupture between your mother on one hand and Nina and Grandma Tenja on the other, and Sandro and I in the middle. On the plus side, the row marked the start of my mother's recovery. Announcing that she was cured, she went on to do all the things that parents and marriage and motherhood had stopped her doing. By the time she died, she was acknowledged as the empire's expert on Aleksandrov's Cats. I'm allergic to cats of any breed but I think what she did was brilliant.

"The minus aspect of the quarrel was the separation from you."

They stopped at that kind place.

7.

Inika slept very well in a small single bedroom in the abbey's guesthouse, and enjoyed a leisurely breakfast with the three other guests who spoke English, a teacher from Arbitsk, a black American pastor who wanted to have his crisis of faith far away from his congregation, and an ex-hippie from Morpeth whose search for a spiritual path had begun in Kathmandu.

In the middle of the morning, Pavl invited her to accompany him and half a dozen of his students on a walk to the House of Roses.

"How far is it?" Inika asked wondering which of her shoes to wear.

"I don't know in English miles... about the distance from Westminster Abbey to St. Paul's Cathedral."

"You've visited London?"

"Often until..."

"Until Dad died?"

Pavl nodded, before he realised he had caused distress. Either wisdom or inexperience with women held him back from trying to comfort her. He let her pass out of the refectory into the garden, where she sprawled on a seat and cried angry bitter tears.

After a while he came to stand near her, talking softly, "Papa and I had lunch in London once a year, as near to my birthday as we could manage, and every year he gave me the most recent photograph of you, and told me how you were doing, when you learned to read, when you learned to ride a pony, the funny things you said. He adored you, you know. He certainly took more interest in you than he had in any of us while we were growing up. The last time I saw him he apologised for neglecting us... A week or so later he broke his neck. And we couldn't even say goodbye to him, because your mother banned us from the funeral. We could have passed ourselves off as former students, we wouldn't intruded into your family, at least Sandro and I wouldn't have, I can't be completely sure that Nina would have behaved quietly..."

Memories of her father's funeral flooded back. It had been the worst day of her life, worse even than the day he died, because she had had to be strong for her mother's sake, she had been on show, she had had to stop herself crying. She still could not stand the cloying scent of lilies that had filled her nostrils while she sat in the front pew of the old stone church and listened to her father's colleagues pay tribute to his achievements. Not one of those speeches had touched on Dad as a real person. She had wanted to scream, and in her imagination her half-sister Nina did what she had been unable to do. Nina stood up in the church, Nina yelled at those desiccated academics, Nina was real. Inika began to smile.

"I'm sorry you weren't there," she said, rummaging in her handbag for a tissue.

Inika did go with Pavl and his students to the House of Roses, the private retreat of an early emperor. Strolling along the country lanes, she discovered how companionable she and Pavl could be without talk. While there was much that she longed to know, she did not want to rush or risk another upsurge of rage against either of her parents.

The students practised their English by telling her about the building's history until Inika told them that her head was swimming with facts, and they left her in peace to enjoy the gardens that gave the place its name.

On her return to the abbey she went to the choral service in the small round church. The music was surprisingly cheerful.

The next day was also sunny and warm. Inika visited the ruins of Tievo castle, the seat of the first five emperors. Her sympathies were with the one who had decamped from the castle's oppressive atmosphere to the House of Roses.

"Not surprising," Pavl commented when she told him. "We are descended from his second son."

"You're kidding!"

"Is an ancestor who was an emperor any less likely than ancestors who were kams?"

"What are kams?"

"Literally those who walk the worlds."

"Like Fahra and her brother."

"Just like them. Known in other parts of the world as shamans. Or is correct usage shamen?"

Inika had no answer.

The third day was showery. Inika spent most of the day in the guesthouse kitchen preparing lunch and supper with Sister Katerina, who had a few words of German, two monolingual monks, and Martin from Morpeth, who preferred his ashram name, Devanand. They laughed almost as hard as they worked.

After supper, Inika asked Mathieu the American and Devanand, "What is it about their faith that makes the people here so... so nice?"

"It be de power of lerve," Mathieu answered, rolling his eyes and exaggerating his Southern accent, while Devanand offered a more serious response, "They know everything's interconnected."

By the fourth day when she had to leave, Inika was beginning to feel that she belonged at the abbey. Wanting to say goodbye, she found Mathieu weeding in the vegetable garden with Devanand, who pulled some folded papers from the back pocket of his jeans.

"We thought you might like this, it's something me and Matt here worked on together, nothing heavy, just an old story about what these people believe... Look after yourself pet," he said giving her a gentle hug.

8.

To her delight, Pavl was to accompany her to the old capital where her indomitable aunt awaited her. She dared not ask him the question that worried her, "Do you think Aunt Fyedora will like me?" in case he replied in the negative.

As they walked across Tievo's town square from the abbey to the station, Pavl warned her, that despite their grandparents' efforts during the Years of Turmoil to bridge the divide between rich and poor, to make society more equal, she was about to discover that rank still had privileges.

"It's a museum piece!" she declared when she saw the gently puffing steam engine and the single coach coupled to it.

"Not at all," Pavl said, slightly offended, "Sandro goes everywhere on this train. It's kind of him to lend it to us."

Inika could not help thinking of Thomas the Tank Engine or perhaps of the naughty engine James, for this locomotive was red gold and black. The coach was also red and gold on the outside. Inside the colours were more muted. Inika was astonished by the facilities - two cubicles with proper beds, a third cubicle with bunks, a lavatory, a narrow kitchen and at the end a lounge with a desk, two armchairs, a sofa and a huge window through which passengers could watch the retreating scenery.

'This isn't happening to me,' she thought as she watched Pavl unpack the picnic that Sister Katerina had provided from the abbey kitchen. The coach lurched. They were off to the old capital.

She lay curled on the sofa gazing through the picture window. The dark ridge of the Manahantjil hills that dominated Tievo's eastern horizon faded into distance as the train 'owned by my half-brother' as she kept reminding herself, headed north and west across the plains, through woods so huge that maybe they counted as forests, past fields where labourers stopped work to watch the quaint old locomotive, in and out of villages where children waved, over streams and rivers.

Pavl touched her arm, pointed at a large dilapidated house. "That used to belong to Mikel Sillin, who was chief councillor to the last of the autocrats. It's sad to see it run down, but I suppose the Sillins have other things to spend their money on. Most of the land from here to the coast was once either Sillin or Sillin-Vrekov."

"What about the peasants?"

"Nowadays they farm cooperatively. Back then they belonged to the land, and the land belonged to the Sillins and the Sillin-Vrekovs until Grandma lost her estates and the peasants like the land passed to the Tereshkovs."

"How did she lose them?"

"During the Years of Turmoil I think, or maybe before. I'm useless at family history. You're better off hearing it from Aunt Fyedora. She's the expert. She met most of the people involved, interrogated them in fact, and wrote down what they told her."

"She sounds ferocious."

"She is," Pavl agreed, which did not help Inika relax. Feeling as nervous as an interviewee, she had little appetite for lunch. For something else to think about, she asked Pavl, "What does Sandro do?"

"I don't suppose you have an equivalent in Britain. I'm sure your Queen and your Prime Minister have confidential advisers, Nancy Reagan had her astrologer, and I read that the Dalai Lama consulted the state oracle for the right time to leave Lhasa... That's the sort of role Sandro plays, a mixture of futurologist and hand holder to the most senior members of government. Papa did it before Sandro, Grandpa before that... It's why there was such a fuss when Papa moved to Britain. The Council of Ministers wanted to prosecute him for dereliction of duty as if he had absented himself from the army without permission. Grandpa had to prove that he and Papa and Sandro offer their services on a voluntary rather than contractual basis."

Thoughtfully, Inika cracked and peeled a hard-boiled egg. 'Peculiarly well-connected' was how the Empire's representative in London had described her, and the more Inika heard, the more peculiar her connections appeared - one half-brother who wore skirts, another who told fortunes, a sister who studied bog insects, a grandmother who was careless with her lands, a great-grandmother who was a shaman, or perhaps a shawoman. Giggles bubbled in

Inika's throat at the thought of telling her mother about her crazy relations.

Then she remembered that her mother already knew, perhaps not about Pavl's robes or Nina's bugs, but definitely about the rest. Her mother knew and had said precisely nothing. Inika pushed her plate away from her with such force that eggshells and breadcrumbs scattered over the carpet.

"What's the matter?" Pavl asked on his knees to pick up the bits.

"Mum," Inika said through clenched teeth.

"Ah," said Pavl, adding a moment later, "I'm glad I'm not a parent, being an uncle's much more fun."

Inika discovered that she had one niece, three nephews and a great-nephew, for Nina had produced her daughter within a year of her early marriage, and the daughter had also had her firstborn before the age of twenty. Long before Pavl ran out of things to say about the next generation, Inika was confused. For quite a while, she watched the scenery.

When she was tired of her thoughts, she unfolded the sheets of handwritten paper that Devanand had given her and read.

VRONJA'S TESTIMONY

Late night in my parents' walled garden, the latest I'd been allowed to stay up. Torch flames flickered on the faces of my mother, father, older brothers, aunts, uncles, cousins and servants and their shiny eyes were fixed upon the man in the white robe. Nobody cared I was there too, bored and tired and thirsty.

The man said, "The divine spark that is eternal is in everyone and everything that lives, and because the spark is eternal everyone and everything that lives, dies and is reborn..." So what? I wanted a drink, cool sherbet on a hot summer night.

He stopped talking. He looked straight at me. He said, "I know what you'd like," and with his own hands he picked up the jug from the table beside him and poured some of the juice into a glass. I couldn't believe my eyes, a man doing the work of a servant! "Better than nothing, if not quite what you wanted," he said holding the glass out to me. Mother intervened, "You should be in bed, not bothering the holy man."

"Let her come to me," he said so firmly that Mother stood back. I went to him and as he placed a hand on my head I felt his warmth spread through me and I knew that I would love him forever.

Two days before my wedding I went to the house where the holy man lived. "I must see him."

"He's at his prayers," the women said.

"I have to see him."

"He's at his prayers and besides there are fifty people in the courtyard already."

"But I love him."

"So do we all."

Then he appeared. One moment he was not there, the next he was. I could not tell whence he came, just that he was beside me, and that my heart was full. He beckoned so I followed him into a room empty of furniture apart from simple mats and stools, but full of the radiance of his being.

"You wished to talk with me."

"Now I'm here I don't know what to say."

"You are to be married soon, but you do not want to be a wife."

"I'd rather be a servant to you. I love you, not the man my family want me to marry." The words fell out of my mouth.

"See the divinity manifest in me also manifest in your husband, in your family, in the children you will bear, in everything around you and in your own self. Hold true to all you know in your heart. That is how you serve me." He placed his hand on the crown of my head and again I felt the warmth flow from him. "Go home and prepare for your wedding."

At the door I turned and asked, "Will I ever see you again?" but I did not immediately understand his answer, "No and yes, yes and no."

In time I understood. The night I was first joined to my husband, four soldiers took the holy man from his house. They dragged him through the streets of the city and out of the gates, and in the desert sands beyond they beat him to death. His body was found by a merchant the next morning.

The holy man's devotees were afraid of reprisals. They met furtively, they mourned, they argued, because some believed that he would be reborn, some doubted. My husband went to the temple and repented of his deviation from the religion of his forefathers because he worked in the city's administration and he had ambition. Towards me he was considerate. He allowed me to hold to my beliefs in the privacy of my heart, indeed I think he envied me my steadfastness.

I gave him five children, of whom four survived and grew into fine healthy youths, I ran the household as competently as I could and strove to be the best wife and most loving mother I could be, and I did not talk about the holy man who had taught that everything contained the divine spark, that everything that lived and died would be reborn, that his divinity would manifest again in a new form. As patiently as possible I waited for his promise to come true.

Years later, two of the servants whispered of a young man who was preaching in the slums. "He calls himself the Second Incarnation"

Wrapped in a plain cloak, I crept from my husband's house into the poor quarter of the city. There in a wooden shack, I met the young man, and he placed his hand on my head, and I felt for the third time the warmth of his power.

"Thank you," he said.

"You? You thank me?" I said, quavery with unshed tears.

"Of course. You have kept faith with me."

Several days later, my husband remarked, "You look cheerful."

"He's come back, the Second Incarnation."

My husband's face changed. "Stay away from him. The priests and the city authorities will not tolerate his heresy for much longer."

"You knew he was back and you did not tell me?" I was angrier than I had ever been.

"*For your own good.*"

"*For yours, you mean.*" We did not speak to each other for several days.

The authorities waited a few months, until the Second Incarnation was drawing crowds of several thousand each time he preached in public. Then they arrested him and tried him for heresy. My husband attended the trial, he had to be seen to condemn. He came home from the court and wept, his face buried in my lap. I stroked the greying hairs of his head, though I did not weep. "All that lives must die, and will be reborn. So it is with him, so it will be with him."

Next morning I went to witness the execution. The Second Incarnation needed at least one friend in the crowd. The senior priests stood on the temple steps and watched while soldiers built a massive pile of planks, which they topped with brushwood. Then they poured huge flagons of oil on to the pyre. All the while, more and more people arrived in the city square. I was terrified when I was jostled and pushed back from the place I had chosen. Worse than the physical pressure was the assault on my sensibilities. The common folk were loud and aggressive, wanting to see someone suffer and die.

A thought came into my mind, as if spoken by another's voice, 'They are manifestations of the divine.' In the crush of angry people, I became an island of calm, and I remained at peace until the prisoner was brought out of the temple.

He was made to stand on the top step while the chief priest took the aggression of the crowd and worked it to fury. They shouted abuse at the half-naked young man who had dared to have a kinder, more tolerant belief. Somehow I was unaffected by the chief priest; I could feel what he was doing and I could feel how the love which flowed from the Second Incarnation wrapped everyone and everything in the same soft blanket, and how feeble the chief priest was and how utterly unafraid the Second was.

The soldiers hauled him to the top of the pile of logs and tied him to a stout post. The chief priest thrust a flaming brand into the heart of the pyre. The crowd screamed and yelled and stamped while the flames leaped and the brushwood crackled. For a moment the heart of the fire burnt brighter than the merciless sun overhead, as if the soul of the holy man, freed from the body it had worn, were manifest in this world.

I returned home, empty and quiet, and I waited for the return. My daughters married, decent men chosen by their father. My firstborn son joined the city's administration, my second son, a more adventurous spirit, went to work for a merchant. On his infrequent visits home, he brought exotic gifts and told stories of strange lands and barbarian tribes who knew nothing of civilised life.

In my fiftieth year, the rains did not come to the mountains; the rivers which fed the farms and the city itself shrank to muddy trickles and the crops withered under the pitiless sun. Malnourished, the city's population was vulnerable to disease. My beloved parents numbered among the dead, and I was rather ill too.

My husband, who loved me, was desperate to save me. He brought to the house a twelve-year-old boy, whom some hailed as the Third Incarnation. I'm told that the boy placed his hand on the crown of my head and prayed. I woke from feverish sleep and looked deeply into the wide brown eyes of the child. Before I could think how rude I would sound, I said, "You are a great healer, but you are not the Third."

The boy grinned like the child he still was. "No, I am not the Third. I am the Shield. You will live to meet the Third."

Some months later, my merchant son came home. He was at peace within himself. When I asked what had happened to him, he confessed, "I have found love."

"You will be married after all these years of refusing the girls your father suggests."

"She is not the kind of girl I could marry. She is only twelve but she is wise beyond her years."

"I have to meet her."

Never before had I ventured beyond the walls of my city. Once or twice I had been to the harbour, but the ocean which stretched to the northern horizon looked too large. I preferred to remain within the walls of the house and garden. Out in the deserts I felt sick; from the swaying motion of the horse litter or from inner turmoil, I could not tell. I was awed by the sea of stones and sand, and I shivered in the coldness of the nights and sweated in the heat of the days, and I marvelled that a child of my body was able not only to endure these conditions, but to enjoy them. When I remarked on how at ease he appeared, he said, "I am travelling towards my love."

At last the caravan reached its destination, a city which stood at the confluence of two rivers. It smelt like home, of sewage, of flowers, of cooked breads and meats. It was familiar, and it was strange. I was taken to stay with the sort of people I would not usually have spoken to, a baker and his wife, but once I had got used to their strange accent, I found unity with them. They had heard and accepted the message of the Third Incarnation.

Early in the morning, earlier by far than I would have wished, the baker's wife led me along narrow streets to the home of the Third's family. The girl was tall for her age, and graceful. She greeted me as if we knew each other, which of course we did. I did not need her touch in order to be sure of her identity. For hours we sat together in shared and silent harmony, which was broken only when my son arrived. His devotion shone in him and I found myself wishing that this wise girl-woman could marry him.

The way the Third looked at me reminded me of the time before my marriage when I had asked to be a servant to the First. She murmured, "And you have been a servant to us all, a faithful and beloved servant. We thank you for everything you have done and we would ask more of you in the years to come."

"Whatever you want of me, I offer, though I don't know what I have to give apart from my love."

I visited the Third Incarnation every day I stayed in the city. Sometimes we sat in silence, sometimes I listened while the Third talked to people who had not known her predecessors, and shared with them the simplicity of her *message. The peace that I experienced with the Third stayed with me on the long journey home across the desert.*

In due course, the Third came to my city, and lodged with her devotees, quietly teaching small groups. Her Shield, the boy who had healed me, was grown to manhood, and was often beside her. Eventually they were married in accordance with the rites of the official religion. This marriage caused many of the Third's followers to desert her, although she repeated gently that there was no real conflict between anything she said and the doctrines of the state priests.

Gradually the Third's following grew once more until she had thousands of adherents. My husband and the Shield talked privately many times. They were plotting something.

"I'm too old to travel," I protested when finally my husband divulged the nature of their plans. "What's more, so are you."

"She wants us to go with her, especially you, because you knew the First and the Second."

"So did you."

"Ah, but you were always loyal, whereas I ... I wavered."

Thus my husband, my son the merchant, my widowed daughter and her children and our servants and I left our house and our city and our land. We took ship upon the wild ocean. We sailed with a fleet of other ships under the direction of the Third to an empty northern land. There we settled. There we stayed.

"Is it true or is it only a story, this *Vronja's Testimony*?" Inika asked Pavl when she finished reading.

"It was carried by word of mouth from the Third Incarnation to the Eleventh. Then it was written down in the first book of teachings, *The Sayings of the Blessed Entoni*," Pavl replied.

"Is what the holy man says here at the beginning about the divine spark in everything part of your faith?"

"It is the heart of it."

"You believe in reincarnation?"

"It is more than a belief. The Most Holy demonstrates it."

"That means the divine spark that was in Dad didn't die with him and could be alive again in someone else."

Pavl nodded.

"It's easier than thinking he survives only in our genes," she said despite the lump in her throat.

9.

She stayed silent and thoughtful until the train reached what appeared to be the seashore, but was in fact the southern bank of the Olnish estuary. The northern side, some twenty miles over the water, was hidden by cloud. In places, the single railway track was squeezed between the high tide mark and reddish brown sandstone cliffs.

"We're out of our ancestral lands now and not very far from the old capital," Pavl said, and he embarked on a description of the city of seven rings. It was designed by Fyedor the Great ("Our ancestor who built the House of Roses") who died before construction could begin.

"The rings represent the layers of the Upper World in Shoshanu tradition, or perhaps Nilenish, I'm not sure. They are not complete rings, more like concentric semi-circles separated by canals. The outermost or Seventh Ring was meant to be the site of abattoirs and tanneries and the sorts of factories that stank or were liable to catch fire. By the time Grandma was born, the seventh ring was our equivalent to the mill towns of Britain's Industrial Revolution or Dickens's East End of London, an appalling dangerous place where a man of my age was old.

"The Sixth Ring is slightly better. The buildings there are stone and brick, and the wrought iron market halls are wonderful feats of engineering. The Fifth Ring is row upon row of four and five storey tenements that provide homes for craftsmen and shopkeepers and clerks, people of that sort. The Fourth Ring, where the railway terminus is, is the commercial heart of the city and where most of the government offices were. The middle classes, officials, bankers, doctors and people of that sort had apartments above the offices. The Third Ring is a long thin park dotted with buildings like the Empress Ylena Hospital and the Imperial Theatre. The imperial art collections used to be displayed here too, but they were transferred to Arbitsk when it became the capital, and their places have been taken over by the university. Our destination the Second Ring was once called the Nobles' Ring because certain titled families, such as the Boiyenabstys, the Sondlikovs, the Baranovs and of course the Sillins, had the emperor's permission to maintain houses there. Tenure depended on the emperors' whims. At one point, the Sillin-

Vrekovs were evicted in favour of the Tereshkovs, but in the wake of the Years of Turmoil, Grandma was permitted to return to her family house. These days, Aunt Fyedora has a flat in the house for her and her three full-time staff, while the rest is open to the public.

"Finally there is the First Ring, which is actually an island composed of a single slab of stone. Long before the Settlers conquered the empire, the local tribe, who according to the archaeologists, lived in round houses, ornamented their pottery with wave patterns, cultivated grains and ate shellfish, dedicated the island to their goddess. She must have been the gentle dreamy sort because she forbade bloodshed at her sacred place. She wasn't much help to her people against the Descharnays, who defeated them and rededicated the island shrine to Mu-Mumis. Despite Mu-Mumis's bloodthirstiness, the ban on bloodshed remained. It is still enforced. The monks of the Monastery of the Most Holy Incarnate cannot eat eggs unless they are cooked off the island, let alone catch fish or harvest shellfish.

"In Fyedor the Great's original plan, the monastery was meant to be the only building on the island, but Emperor Wratislaw built a palace there. He earned the soubriquet The Bad for killing his empress because she had dared to smile at a handsome lute player. Because he had murdered her on the island, his ministers rose up against him. They were careful not to break his skin until they had ferried him off the island. Then they each drew their daggers and stabbed him once so that none could say who of their company had delivered the fatal blow. Wratislaw's successor spent his spare time experimenting with methods of execution that killed without loss of blood. I believe he came to favour poisons."

By the time that Pavl finished his gruesome tales of medieval emperors, the train had reached the edge of the city. Inika saw scenes of dereliction – huge factories with boarded or broken windows, barren waste grounds littered with piles of rubble, unpaved roads, a functioning sewage plant surrounded by high metal mesh fences. First impressions of the old capital were unfavourable, but then, she reflected, the rail approaches to cities like London, Birmingham or Manchester are every bit as ugly.

Pavl was annoyed when they got off the train, "Van should have been here."

"My husband?" said Inika incredulous.

"Aunt Fyedora's grandson. A charming fellow but feckless ... I pray that he puts his talents to good use, but last I heard he was writing a play." Pavl sounded middle-aged.

They walked across the station concourse and out on to the street that was noisy with trams, electric vans and horse-drawn cabs. Inika who had read and reread *Black Beauty* noticed that the horses appeared plump and well kempt, but none of the ones that waited in line for passengers off the trains was as smart and glossy as the four chestnuts that were approaching at a high stepping trot. Pavl groaned, "I should have added exhibitionist."

The driver halted his team in front of Inika and Pavl and saluted them with his whip.

"My new job," he announced, "Giving tours of the city to welcome guests. One day only, so make the most of it. Climb aboard."

Van Nallikino drove through the Fourth Ring with such reckless panache that pedestrians stared. Inika did not want witnesses to her terror as she gripped the frame of the open carriage and despaired of reaching her destination intact. With Van yelling the names of important buildings over his shoulder, they swept through the park of the Third Ring, and over the bridge on to the wide tree-lined avenue of the Nobles' Ring, where the upper storeys of white, ochre, turquoise and jade green stuccoed mansions reared above garden walls.

"These days," Pavl said, "Most of these houses are divided into apartments for the university staff."

"Sometimes they are film sets," said Van as he steered the horses through imposing gates and round to the stables at the back of the house.

The rest of the day dissolved into a party. Whether Van had organised it for her or whether it marked the completion of a significant phase in the making of the film or the director's birthday, Inika did not establish. Drink in hand, she wandered from the stable where the coach horses munched on hay and something unpleasant had happened to the leading actress, through the vast kitchen where two sweaty cooks were chopping and slicing, to the hall where she was asked for her opinion on the state of the British film industry. She was made to feel horribly uninformed and shallow because she regarded cinema as entertainment, not art.

A gong to rival J. Arthur Rank's reverberated through the house as a summons to dinner. The long table was laid for forty people and Inika was seated between the lighting man, who had once worked at Pinewood, and Van, with Pavl opposite her. Her half-brother was not entirely sober but unlike everyone else he did not become obviously drunker.

After supper Inika escaped outside. The lawns ran down to the water's edge. The colours of sunset streaked the sky and reflected back off the river. She said aloud, "Tomorrow's my last day here." It did not sound good. "Tomorrow I meet Aunt Fyedora," sounded worse.

Nervousness that amounted to dread could not prevent tomorrow's arrival. Heavy-footed butterflies danced in the pit of Inika's stomach as she walked beside Pavl and Van the few hundred metres to the house which had once been Sev Sillin-Vrekov's and was now a museum dedicated to the memory of Bogan and Tenja. The short queue of people waiting for admission watched enviously as Van opened the front door with his key.

Inika entered her grandmother's home.

A smart young woman asked if she wanted to join the official tour. Inika looked to Van who shook his head. "We'll just have a look at the ballroom before we go up to Gran's apartment."

The guide moved to the foot of the grand staircase. "This is where the steward used to stand once a year to announce the guests who arrived for the First Summer's Eve ball. They would climb the stairs to be greeted by the members of the family, Count Sev and Countess Verja, later Count Bogan and Countess Fahra, later still Countess Tenja too. Three to four hundred guests came, headed by the emperor, his empress and sometimes his official mistress too, the grand dukes and grand duchesses, counts and countesses, barons and baronesses, and because this was the Sillin-Vrekov house, untitled people like soldiers, churchmen, businessmen, and in the days when Countess Verja wrote the list of invitees, composers, artists and writers too. Countess Fahra did not learn to read or write until she was in her twenties and the fine arts did not appeal to her. She tended to invite professors of practical subjects like engineering rather than the stars of the Imperial Opera. Invitations were prized except by some of the high nobility who refused to mix with commoners. As you climb the stairs, imagine the splendour that once was here."

Inika remembered an interview with a famous actor who had claimed to build his characters from the feet up. "Find the right shoes first, because they give one the walk, and the walk gives one the voice." She wondered what sort of shoes Tenja might have worn and decided on flat soft-soled pumps made of satin, fastened by a button of tortoiseshell or mother or pearl. Obviously the dress would have been long, probably silk, and she would have had to have lifted the skirt in order to walk safely up the stairs. Inika could almost feel the fine material between her fingers, could almost see the colour of it that was rich wine red to match the rubies at her throat and in her hair.

As if he knew that she was halfway into the past, Pavl flung open the double doors of the ballroom and bowed as she passed him. Sunlight poured through the huge windows. Rainbows glittered in the prisms of the glass chandeliers. Inika began to move in a waltz, ONE, two, three, ONE, two, three.

Van said, "May I?" and holding her close, led her in the slow dance.

They found it easy to move together, and were dancing dreamlike in the middle of the room when the spell was broken by three sharp bangs on the floor.

"No, no, no! Not a waltz. Never a waltz here. This is Sev's house on First Summer's Eve. This is a peasant celebration. The instruments are not fine violins or flutes. They are fiddles and pipes, tambourines and drums played by folk musicians who wore baggy trousers tied at the ankles like peasants. Their tunes have the rhythms of horse hooves and the patterns of bird song. Van, you should know this, you also Pavl."

Sheepishly, Van released Inika's waist and led her by the hand towards the tiny but commanding woman who lent on an ebony cane in the doorway.

"Gran, may I present Inika Smith?" he said.

Her aunt's gaze was as direct as the Miacharnay woman's had been, and much more critical.

"Shira Marmasye was quite correct. You do look like my mother. I hope for your sake you do not have her temperament."

"I'm afraid I don't know how alike we are. I was hoping that you would tell me about her, and my father of course," Inika said.

"Such is my intention… This is a good a place to begin, and First Summer's Eve in the imperial year 605 is a good time. You see, almost everyone who became important in my mother's life was here that night, her parents of course, her first love, her first lover, her husband, several of her allies and most of her enemies… Come upstairs all of you and I will tell you what happened.

PART TWO
TENJA'S FIRST LOVE
Imperial Years 605 to 614

1.

Everyone at the Sillin-Vrekov's ball on First Summer's Eve 605 was marked in some way by the Western War. On his cheek, Erwan Filowet wore the track of the bullet that had grazed him and killed the man behind. Of those born during or soon after the war, Ani Marmasy grew up fatherless, Istven Boiyenabsty might as well have because his father was an emotional wreck, baby Voldimir Shennikov was dedicated to the church as his mother's thanks for victory, and Tenja saw her uncle's body swinging from the rafters. Fortunately she was only three when Maro chose suicide over recurrent nightmares, and she did not remember.

By 605, the time before the war had acquired a golden glow, as though the normal collective hardships of life, such as epidemics and poor harvests, and individual tragedies, such as stillbirths and crippling injury, had not happened, as though the people of the empire had lived happily ever before. The one truth of the golden age was the length of the peace – the last war with a neighbour, in that case the Kingdom of Nilens, was ended in 471 by the Second Treaty of Kitak, and the last armed rebellion by the Kohantsi tribe was suppressed in 512. The armies, the First Army or Imperial Guard, the Second Army on the western border, the Third in the Don basin – the area once dominated by the Kohantsi – and the Fourth on the Nilentin border grew complacent. The Church was complacent. The court was complacent. The peasants were not, but they were worked too hard to do more than grumble, and whenever the local minister of religion heard complaints, he reminded the discontented of the better life to come.

Before the Western War, the pace of change was imperceptible.

After the Western War, the pace of change was rapid. Emperor Fyedor the Third decreed that never again would enemies find the empire ill-prepared. He had just started to reform the armies when he died. His successor Nikolka the Sixth decided to lift the country into technological parity with Katoria in the west and Nilens in the southeast, and he gave Bogan permission and a large sum of money to start building railways.

In the wake of the railways came new demands for raw materials – timber, steel, coal – new factories to process the raw materials, new homes for the factory workers, and so on and so forth on the headlong rush to industrialise.

Bogan loved his railways. He loved the role of pioneer. He loved the gangs of ex-soldiers who hacked through forests and dug through mountains and bridged the streams, who built the shiny engines and drove them. They were his tribe and he looked after them. Bogan and his railmen came to symbolise progress. Not everyone in the Empire liked or valued it.

Every story needs conflict between opposing forces, and at one level this tale is the struggle between progressives and conservatives, in which it is too easy to label the Sillin-Vrekov faction as good and heroic, and the Filowets as villainous. Here as everywhere else both sides have their merits and their faults. The hostility between them was more than an intellectual disagreement about the Empire's route to a secure prosperous future. It was also personal.

2.

"He's jealous," said Bogan's detractors when the public adulation that had once been his passed to the younger handsomer soldier.

"Count Bogan can prove that Colonel Filowet is a thief," Bogan's supporters murmured to the Emperor's aides in the middle months of the war. For reasons of his own, Fyedor the Third refused to punish the offender.

At midwinter 588, a new dimension was added to the rivalry. Fahra's brother Maro was working as a medical orderly in a field hospital southeast of the Goroki ridge. On a rare afternoon of rest, he was disturbed in his tent by an intruder, who announced, "I have a message from a guardian spirit for Bogan Sillin-Vrekov. You will introduce me to him." Maro's visitor was Nilhri, the last living kam of the Shoshanu people.

Army rules, regulations and red tape meant nothing to Maro. He quit his job and walked unnoticed from the hospital. Nilhri and Maro travelled half the length of Goroki ridge along the rough roads and tracks regularly tramped by soldiers, and though they did not flaunt themselves they did not bother to hide. They were kams who did not wish to be seen, therefore they were not seen, until Sergeant Konstanti Rylov saw them and begged for their help.

Rylov was a man driven crazy by a little red bird that had twittered at him, telling him that the future of the empire rested in his hands. When Rylov tried to ignore the bird, it had fluttered round his head. When he brushed it aside, it had pecked his ear.

"What do you want?" he had demanded.

"I'll show you," the bird had replied, but Rylov had refused to learn to fly. Enraged, the bird had flapped its wings in his face, and the more Rylov resisted, the larger it had grown. Once it reached the size of a hen, Rylov ran from it. He ran until he collapsed. The red hen caught up with him and attacked him with beak and claws. Weakly he called to Nilhri and Maro.

"Leave him alone!" Nilhri commanded. With an indignant squawk, the bird backed away from its victim. "I promised to deliver your message. You didn't have to persecute him."

"I didn't expect you to live long enough," the bird retorted. "Besides, tormenting him was fun."

Through the blood on his face, Rylov saw how Nilhri became larger and less substantial than a human had a right to be. A single gust of wind swept the bird into the sky, and a single red feather floated to the ground, before Nilhri shrank back to his normal wizened shape. Maro wiped Rylov's face and said, "Come with us. We'll keep you safe from the bird."

Together the Miacharnay, the Shoshanu and the deserter arrived at Bogan's office. The story they told him was on first hearing utterly incredible, yet the feather and the deep gashes on Rylov's face convinced him. Bogan undertook to present their information to the commander-in-chief in person.

Fyedor the Third was a stickler for procedure, whereby nobody, not even a general, was received at the palace without an appointment. Bogan's arrival provoked consternation. The chief of staff barked, "You've left your post without authorisation. Why in the name of all that's holy have you done that?"

"I have a proposal that could win us the war."

"You should have written."

"Could I have been certain that my letter would have been read?"

"Ah," the chief of staff began to soften. "I had hoped... The small matter of Colonel Filowet I presume."

"Small?" Bogan's eyebrows arched. Supplies destined for other units were still disappearing in transit and Bogan blamed the thefts on Filowet's cohorts.

The chief of staff polished his spectacles on his handkerchief, "Personally I agree with you. Colonel Filowet is a menace. I'd gladly shoot him. Problem is, Filowet is a successful menace. It is considered at the highest level that his élan, his courage, his luck, call it what you will, outweigh his disregard for the rules. He's a hero, and at the moment we need heroes. Good for morale... Why don't you tell me your proposal?"

"If I tell you and you tell the emperor and he hates it..."

"Ah," the chief of staff said again. "A radical proposal." Bogan watched him choose whether to risk a share of the credit or a share of the blame. "The schedule is very full today, but I will inform His Imperial Majesty that you are here."

Responsibility was Bogan's alone.

The emperor waited from midday until almost two the following morning before he summoned Bogan to his study. The red of his velvet dressing gown did not match the reds of his cap and slippers, but Fyedor remained daunting despite the jarring colour scheme.

Nervously Bogan unrolled his maps and began to explain, "The enemy is already weak here and here. The Spears of K'fir are poised to attack the main Katorian army here and here. I suggest we launch a simultaneous attack on each of the four vulnerable points."

Fyedor pursed his thin lips, "For this nonsense you deserted your post?"

The clock on the mantelpiece above the fire chimed twice. The peasants call the time between two and three in the morning the hour of dreams, when a sleeper may walk in the gardens of delight, or struggle in the clutches of a nightmare. Bogan squared his shoulders, took a deep breath and said quietly, "Not nonsense. A bird's eye view of the enemy's positions you might say... which incidentally explains why the Spears of K'fir turned south to the Abkhar instead of marching north to the capital."

Fyedor harrumphed, reluctantly intrigued.

"As Your Imperial Majesty no doubt recalls, after your namesake Fyedor the First had defeated the Knights of Kator in 87, the surviving Knights swore to avenge their fallen comrades. Their successors, the Spears, were bound by that vow to destroy both the Shoshanu and the spirit of the Abkhar. A kam named Nilhri has seen his people almost destroyed and anger gives him strength beyond his age. As kams can, he journeyed in other worlds, and the anger which he carried from this world drew to him a vengeful being. At first, he saw it as a bedraggled bird so tiny that it could sit in the palm of his hand. Once she was a goddess, the equal of the Spears' god K'fir, but while his devotees feed him, the loss of belief in her has diminished her to her current state. Nilhri says that a few minutes of his attention sufficed to bring a blood red glow to her feathers.

"Nilhri claims to have mastery of the air, so he can fly above our world. The red bird showed him an opening through which he looked down upon the region between the Abkhar and the Goroki ridge. He saw not only how the enemy is currently deployed, but also how they plan to move and how we can move against them... I didn't believe it the first time I heard it. However, when Nilhri's descriptions of the landscape are translated into map references, they are absolutely accurate. Once one accepts that he saw the land from above, the rest is easier." Throat tight and dry, Bogan paused and glanced across at the emperor.

Fyedor sat upright in his armchair. A tear glittered in the corner of each of his closed eyes. From a long way away, he asked, "Have you ever met Pavel Chrezdonow?"

"No," Bogan answered.

"He's something of a recluse, but I thought perhaps he'd introduce himself to your wife, he'd be interested to meet her." Fyedor wiped his eyes on his sleeve and glared at Bogan as if to say, 'If you so much as breathe a word of this, not only will I deny this conversation took place, I will make you wish you had not been born.' Aloud he continued, "Pavel Chrezdonow tried to talk to me of a goddess who can take the form of a giant bird... His mysticism annoys me. I never listen to him... If only I had listened... So many lives lost... I am too stubborn, too old..."

Suddenly Fyedor's usual acerbic persona reasserted itself, "The generals will have to be persuaded of the merits of our attack without knowing its true source. I expect they will readily attribute its audacity to the devious mind of Colonel Filowet, in which case you do not need to be associated with it any further. Leave your maps and get back to your duties... And thank you. Thank Nilhri."

Tenja was conceived during what remained of the night.

While Bogan understood intellectually why the red bird could not be mentioned, it stuck in his craw that Filowet was given the glory and the material rewards, the estates and the revenues from the diamond mine.

3.

Miacharnay tradition taught cooperation, harmony, and how to resolve argument by negotiation rather than combat, so Fahra tried not to hate Filowet's uncle Wassil. To her, he resembled a heron motionless on a riverbank, tall, stooped, elegant, malign. She claimed that in her practice as a kam she brought comfort to the sore of heart and healing to the sick in body and mind, whereas he was convinced that nothing helpful came out of the darkness of the Below. Thus in his opinion, she endangered the immortal souls of the patients on whose behalf she journeyed into the Underworld. He also resented her relationship with the Twenty-Third Incarnation. Not only had the Most Holy married her to Bogan, but He continued to receive her in the monastery two or three times a year, until He grew too old and doddery to look after Himself. The day after Father Wassil replaced the Most Holy at the helm of the church, he preached against Fahra, threatened to close church doors against her and her patients, and refused to discuss her beliefs or her actions face to face.

She was understandably annoyed when Grigor the house steward called from his place at the foot of the staircase, "FATHER WASSIL."

"We didn't invite him," she muttered.

"Now he's here we can't turn him away," Bogan replied quietly.

Villain number one climbed the stairs to where the Sillin-Vrekov family waited by the ballroom door to greet their guests.

"Forgive my intrusion." Wassil did not sound apologetic as he shook hands with Bogan, and carefully avoided physical contact with Fahra and Tenja. "I want a word with my nephew. I gather he is the guest of honour tonight."

"Not the most honoured guest," said Bogan, "That place is reserved for His Imperial Majesty. Would you care to wait in the library? I'll ask your nephew to join you there."

Shortly afterwards Grigor called out a string of names, "ERWAN FILOWET, ELYDA FILOWET, ALEKSANDR NALLIKINO, VIKTOR ZHARALOV, VOLDIMIR SHENNIKOV."

"Did he have to bring his entire entourage?" Fahra snapped.

"We've room for extras," Bogan murmured.

Up the grand staircase came two more villains, or perhaps one villain and one dupe, a hero, a heroine and a man who was less straightforward than he appeared.

Social mask slipping from its place Bogan said, "Welcome to my house, General."

"Marshal actually," Filowet replied.

"I do beg your pardon, Marshal, I forgot, your investiture was this morning wasn't it? Your uncle wishes to speak to you in the library. Down the stairs, second door on the right." Bogan conveyed the smugness of a child whose sibling is about to be punished.

Information is power they say. Bogan believed and acted on that maxim. He maintained a network of informants that surpassed the government's because he paid better. Much to his amusement, he had heard how uncle and nephew had lobbied for both the important army posts that had by chance fallen vacant at the same time. Father Wassil had used his new standing in the church to press the Council of Ministers to appoint Erwan to the Captaincy of the Imperial Guard, whilst unaware of his uncle's efforts, Erwan had asked for command of the Third Army. Bogan admired Erwan's choice, but guessed that Wassil could not appreciate why his nephew wanted to go two thousand miles from the centre of power.

Based in Donsgrat, the Third Army controlled the vast swathe of land from the Manahantjils east to the gold fields of the Okhpati marshes. Originally, the Third Army's role had been to contain the Kohantsi, but after the victory of 512, it paraded and drank and diced in idle fashion up to the outbreak of the Western War. In the few years since victory, it was showing signs of relapse in old habits. As builder and owner of the railways Bogan knew better than most the economic potential of the Don basin, and wondered how a man as rapacious as Erwan Filowet would seek to profit from his position as the emperor's representative in the area.

Marshal Filowet turned on his heel and went back down the stairs, with a casual over the shoulder remark to his three male companions, "Be so good as to entertain my wife."

4.

Young Cadet Shennikov did not hear his commander's request because he was fascinated by Tenja's green eyes.

At the Donsgrat horse fair in the autumn of 604, Shennikov had noticed a Que-Que man who looked and smelled like the rest of the tribe - fair-skinned, fair-haired, small, horsy, none too clean, but who was qualitatively different. Shennikov decided that the difference had something to do with authority. Though the tribal did not wear badges or a uniform, though he did not shout or appear to give orders, he was a leader, and Shennikov longed to lead as effortlessly.

Minutes later, the man had tapped his shoulder and said, "You have a decision to make soon."

Shennikov was taken aback by the accuracy. "Not that soon. When I'm seventeen."

"Then we speak of two decisions. The one I see, the one you expect. Show me your hands."

Intrigued, Shennikov did. For a moment, what the tribal saw in the bumps and lines scared him, but he spoke calmly, "You will have a most interesting life, surrounded by people of power... You think you must decide between the army and the church. Rubbish. Your big decision is how you use power. Are you a wise and good man or a clever bad man? Your decision is very important.

"It is also unimportant. See here, where the lines that split come back together. They show you get to the same place, but do you get there by love or by hurt? In all my fifty years I have never met anyone else with the possibility to do so much hurt or to do so much love."

"I'll do all the love I can," said Shennikov, with a soldier's bravado.

"You want the love, you wait for the green-eyed girl. She is all the love you'll need in this life."

"Sounds like I stay in the army then. If there's a girl."

"The girl and the church go together better than you think," said the tribal, holding out his hand for money.

When Shennikov invited the girl of his future to dance, he was of little consequence to her. She wanted a little diversion from nervousness while she waited for the arrival of the emperor's page with whom she was in love.

Would Istven ask her to dance? Would he even notice her in the green dress she had chosen because her confidante Alizette had told her it was his favourite colour?

"That green does not suit you," Fahra warned when she and her daughter had inspected the dressmaker's fabrics. Tenja had insisted. The dressmaker knew better than to take sides. Lovely in itself, the green gown did not flatter its wearer.

For Shennikov, the shade of the dress was nothing compared to the green of Tenja's eyes as their conversation bordered on flirtation. She overstepped the bounds of proper behaviour by asking too personal a question, implying that the distance between Donsgrat and the capital was a problem for her, "Are you going to stay with the Third Army or are you going to ask for a transfer, to the Imperial Guard for instance?"

"I regret to cause disappointment, but I wish to serve under Marshal Filowet."

"The hero of the Western War," she said sarcastically, but he missed the irony by launching into a paean of praise for the marshal's achievements. When he reached the plan for the empire's final offensive, Tenja interrupted him, "Filowet claims it was his idea?"

"Of course he does, because it was," Shennikov retorted.

"No it wasn't."

"Well if it wasn't his plan whose was it? Your father's?"

"More my father's than Filowet's, but not really his. Come, I'll show you something you won't have seen before." She stood up and pulled him to his feet. The manners instilled in him at the cadet school finally prompted him to say, "Shouldn't you be entertaining your guests?"

"Probably, but if it's a choice between correcting your education and agreeing with the Grand Duchess X that it's a bit chilly for the time of year or speculating with Countess Y that Baroness Z's diamonds are fake, which they are because everyone knows she had to flog the real ones to pay the furrier for the sable coat she needed because she could hardly carry on wearing the rag of fox fur she's had for the last two years, and her husband was too mean to buy, I'd rather correct your education if it's all the same to you."

"But my dear it *is* chilly for the time of year," Shennikov warbled. He saw the marshal, one arm possessively around his wife's waist, the other clutching a brandy glass, guffawing at a joke - a man in middle age, loud, immoderate and imperfect, not the man of courage and vision. "Educate me," he said.

Tenja led her companion through the maze of supper rooms and card rooms to the servants' stairs, then to the passage outside the library where the walls were lined with sepia photographs. Of the first Tenja said, "This is my uncle Maro. My mother's twin brother and also a kam. You know what a kam is?"

"I had one read my palms. He warned me about you."

"Me?"

"How many green-eyed women are there?"

"Plenty. Besides, fortune telling is the least of what kams do. This picture is of my uncle and the last of the Shoshanu kams Nilhri." She told the story of Nilhri, Maro, Konstanti Rylov and the red bird, and just as she reached the end, she heard Grigor's stentorian voice announce the arrival of the emperor.

"Consider yourself educated," Tenja said to Shennikov. She picked up her skirt and ran back to the ballroom via the servants' stairs.

Shennikov remained outside the library examining the photographs. His mind was spinning: the green-eyed woman, her proximity to the monastery, disillusion with the marshal. Perhaps it would not be so bad to honour his mother's promise by entering the monastery.

5.

Fahra recognised the kinship between Voldimir and Tenja the moment that they met. Although he was obviously not pure, she could not see anything dark or shadowed in or around him, and she was delighted to see them dance together at the start of what she was sure would be a lifelong relationship.

Almost simultaneously, she watched the beginning of an affair. Major Nallikino responded to the Marshal's order to entertain his wife by requesting the pleasure of a dance with her.

Waiting beside Bogan to greet their guests, Fahra was able to observe the dancers. The major and Madame Filowet were the handsomest and most stylish couple in the room. Suddenly she felt like an intruder.

No more than three years older than Tenja, Elyda was already a woman and second wife to a man whose first wife had died in circumstances that could have been murder or suicide. No more than three months married, Elyda had already acquired the nervous demeanour of a woman whose man is unpredictable and sometimes violent. Vulnerability enhanced her beauty.

'No wonder the major is smitten,' Fahra thought, before she turned her gaze on her daughter, who still moved with a child's enthusiasm, not a woman's grace.

Grigor called out another group of names, "ALINA MARMASY, ANI MARMASY, ANTONI MARMASY, GENRIK LASARYK, ELIZVET ROKOVSKY." Widow of the last Lord Steward of the Abkhar, Lady Alina was a genuine friend of Fahra's, though Tenja was less fond of Alina's daughter Ani. Both Sillin-Vrekov women were wary of retired General Lasaryk, estate factor, companion to Alina, and father figure to Ani, because he was too hungry for information about Miacharnay culture. Fahra did not think it any of his business while Tenja tried to ignore that side of her heritage. Fahra had not met the distant cousin Antoni before and first impressions were unfavourable. About to enter the monastery, he had already acquired a sneering disapproval of joyful frivolity. Fahra did not have any intimations of the role Antoni was to play in Tenja's future.

The last to arrive of the characters destined to influence Tenja's life was the emperor. Nikolka Chrezdonow, the sixth of his name to reign, had too much and too little. Expert in the cultivation of roses both floral and human, he preferred his gardens to his council room, and the secret chambers of his mistresses to the empress's bed.

Every year he danced first with the Countess Fahra, and then with the Countess Tenja. Neither mother nor daughter appreciated the honour because he was careless with his feet.

As soon as the emperor released her, Fahra looked for an opportunity to speak to Major Nallikino. Having observed how Elyda's grace was reduced to awkward girlishness by the roughness with which her husband reclaimed her from the major, Fahra was resolved to interfere.

Eventually she managed to corner Nallikino in the supper room, "A word if I may, a word of... encouragement perhaps."

"Certainly you may," he replied, politeness overcoming innate caution.

"In the months and years to come, Madame Filowet will need a friend. A loyal friend, a man friend, you, I think... Love her, because her husband does not." She touched his sleeve, smiled and was gone into the crush of people before he could speak.

Eventually the ball was over. Shortly after dawn, Fahra and Bogan sat together in the breakfast room. While Grigor poured the tea,

Fahra asked, "Shall I reveal the identity of the Emperor's next mistress?"

"Ani Marmasy?"

"Close. Elizvet Rokovsky."

"Each one's younger than the last. Let's hope his roving eye never alights on our daughter."

"She wouldn't have him."

"She wouldn't be able to refuse, any more than Elizvet and her family will be able to refuse. Where is Tenja by the way?"

"She must have gone to bed."

6.

After her obligatory dance with the emperor, Tenja limped down the stairs and out into the garden. She took off her shoes to let the grass cool her poor feet. Her progress towards the summerhouse was halted by the sound of voices. The male one was Istven's, the female Alizette's. Tenja could not help overhearing their conversation.

Her best friend said, "Dear cousin, it's so unfair I have to marry money. I'd much rather marry you."

"I'd rather marry you too, except most married people stop liking each other after a while and I don't want to stop liking you. Sadly, we both have to be realistic. We must marry money, very soon in my case. Such a sordid scene yesterday. A grubby little Fifth Ring type, the type Mamma tends to go to when she's short, barged into the house asking for ten thousand in cash. Cash! I ask you, where is Mamma going to find ten thousand in cash? I tried to palm him off with the emeralds Papa gave her for her last birthday before he died, but the frightful little man delighted in telling me she'd had them copied to pay off her last crop of debts, the ones she didn't tell me about... I managed to clear him from the house by promising him fifteen thousand crowns the morning after my wedding. I really do have to marry very soon."

"It's a good thing she's so in love with you she won't notice you love her money more than her until too late. I wonder how huge her dowry will be."

"Who cares about her dowry? She has millions in her own right, left her by the grandmother who was killed before she was born. Her own right becomes hers and her husband's the day she marries."

"You will think of spending some of your millions on your poor little cousin won't you?"

"Of course I will my dove."

Tenja was rooted to the ground, upset and curious about Istven's unfortunate bride-to-be. She finally realised that they meant her when Istven said, "All the millions in the empire do not compensate for the shame of having a tribal as my mother-by-marriage."

From her place in the shadows, Tenja bellowed a roar of protest, a howl of despair. She fled to the house, entering through the kitchens and racing up the servants' stairs to the privacy of her room. She locked the door, flung herself on her bed and sobbed.

Just before lunch on First Summer's Day, Tenja's maid spoke to Grigor, Grigor spoke to the Count, the Count spoke to Fahra, who said, "I don't care if she has the worst hangover anyone has ever had. She can't lie in bed behind a locked door all day."

Bogan knocked on Tenja's door, called out to her but she refused to answer.

"She hasn't eloped has she?" he asked in more than jest. Grigor handed him the tool he needed to take the door off its hinges.

Tenja was not asleep. She heard her maid, and Grigor, and her father. She heard the sound of the screwdriver in the wooden doorframe. She heard but could not quite connect sound to meaning because she was not in the ordinary world, nor was she part of another world. She was adrift somewhere in between, and in the emptiness she was nowhere at all.

The door dismantled, Bogan strode across the room and reached out to shake her shoulder.

"No!" cried Fahra. "Don't touch her."

"Look at her. She's sick. She needs help."

"We cannot help her. She has to find her own way through this. Leave her be." Gently, Fahra shepherded Bogan from Tenja's bedroom.

Out on the landing, Fahra began, "I didn't think this could happen because she's an only child."

"She's ill, that's all."

"She's not ill. She was conceived the night the Shoshanu kam Nilhri died, remember? It's possible the soul that lived in him found its next host very quickly."

"Nonsense."

"The new Incarnation of the Most Holy Incarnate is conceived as soon as the old one dies."

"The Most Holy is different. My daughter is not the Twenty-Fourth. My daughter is not a kam."

"No she isn't. Yet. You'd better hope she becomes one, because if she doesn't she will continue to react like this to any setbacks she meets. Episodes will be more frequent, and will last longer."

"Are you telling me she'll go mad?"

"Unstable and unhappy, definitely. Mad, well, people call me mad."

"They call you witch as well and it's not a name I want attached to my daughter."

Rather than argue, Fahra walked away from her husband. They did not speak again until dinnertime. He said, "I admit, I do not want Tenja to be a kam."

The telltale red spots glowed on Fahra's cheeks. She was still very annoyed. Bogan held up his hands in a placatory gesture, "I can see how hard it is for you to walk the roads of healing. I suppose I want Tenja to have an easier life."

"Do you want an easy life?" Fahra asked with a dangerous edge to her voice.

"Of course not. I thrive on challenge."

"Perhaps she will too. She's your daughter as well as mine."

Through the heat of the summer, when most aristocrats deserted the city for their country estates, Tenja lay between the worlds. She was aware of her mother and her maid when they fed her, bathed her, sat her on the lavatory, dressed her in clean nightdresses, massaged and moved her limbs to exercise them. It was embarrassing to be treated like a floppy doll, but not so embarrassing that she had to attend to her own needs.

Her father sat with her for a few minutes every day. He was worried and she wanted to reassure him, but not so desperately that she bothered to communicate with him. She felt too vague to speak.

Fahra only agreed to consult the nerve doctor who specialised in the treatment of hypochondriac and miserable noblewomen because Bogan accepted her bet on the precise phrasing of the diagnosis.

Tenja was aware that a strange man with a gold watch stood over her because the bright shiny metal flashed in the afternoon sun. The man asked her questions but as she could not think of the right answers or any wrong ones she did not reply. She was much more interested in the flashes of light as the watch swung. They were telling her something that she was too dense to understand.

"I told you he'd call it hysterical paralysis," Fahra said holding out her hand for Bogan's payment.

"How much longer will she lie there like that?" Bogan said. He sounded like a small boy. His worry was stretching him to his emotional limits: seeing Tenja's condition as unchanging, possibly permanent, he was unable to trust that it would change when she was ready for it to change.

"There'll be a thunderstorm soon. If she doesn't find her way back during the storm, I'll bring her back after it," Fahra said.

"Do you mean you've let her suffer when you could have brought her back right at the start?"

Fahra stepped several paces away from her furious husband, but was unapologetic. "Of course I've wanted to bring her back. It has taken real discipline not to chase after her. I have let her have the time she needs because it is her life, her choice, and if I have to rescue her, I will not be doing it for her, I'll be doing it because you can't trust her." Bogan held out his arms and they hugged each other for a long time.

The change in air pressure as the storm approached made Tenja restless. She shifted in her bed and moaned as if in pain. Bogan could not bear to watch what Fahra regarded as a hopeful sign.

In the growl of the thunder Tenja heard the growls of a bear. As the lightning flashed and its reflections flickered in the mirrors in her room, she saw a white bear up on the ceiling. When the thunder boomed and crashed, Tenja heard the white bear's song, the same six notes, repeated over and over again, and in the repetition was the idea that if she sang the same song she could walk in all the worlds instead of drifting between them.

The next time the thunder rolled, Tenja sang the six-note song with it and she continued to sing after the storm had passed. Six notes over and over and over. She sat up and while she chanted she was fully aware of her surroundings and wondered why her things had been moved. The chant was boring. She stopped, but when she stopped she began to slide away, so she started again and her hold on the ordinary world grew firmer. She chanted the six notes, her six notes, and the feelings they evoked changed.

She felt anew, as intensely, the anger and the shame of Alizette and Istven's betrayal, until the chant melted the feelings so that she could think of the experience as a gateway. She relived the embarrassment of her mother's and her maid's intimate care for her body and the chant slowly changed the feeling into gratitude that they tended to her so gently. In recognising the loving connection to her mother, the six-note song brought her to acceptance of her Miacharnay blood. She imagined, or perhaps sensed, that all the Miacharnay kams who had ever lived sang with her, so that her throat was no longer tight or sore. She sang her song loudly and with pride. She stood up and opened the north-facing window and shouted her song to the departing storm, to the cloud-wracked night and to her mother's birth land.

Waiting in her bedroom out of earshot of Tenja's room, Fahra whispered to Bogan, "She's done it. She's found her song."

"You mean she's a kam now?" Groggy with sleep, Bogan was nevertheless delighted.

"She's further to go before she's a kam, but she's on the road."

When Tenja realised that she had merely completed the first stage of a longer journey, the newfound acceptance of her Miacharnay heritage deserted her. She yelled, "I don't want to be like my mother! I don't want to be a kam."

"It's be a kam or be crazy," Bogan said brutally. "And if you have it within you to be a healer like your mother, how can you be so selfish as to deny healing to other people?"

Tenja hung her head, "I was scared. I sang my song so I could get back to the ordinary world. I don't want to have to get lost again."

"Then you need to prepare for a proper initiation."

7.

Just over a year later, Fahra deemed Tenja ready for her initiation. They went to one of the Imperial New Islands Territories during a week of rare soft weather around the autumn equinox. Bogan chartered a steam yacht to ferry them to the island, and while Tenja endured the preparations for the ritual and the ritual itself, he enjoyed three days of sea fishing.

Though as a youngster Tenja had accompanied her parents on their expeditions to railway construction camps, she had forgotten those experiences of the simple life. Privileged and soft, she did not enjoy sleeping on board bunks in the fishermen's shack. She did not like finding, carrying or chopping driftwood, though tending the fire during the long northern twilight was quite fun. She was nervous about the coming ordeal, because her mother's answers to questions were evasive: "It depends," or "How long is a piece of string?" or "It's your initiation, not mine. Mine's irrelevant because the one sure thing about yours is it will be different."

At least Tenja did not have to cook over the open fire because part of the preparation was a fast.

When the rim of the sun sank below the western horizon, Fahra picked up her drum and began to beat a slow steady rhythm. Half chanting, half speaking in time with her drumbeats, she told the story of how First Kam found her song.

Safe in her lair beneath the winter ice, the Great White Mother gave birth to three fine cubs. She licked them clean and while they suckled from her teats she sang to them. She sang three notes three times to teach them everything they needed to know to live as white bears must, and the cubs sucked in the knowledge from each of the three notes as they sucked in their mother's milk. When they were full of music and milk they curled up beside their mother and they slept. They ate and slept, slept and ate until the darkness of winter was broken by the return of the sun.

Lean and hungry, the Great White Mother led her cubs from their winter den on to the tundra in search of food.

The woman, wisest of her people, also walked the tundra in search of food and as she passed the Great White Mother's lair, a shaft of sunlight unfroze the notes that the Great White Mother had sung to teach her cubs how to live as white bears must. The woman heard each of the three notes three times. The first time she listened in wonder, the second time she listened in understanding, the third time she listened in thankfulness, for now she knew how to live as kams must. She knelt on the snow-wet ground, and she promised to honour the Great White Mother, she promised that the People of the tundra would forever and beyond honour Her for the gift of understanding how to live as People must.

Fahra's voice faded, the drumbeat grew faster, louder, stronger. It pounded through Tenja's body as she sat cross-legged, shut-eyed, on the floor of the fishermen's shack. It pulled at the pit of her stomach urging her down through the planks of the floor.

Tenja stood on a step of ice, a rung of the endless stair, and still the pull was downwards. Cautiously, in case the icy steps were slippery, she dropped two turns of the spiral. Her foot reached for the next tread on the stair below but landed upon hard-packed snow.

She shivered. The air was chill, but it was not the cold that caused her shiver. It was the desolation, the immensity of the emptiness, where the sun was a bloodstain on the southern horizon, where the land and the sky were steel grey, where she was alone, a puny little human soul in a body that was not quite hers, in reindeer-skin clothes that were definitely not hers, in the first realm of the underworld.

Her mother had given her three pieces of advice, of which the first was, "The underworld reflects what you are inside."

'So,' thought Tenja, "I am lonely and empty.' The sky seemed to lour. 'No, I am new. This... this vastness is everything I have yet to discover. As I change it will change.'

She remembered her mother's second piece of advice, "What you think manifests."

"The light will come," Tenja said and the rays of the sun fanned across the sky.

The third piece of advice was, "What you ask for you receive." Tenja faced the rising sun and called, "I invite my companion to come to me, to guide me through this realm and to teach me its ways."

Nothing happened for so long that she decided that her mother's advice was useless. Requests, prayers, whatever they were called, were not answered. A dark cloud obscured the sun, and she heard the faintest echo of a howl.

In the flat emptiness where the wide land merged into a huge heavy sky, she was lonely and close to despair. She wanted to escape from this terrible place but she did not know how to find the door to the endless stair. With a depth of need that she had lacked earlier, she cried, "I wish I had a friend beside me."

Something was behind her. She heard it or smelled it. She whipped round. A wolf grinned at her, eyes glowing like the heart of a fire. He thrust his muzzle into her hand and melted into her, so that she became wolf.

In every cell of her being, she felt how it was to be him, yet she retained just enough of her humanity to register and to name the sensations:

- the smells of urine and faeces, of the pack, of strangers, of the winds, of the sea, of the coming of storms.
- the smells of reindeer, strong/weak, healthy/vulnerable
- the smells and tastes of blood, fresh meat, marrow and carrion
- the feel of an empty belly and a full belly, of exhaustion, of the languor of sleep
- the hunger.

She knew too the sharpness of instinct which informed the decisions to spend or to save strength in the chasing of prey, to protect and to play with cubs, to accept the members of the pack, to be wary of others.

Above all, pampered Tenja who had always known plenty, shared the hunger, which drove the wolf to follow the reindeer thousands of miles north to south, south to north, on the move most of his life.

She was one with the wolf.

"Always we are one," the wolf agreed, for he was her as much as she was him.

Stupid! Wolves do not talk. Tenja was cross-legged on a hard floor. A wind was blowing outside the hut. Fahra was still drumming. The rhythm pushed Tenja far down in her being. She was falling, falling. The wolf howled. She crashed into his realm and drowned in the liquid fire of his eyes.

She was in a river, the river, swimming upstream, swimming underwater. She thrashed tail and fins to try to reach the surface to breathe, though she could already breathe well enough to swim. She was salmon; she was human. Fish in form, herself in consciousness, she was in the second realm of the underworld where the waters flowed. She struggled to free herself from the fish. The water was cold, she swallowed some and spluttered. She was choking, suffocating. She had no air in her lungs, only water, cold, cold water. She was not a cold slippery fish, and she would not, could not, change her awareness for his.

The salmon was more determined than she was. He had to swim up the stream, this stream, no other stream. He dragged her with him, into him, so that she came to appreciate, as he did not, the perfection of form, the subtleties of flow and taste that identified this water as his water, the instinct that forced him to go against the current and to leap up the falls.

He/she misjudged the height and fell back into the pool. Together they gathered the power in a great sweep of the tail, then arced into the air. They cleared the fall, but could not resist the downward rush of the water that tumbled them down to the pool once more. Again the sweep of the tail provided the strength to leap, and this time they overcame the obstacle and swum further upstream.

At last they came to the shallow gravelled pool where a tiny alevin had first tasted the water of this river. The gravel grated against his scales. Separated from the fish, Tenja was sucked below the stony riverbed.

In the third realm of the underworld, she scrabbled at the stones, clawed at the thin soil, anything to escape the tangle of roots that wrapped around her legs, her arms, her neck, that stopped her from reaching light and air. Slowly, resistance was squeezed out of her. She became still, and in the stillness was able to feel the tiniest pulse of life that sustained the plants through the long dormancy of winter so that they could burst above the surface in the brief weeks of summer light and warmth to carpet the tundra in a riot of colour. She was held by the net of roots until she understood enough of their tenacity to recover her determination to be a kam.

She became heavier and heavier until the fragile roots could not support her weight. They released her into the fourth and lowest realm of the underworld, the lair of the Great White Mother.

The bear pinned Tenja to the floor of the den with huge paws, while She licked and licked and licked. It was affection of the kind lavished on a cub. The Mother's tongue was pleasantly warm. Her breath reeked of rancid milk and rotten fish. Lick, lick, lick. The Mother scoured Tenja's skin. It hurt to lose the layers. Lick, lick, lick. The Mother flayed the flesh from Tenja's bones. She was raw. She was pain. Lick, lick, lick. The Mother curled Her tongue and swallowed Tenja into Her belly.

In the warm dark was relief. Tenja lay soft, and unformed, and at peace. She floated as aimlessly as she had floated through the summer. Time passed uncounted in the easy comfort, until the time came for her to leave the place of bliss.

The walls of her special place closed in upon her. She pushed against them with her fists. She kicked at them with her feet. They retreated a fraction. Thinking she was safe, she relaxed in the warmth. Again the walls pressed in on her. She punched at them, pushed at them with all her might, but she could not stop them closing in on her, squeezing the life out of her. She screamed and screamed louder while the prison folded about her. Stopping the screams because they used too much air, she snatched the last breath into her lungs and held it there. Her head was compressed against the walls and ceiling of her tomb. She was about to break under the pressure.

She was about to die.

She released her last breath in the six notes of the song which had brought her home to the ordinary world. She sang the six notes, and with one last massive contraction, the walls of the Mother Bear's womb thrust her headfirst out of the tunnel to rebirth as a kam.

She knelt at the Great White Mother's feet and the Great White Mother Bear sang to her. Just as First Kam had understood the three notes, so Tenja now understood the Mother's song.

May your song sound through the realms and the worlds, Tenja-kam. Sing it to heal and to comfort. Sing truly and my blessing is with you. Enter my realms at need. Wolf salmon and root will guide you and at the end I will call you home. Sing truly, for the north has no place for lies. Sing truly and hold the Great Mother in your heart as you are in hers.

Like First Kam, Tenja touched her forehead to the ground in thankfulness. The ground was no longer the White Mother's den but a step on the endless stair. Up and up the spiral she climbed, winding her way in search of a door into the ordinary world. Her legs ached. She was short of breath and dizzy. Perhaps she had come too high, perhaps she needed to return to the Great Mother to ask her where to find the door. She descended one full turn of the spiral before she realised that in the decision to go down she was singing a false song. The Mother who gave birth also destroyed false singers.

Wearily she resumed her climb up the endless stair. Then came a lurch when instead of the expected step she was borne aloft on the wings of an eagle. The fragment of her mind that remained Tenja was nauseous. Heights had always terrified her. The part that was bird wheeled in the thermal and scanned the summer grasslands below for the quick movement of lemming or baby hare.

Food! The eagle swooped, and as they plummeted towards the earth, Tenja let go rather than crash to the ground. She landed hard in her body in the fishermen's hut. The drumbeat was as harsh as the eagle's cry, and disapproving. She had time to think that she had failed before the wind gusted through the planks of the walls and carried her up to the skies.

She tried to resist it but it had no substance against which to kick or punch. It had strength enough to carry her higher and higher until it spilled her into a place as empty as the void between the worlds where she had passed the summer, which could not possibly be where she was supposed to be. To correct the wind's mistake, to help her find the next realm of the upper world, she sang her six-note song but in the thin air it sounded ugly and useless.

A voice warned, "Wait! Please wait until you can see me."

Tenja peered into the mist that surrounded her. She could not see anything but she was suddenly sure that something could see her, and it was not impressed. A not quite audible whispering was dismissive, "Goway, goway, goway. Notwant. Goway."

The warning voice spoke more kindly, "Don't mind them. They're upset because you've come alone. They expect twins. I've tried to tell them one's better than none, but they're traditionalists. They don't like change. They don't quite believe the Great White Mother Bear can give a song to anyone on her own. That's better. I can see you properly. Can you see me?"

The mist in front of Tenja solidified into the shape of a small bent Miacharnay woman, who said, "I can see your mother in you. I used to be her teacher, you know, hers and Maro's. If you win the Great White Father's permission to journey in His realm, I will mediate between you and your ancestors. I don't suppose you'll call upon them much. Your mother doesn't. There's not much call for our wisdom among the Settlers. We know all there is to know about the diseases of reindeer and cloud formations, that sort of thing, but we're not sure about your father's people. They do not behave like People.

"We can't stand here chatting. The Great White Father is not to be kept waiting. You'd better go to him, but please, if you see her again, tell your mother we'd like to see her more often than we do."

Tenja seized upon the word 'if.' Nervously she asked for advice on how to face Him as her mother had not said anything useful. The reply did not lift her confidence, "Fahra was wise not to influence you. The Great White Father has as many faces as the Mother. Whatever you expect, He will be something else. Go to Him. He's waiting."

Tenja missed the transition from the realm of the ancestors to the fourth realm. One moment the spirit woman was there, the next she was not, and in her place an enormous white bear sat on his haunches, aloof and austere. Tenja was unsure whether she was supposed to greet Him or wait until He deigned to notice her. The blue haze around His head expanded as He exhaled. Tenja waited and the blue haze grew to envelop her.

It was ice blue and ice cold, so cold that it burnt her nostrils and the back of her throat as she breathed it in. She held her breath rather than draw in more of the burning coldness. In the end she had to breathe and the freezing air hurt her.

She began to freeze from the inside out, the tissue of her lungs hardening to solid ice. Opening her mouth to scream, a high inhuman noise emerged. She thought of the six notes of her song, she tried to force them out of her voice box, and they came out clear and dry as glass, the overtones to complete her usual chant. She sang the whole of her song and the ice inside melted as if it had never been, and the air around her warmed, and the blue haze vanished, so that the Great White Father was revealed in His magnificence. He turned his gaze upon her and in His small dark eyes was recognition.

Her song was but a part of His, yet she understood the meaning in His music, *May your song resound through all the worlds, Tenja-kam. Sing truly, sing to create and you may enter My realms at need. Sing falsely, sing to destroy and I will destroy you, for the north has no place for lies. Go with the blessing of the Father in your thoughts.*

She knelt to touch her forehead to the ground and found that she pressed her head to the earth floor of the fishermen's shack.

Fahra let the drumbeats fade to nothing, and said severely, "You came back to your body twice. It is dangerous to flip between the worlds like that. You were lucky to survive."

"Aren't you going to congratulate me?"

"Petulance doesn't serve you. The Mother and Father might have accepted you as a kam in their realms. You have yet to convince me you can be trusted as a kam in this world. This is the one that counts. This is the one where you use your knowledge and the gifts of the other worlds to serve others and to heal. Let's see if you learned enough to compensate for your lapses in concentration."

Fahra questioned Tenja mercilessly about the guides she had met in the other worlds and about their teachings. When Tenja spoke of the spirit woman and the ancestors, tears trickled down Fahra's cheeks but she continued her questions until at last she was able to say with satisfaction, "Welcome to the ordinary world, Tenja-kam."

In the deceptively summery weather of the next morning, Tenja sat on the wall of the small harbour to wait for the steam yacht's return. Seaweed stirred in the lilt of the incoming tide, silver pinpricks of light danced on the water. Sure of her new place in the web that joins the worlds, Tenja felt peace of a profundity that she had never experienced before, and as the waves lapped gently at the land and the harbour filled, it did not occur to her that the peace was as transient as a summery day in a northern autumn.

8.

Cool and composed, Fahra repeated for the thousandth time, "The other worlds are not a refuge from the ordinary world. You cannot use them as a private hideaway."

"Don't you understand?" Tenja wailed. "It's too... too difficult for me to stay in the ordinary world. Too much ugliness."

"The contrasts make it what it is, this world we live in. Do not journey again until you have found the beauty and can keep awareness of it in your heart."

Tenja wrapped herself in a fur coat that had once been her grandmother's and went for a walk across the parkland of the Third Ring. It was a day early in 608 when the light was returning, and the winter was pretending to be spring. In the lea of the wind, the sunshine was almost warm on her face.

She could see the beauty of nature in the tight buds on the bare trees, in the rich blue of the sky, in the play of light and shadow. She could accept that nature was also as ugly as the debris floating in the canal that divided the Third Ring from the Second. What she could not cope with was the nastiness she perceived in people and in herself.

She had got into the habit of running from it to the emptiness of the tundra where she found clarity, truth and the absolute loyalty – love – of a friend. The problem was that she applied the knowledge of the wolf that properly belonged in the underworld to this world. When she looked on her fellow humans with his eyes, she saw through their pretensions, their jealousies, their competitions to the weaknesses beneath, and she forgot compassion for others and for herself because compassion was not part of the wolf's nature.

Watching the emperor through wolf's eyes, she knew that one snap of strong jaws would kill the vainglorious cockerel that crowed from the top of the dung heap. She longed if not to break Nikolka's neck, at least to shake him, to alert him to his responsibilities. He preferred to drain the energies of his courtiers in intrigues, rather than encourage them by example to care for those less fortunate. She knew this, yet at parties or balls or soirees with her own class she joined in the analysis of every smile or frown that passed across his face, despising herself for it, doing it just the same.

And what, conscience demanded, had she done for the poor?

She went once to the Seventh Ring soup kitchen run by the monks and nuns from the Monastery of the Most Holy Incarnate. The ragged people who came for free food smelled awful, a drunkard's sexual advances frightened her, the nun in charge treated her as though she was useless. Tenja was too disgusted and scared to return.

She told her father how guilty she felt to have so much when others had so little. Her father replied, "You have money of your own. Give some to charity."

She ordered her bankers to transfer ten thousand crowns from her account to the Church's Relief Fund.

She still felt guilty. She talked to her mother who advised her to practise the healing chants and work with the people who came for help.

Tenja snapped, "It's not enough. Nothing we do makes a real difference."

"We make more of a difference than you think," Fahra offered calm, unacceptable reassurance.

On that winter day in 608, Tenja's mind churned round and round the issues of beauty versus ugliness, rich versus poor, guilt versus acceptance, while she strode past the Imperial Art Gallery, the Imperial Opera House and the Ministry of the Interior, until she reached the gravelled circle in the middle of the park that is dominated by the bronze statue of Emperor Fyedor the First and Great.

She stared up the long greenish brown nose of the rearing horse and the horse stared straight ahead with empty eyes, as arrogant and haughty as the grandest grand duchess at the imperial court, but for the seagull perched between its ears. Tenja laughed aloud. Ruffled, the seagull fluttered to a place of greater safety, the emperor's head.

She sat down on the bench from where she could see Fyedor's profile. Ever since childhood she had found the vast bulk of him reliable, somehow reassuring.

When she saw someone, a brown-robed work brother from the monastery, walking towards her, she was irritated, for she did not want to share Fyedor with anyone else. She glared at the young man in the hope that he would be intimidated. He was not. He moved with grace and confidence as if he expected to be noticed and admired and welcomed. He came close to her and said in greeting, "You've changed."

"So have you," she replied, recognising the voice. "You weren't wearing a skirt last time we met. Red and gold suited you better, I must say."

"The red and the gold would have kept me in Donsgrat whereas the brown lets me live quite close to you."

Tenja remembered some nonsense about the green-eyed woman who would be the love of his life. She sat in what she hoped was repressive silence. Uninvited, he sat down on the bench beside her.

"Something has happened to you since last we met. You're deeper, more like your mother, and him too." He nodded towards the statue. "Were you aware he was also a kam?"

"Was he?" Tenja almost squeaked. She was full of questions but beyond the bare fact, Shennikov knew very little. Keen to consult the books in her father's library, Tenja set off for home. She did not pay her companion much attention, and parted from him at the gate without regret. Afterwards, she thought about him frequently, wondering if and when they would meet again and hoping that it would be soon.

Winter storms blasted across the capital city. One of Tenja's cousins, Dorotja Sillin, unmarried and at thirty something unlikely to marry, visited.

"One soup kitchen. That's all the Church's Relief Fund provides. One soup kitchen. Do you think it's good enough? I don't."

Dora Sillin had plans and she drew Tenja and some of Tenja's money into them. In the spring, they bought premises in the Fifth Ring where they established a school. Dora took up residence in the apartment above the school while Tenja spent a day or two a week there, learning how to teach scrawny cheeky children to read and count.

Through the school, Tenja became acquainted with the sorts of people she would never have met had she remained safely cocooned in the Second Ring. One of them, a sculptor, became a close friend.

Despite the new activities, Tenja had time to think about Brother Voldimir, to wonder when they would meet again, to daydream of how it would be when they did.

Shortly before First Summer's Eve, they met near Tenja's bankers in the Fourth Ring.

"Father Wassil finds me useful," he explained when asked what he was doing in the commercial sector of the city.

They lingered in the park by the statue of Fyedor the Great in heated debate about his current essay topic *Belief fulfils itself. Discuss.*

Intending to illustrate the accuracy of the proposition, Tenja told one of her mother's tales about the battle between a kam and a demon for possession of a child's soul. If she blurred the distinction between fiction and personal experience, at least her descriptions of the background were authentic, and Brother Voldimir was fascinated. They went deeply into discussion of the Below, which was forbidden territory for a novice taking his first steps along the Esoteric Path.

Every time they met thereafter, he encouraged her to tell him more about her journeys, especially those which took her into the underworld, and she was happy to have found someone with whom she could share adventures that most other people dismissed as mad imaginings.

Once while Tenja was waiting for Brother Voldimir by the statue, she was embarrassed to meet her mother who had just visited a friend in the Empress Ylena Hospital. For Tenja embarrassment deepened when she had to introduce Mamma to the handsome young novice priest. Fahra surprised her by remembering his name.

Afterwards, Tenja had to be grateful that her mother did not refer to the encounter. Fahra held her silence, not because the incident was too trivial to mention, but because it was too important, for in Brother Voldimir she saw the twin who had not been born of her womb along with her daughter. Why they had been woven into the web, separate but joined, Fahra did not enquire. The nature of their bond was theirs to unravel.

Summer came. Fahra and Bogan left the city for the cool and quiet of their favourite of their country estates. Tenja remained in the capital, ostensibly to teach at her cousin's school.

"Fifth Ring people don't have the luxury of escape from the heat," she declared, "They can't leave so I won't either."

The real reason she stayed was to continue her affair. By this time, she was convinced that she was Voldimir's green-eyed love, and not all their meetings were in public. Once they borrowed Dora Sillin's apartment, then the sculptor willingly lent them his room. Occasionally, Voldimir missed a tryst and Tenja was frantic until she saw him again. The sculptor tried to reassure her, "It can't always be easy to get out of the monastery."

One humid afternoon, Tenja lost her virginity to Voldimir. Although unwed girls of her background were no more supposed to indulge in sexual intercourse than novice monks, neither admitted to the least twinge of guilt. They told themselves theirs was true, enduring love, its consummation outside the bonds of marriage right and necessary. She did not much enjoy the process, though he drew on experience to be gentle. The next time they made love, she began to appreciate the pleasures. The third time in the sculptor's bed was wonderful.

To the close of 608 and into the spring of 609, she and Voldimir continued to meet whenever they could. Sometimes, the frustrating times, they were only able to snatch a few minutes of conversation and the briefest of kisses. Other times, especially during the week of compassionate leave granted to Voldimir on the occasion of his grandmother's death, they managed to spend the whole of a day and much of the evening in each other's arms.

At midsummer Bogan and Fahra travelled east to open the new railway to the Okhpati gold fields. In her parents' absence Tenja dared to invite her lover to her home. Disapproval twisted Grigor's mouth as he announced Brother Voldimir's arrival.

"Show him to the library," Tenja said. "And please do not disturb us."

Eagerly, she and Voldimir made love on the library floor. The rich scents of flowers from the garden wafted by the breeze through the open windows mingled with the dry chemical smell of old books.

In post-orgasmic bliss while he was still inside her, Voldimir asked Tenja to show him the gateway to the underworld. Beneath him, she went rigid. "I can't."

"Can't as in don't know how or can't as in won't?"

"Can't," she repeated. "You're not Miacharnay."

"At least tell me where to look."

"No," she said sadly as she felt love wither. All the talks they had had, when he had appeared to be interested in her and to understand her, seemed now to have been the deliberate extraction of information. She pushed him off and reached for her clothes. "You've used me for what I know, not loved me for who I am."

Shrugging his shoulders, he pulled his robe over his head, knotted the belt and buckled his sandals. "When can I see you again?" he asked, his eyes on his shoes.

"I don't know. I think I'll go to the country for a while."

"You can't run away from me you know. I love you and I'll never stop loving you. You'll come to your senses."

"I'll show you the way out."

In the passage outside the library, Brother Voldimir stopped by the photograph of Maro, Nilhri and Sergeant Rylov that had been the subject of their first serious conversation. He tapped the glass over the soldier's face, "Before Nilhri died, Konstanti Rylov wrote down everything the old chap could remember about the traditions of the Shoshanu kams, and guess what, the soldier became a monk. I reckon I can get the information I want from him any time I choose. I just have to service his desires like I've serviced yours..."

Tenja exploded, "Get out of my house." She ran from him. He made his way to the door and if he was hurt by the loss of his love, he was not prepared to admit to pain.

She sat on the edge of her bed, rocking backwards and forwards, trying not to cry. In her hand she held the crumpled piece of paper that was his one gift to her, the poem he had written, or perhaps copied, because he had not really loved her.

When one is me, and one is you,
One plus one is one not two.

Rubbish! She tore the paper into tiny pieces. Then the tears came.

Less than a month later Tenja was summoned to Father Wassil's office in the Monastery of the Most Holy. Her recall of that interview was fragmentary. Clearest was the dread which filled her from receipt of the summons to the wait outside the heavy oak door, as she expected some kind of punishment for her affair with Brother Voldimir. She remembered how Father Wassil tried to intimidate with rudeness: he did not rise from his chair to greet her nor lift his eyes from his book until he had finished the page. When he deigned to speak, he did not mention Voldimir, and instead harangued her about her work as a kam. She stared at the wall above his head trying to appear contrite when she was in fact relieved, until he said with quiet menace, "You think you journey Above and Below, but how can you be sure where you go when even this world is not what you think it is? Everything you trust as solid - the wall, the floor, that chair, your body - is not solid at all."

As he spoke, it seemed that the objects around her started to liquefy, to dissolve into light.

She had no idea how long the experience lasted, less than a second, more than a minute, because time itself started to fade into nothingness.

She gulped, felt the flagstones settle beneath the soles of her shoes. Wassil smiled a thin-lipped smile, "If this world that seems dense is illusion, what of the Above? What of Below? Why, they exist only inside our minds. They have no other location than in the tissue of our brains. It follows that your journeys are imaginary, at best useless, at worst diseased and harmful. The more you think about what I have just told you, the more you will realize the truth of it."

He dismissed her then and she walked home through the rain. She had to concentrate on putting one foot in front of the other in case the ground beneath her feet shifted again. The world felt unstable.

She tried in the weeks, months, years that followed her interview with Father Wassil to forget how the ordinary world had crumbled before her eyes, but could not. Her failure to exorcize the experience meant that she was never quite sure of the efficacy of her work as a kam, and she began to avoid journeying into the other worlds. Where once the underworld had been a refuge, now it was a fearful place. She busied herself at Dora Sillin's school and led a hectic social life in and around the Fifth Ring, not the Second.

Years passed, years of useful activity in the Fifth Ring and levity in the Second, of friendships and unhappy love affairs, of discussions of how life was and how it could be: in short, years of no particular relevance to this version of Tenja's life.

9.

During the moment of quiet before the First Summer's Eve Ball in 614, Fahra experienced an odd flutter in the pit of her stomach. Something was not right. She left Bogan and Tenja in place by the ballroom door for one last inspection. Grigor stood at the foot of the grand staircase. His uniform was immaculate. In the ballroom, the light from the chandeliers glowed softly in the mirrors, the musicians had their instruments in tune and their sheet music in correct order on the stands; in the supper rooms, the tables were laid ready, and the maids, their own and the ones they had to hire each year, were prepared to circulate among the guests with titbits and drinks; in the gaming rooms, new packs of cards remained wrapped. Fahra picked up the single violet petal that had fallen from a flower arrangement to the floor. Everything looked fine but something still felt wrong. She could not name it.

When the Emperor's mistress Elizvet Rokovsky arrived, Fahra saw the tension underneath the deceptively simple dress and expensive jewels, and she was the only witness who did not freeze in horror when Elizvet screamed from deep in her belly the single word, "NO." The emperor still held out his hand.

"No," Elizvet repeated more quietly, because she already had everyone's attention. She curtsied, as shallowly as she dared, turned her back on her lover and walked out of the ballroom. The only guests to move were those who stepped aside to let her pass.

Raggedly the musicians resumed the dance tune but the emperor gestured at them to stop. He too marched out of the ballroom. Looking from one to another for guidance on how were they meant to behave, the guests decided to take their cue from Countess Ylena Boiyenabsty, whose manners were impeccable despite the shortness of her purse. She thanked her hostess for a marvellous evening, but regretfully found herself obliged to leave early. In her wake, three-quarters of the guests also departed so that only family and good friends were left.

Long experience of the court led them to the conclusion that there would never be another Sillin-Vrekov First Summer's Eve Ball, and a desperate abandon overwhelmed them. The sun was high in the sky before Bogan, Fahra and Tenja gathered in the breakfast room for a cup of tea.

"Why did the wretched woman have to end her affair here?" Bogan moaned.

"Apparently because she's desperate for a baby and our beloved emperor won't let her have one," said Tenja removing her shoes and wriggling her toes.

"Given the trouble he has with his bastard half-brothers, I can't say as I blame him for refusing her."

"Then he should have let her move on to another man's bed."

"But he loves her. Probably hates her at the moment and everyone associated with her, including us. He'll blame us for inviting her or something, any excuse not to revisit the scene of his humiliation. What do you think my dear?" Bogan turned to Fahra.

"I had a dreadful feeling right at the start, and I still have it. Something's happened, or is about to happen, much more significant than a lovers' tiff," Fahra answered.

Bogan had less than three hours sleep before he was roused to meet an informant, Drushku Uleven, who had witnessed something so appalling that he felt obliged to inform his employer in person.

The origin of the trouble in the port was the installation of a huge new machine on the first floor of a small factory without regard for its weight. The floorboards gave way, the machine crashed down on to seven workers. Six died quickly. One lingered for several hours in screaming pain. The factory owner had not dealt kindly with the bereaved families, who spread word of his meanness. After the shops, mills, and manufactories closed for the First Summer's Eve celebration, workers gathered outside the factory where the accident had occurred. Insults were shouted, stones were thrown, windows were smashed. The factory owner panicked and called on the local militia to protect his property.

The militiamen were used to guarding the docks and the railways from fire and theft. They were not trained to face down an angry mob, especially a mob composed of their neighbours in the crowded tenements. The militia captain sent a messenger on the last scheduled train to request assistance from the Imperial Guard stationed in the capital.

Although the mob had mostly dispersed before the soldiers arrived, the officer in charge gave the order to open fire on the stragglers, who ran for cover. A few of the younger angrier men tried to fight back. Two soldiers were battered to death, and their comrades went berserk.

Uleven counted forty bodies, female and male, child and adult, with gunshots wounds to their backs, and there might well have been more.

The soldiers returned to the capital as they had arrived in the port, aboard the train that they had commandeered from Bogan's company. Uleven travelled with men he regarded as murderers, because he had to tell someone the truth of what had happened.

In his youthful dream of a railway network across the Empire, Bogan's main interest had been the technology of the massive locomotives, of bridge construction, of tunnels through the Manahantjil hills, of laying track over all types of terrain. Asked by Emperor Fyedor the Third what benefits the railways might bring, Bogan had suggested quicker cheaper transport of people and goods. To Fyedor's second question, "What of the drawbacks?" Bogan had replied, "There aren't any."

He had of course been wrong.

10.

"A good place to stop for luncheon," Fyedora announced. "I need to be alone for a while. My cook has prepared a picnic for you youngsters. We will meet again here in two hours."

Slightly slower than Pavl and Van, Inika stood up as Fyedora limped from the room. Abuzz with questions, Inika followed Pavl downstairs and out to the garden while Van collected their lunch basket from his grandmother's kitchen.

Pavl walked with her across the lawn to the edge of the river estuary. The tide was coming in gently. To their right Inika could see the island that formed the city's innermost ring. Ahead lay sun sparkled water and the northern bank of the Olnish on the horizon.

"These kams… Was our grandmother really one of them or was Father Wassil right when he accused her of an over-active imagination?" she asked.

"Don't worry, Grandma wasn't mad, nor was Papa, nor are Sandro and I. Of course Nina's a little neurotic… If you'd inherited Tenja's tendency to walk the worlds like you've inherited her looks, I expect it would have manifested by now. Either you'd have gone through an initiation or you'd be quite ill… On the other hand, Father Wassil wasn't altogether wrong." Inika groaned while Pavl continued, "What we think is solid is mostly space… Papa devoted most of his career to proving such things."

"Did he succeed?"

"I don't know. I'm not a scientist. I am content with faith."

Inika decided that she needed to stand on firm ground rather than venture further into metaphysical realms. "Is that the summerhouse over there?"

"There may be one or two original timbers left," her half-brother smiled.

Van appeared with the picnic and a rug which they spread on the grass. Fyedora's cook's version of a packed lunch was much grander than Sister Katerina's.

When he had finished eating, Pavl left Inika and Van in the garden while he visited the monastery. Alone with Van, Inika felt girlishly shy, which was ridiculous because not only was he much younger, he was also her cousin. To cover her discomfort she asked when his film was due for release. He guessed in a year or so.

She fiddled with some daisies that were growing in the lawn. Van packed the remains of lunch into the basket. In an uncanny echo of her thoughts, Van said, "I suppose Gran's talk of the other worlds must sound very strange. You Brits pretend to be so matter of fact, but a rich vein of mysticism runs through your history too."

"Not that I'd noticed!"

"You have to look for it. It's not in the school curriculum, I know because I lived for a year in York with a history teacher, but it crops up sometimes on Channel 4 and in books."

"Like *The Da Vinci Code*." Inika was dismissive.

"I was a little more serious," Van almost snapped. He stood up. "You can find it for yourself if you want to. Meanwhile, would you like me to show you more of the house?"

The room that interested Inika most was the library. She could not help thinking of Tenja and Shennikov and the scent of summer flowers from the garden and the awfulness of that kind of argument.

"Did they meet again, my grandmother and Voldimir?" she asked.

"I don't want to spoil the story. What do you think?"

"I think they must have because Fahra was so sure they were linked. I don't know why I hope they met because he wasn't actually a nice man."

"But very attractive," Van said, while Inika thought, 'Like you.'

"Would you like to see some photographs?"

When she nodded her assent, he stepped over the ropes that stopped visitors from touching the books or the furniture, and hunted through the shelves and cupboards for old albums. He removed the cardboard emblems of a holly leaf from two of the chairs, saying, "As we're family we're allowed to sit down."

Side by side, they looked through the first of the five albums that Van had found. The earliest images were sepia prints of Sev Sillin-Vrekov on his seventieth birthday. Then came a series of landscapes and dead animals that Bogan had shot on his travels. In another photo, Fahra and Maro stared coldly at the camera. They were identical, and powerful, and to Inika's eyes very alien in their clothes of reindeer skins. In a later picture, Fahra wore a jewelled tiara and necklace and a ball gown. Difficult as it was for Inika to believe that they were pictures of the same woman, it was more difficult to accept that she was descended from either of them. Next was the picture that Tenja had shown to Shennikov, the one of Maro, Nilhri and the army sergeant who towered over both of them. A little shiver ran down Inika's back. The Shoshanu kam was shorter than Maro, and wrinkled as a prune, yet he radiated something that Inika could not define. On the following page was an official Victory Day portrait of the Emperor Fyedor the Third in the uniform of the commander-in-chief. Comparing the two, Inika decided that Nilhri was the more truly imperial.

Most of the second album was devoted to the development of the railways. Alongside huge locomotives were pictures of Bogan and his workmen. Inika could tell how much Bogan had enjoyed their company. Van closed the book. "One engine is much like another unless you are a real fan."

The first photo in the third album was of Tenja with a baby in her arms. Inika's breath caught in her throat. "Is that my father?" she asked. Van shook his head. "Aunt Fyedora?"

Very gently Van took the album away. "We haven't reached that part of the story yet. It's time we went back upstairs for the next instalment."

The Don Basin Railways

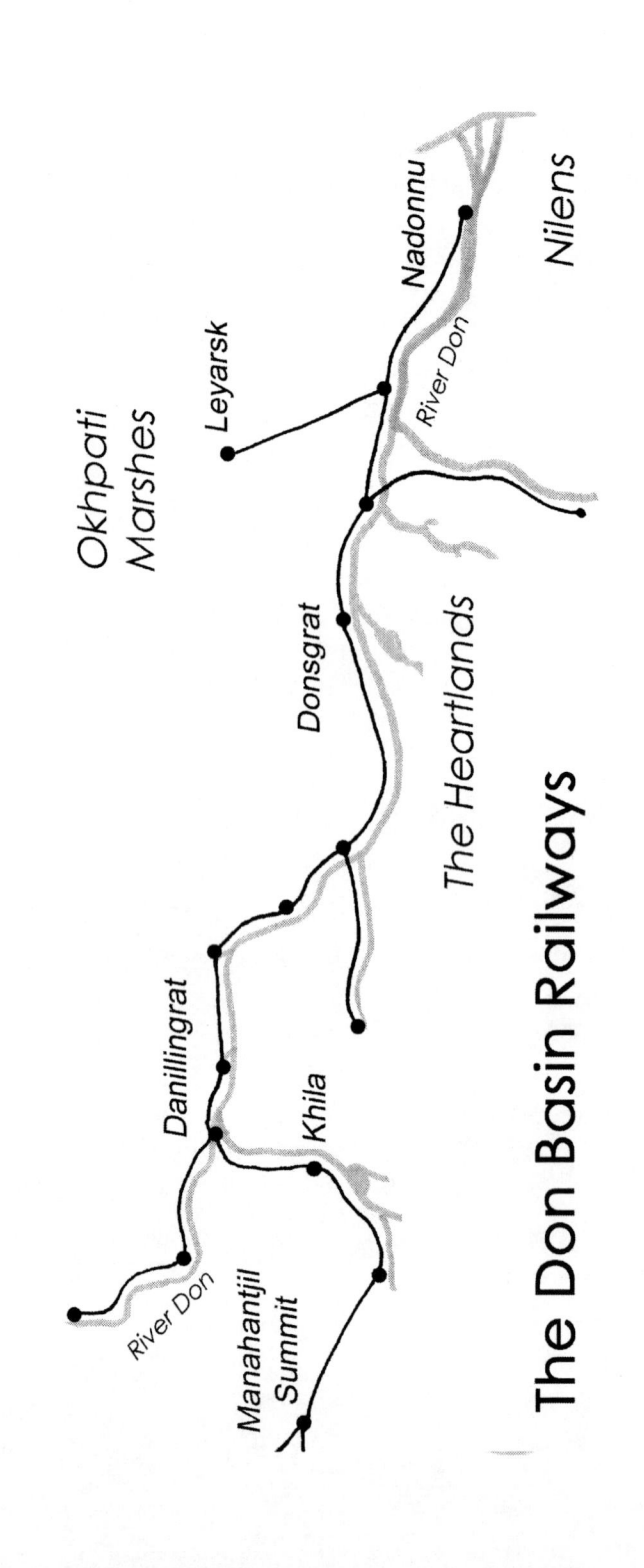

Okhpati Marshes

Leyarsk

Nadonnu

Nilens

River Don

Donsgrat

The Heartlands

Danillingrat

Khila

River Don

Manahantjil Summit

PART THREE
SHADOW HEART
Imperial Year 614 –5

1.

When Shennikov was asked why he did what he did on First Summer's Day 614, he usually grinned and said, "Like the brown bear cub in the Miacharnay story, I behaved in accord with my nature."

On one occasion, Inika's father dared to press him, "Surely you can tell me the truth. It wasn't just mischief, was it? It was politics."

Shennikov threw back his head and laughed, "Politics? People like me didn't indulge in politics back then. Prior to 614, politics was an emperor who decreed at his coronation that technological progress must happen and then travelled with the curtains of his carriage drawn so that he would not have to see the consequences that followed his decision as surely as night follows day. Politics was the pretence that the empire wasn't leaderless. Politics was the Treasurer trying to collect taxes from landowners no longer able to pay them because their peasants had gone to seek their fortunes elsewhere, or from new rich industrialists who kept at least two sets of accounts. Politics was the Minister of the Interior explaining to the landowners of the western plains that their missing peasants could not be caught, whipped, branded and returned because labourers were needed in the factories and mines and mills of the east. Politics was Mishka Sillin's network of informers listening at keyholes in case the government's critics were plotting revolution. Politics was quiet cautions or arrests and beatings for those who would not keep their mouths shut. Politics was not the business of a twenty-four year old lieutenant in the Third Army."

"Your business or not, you must have had political opinions," Alfin said. "You travelled and I expect you kept the curtains open."

In his latter years, Shennikov had a way of folding one corner of his mouth into a self-deprecating smile. It twisted his lips as he said, "Such vehicles as I travelled in didn't have curtains. I also walked... Oh yes I had opinions... mostly parroted from Father Wassil."

"Another politician," Alfin interrupted.

"Never! Father Wassil devoted his entire life to the glory of the Church. The fact that he was ruthless does not reduce him to the status of a mere politician... I've thought long and hard about why Wassil was the man he was, and the best analogy I can come up with is to liken the church to a loaf of bread. Before the Western War, the church was like risen dough – airy and malleable. It got baked in the furnace of war into hard crusty bread, not easy to eat but wholesome. Some men spat it out, others were nourished by it. Wassil was in the latter group. But for the war, he'd have lived a decent life in the obscurity of Tievo abbey. Because of it, he became an army chaplain, exposed to the horrors of Goroki ridge. He had to cope with the enemy's dead and injured as well as ours, and was much influenced by the steadfastness with which wounded Katorians held to their belief in K'fir. During one winter's night vigil, he prayed so intensely for the souls of the dead that he started to sweat. The love of the Most Holy - specifically, he claimed afterwards, the Most Holy in His Seventeenth Incarnation – pulsed through him to give him a direct visceral experience of faith that supplemented his intellectual convictions.

"As I'm sure you're aware young Alfin, each incarnation brings a fresh flavour to the core teachings of the church. Where the Twenty-Third was a playful character, the Seventeenth was austere to the point of severity. Father Wassil reverted in his own practice to the forms prescribed by the Seventeenth and as he rose through the ranks of the church he persuaded others to join him under the reversionist banner. The Reversionists' certainties proved very attractive to everyone overwhelmed by the pace of progress or upset by the Twenty-Third's retreat into second childhood, and utterly unappealing to everyone who valued the Twenty-Third's teachings on the joy of the moment. Early in Wassil's leadership, church attendance fell. At that time, he didn't mind too much because smaller was purer.

"I was far too deeply in love with your mother to appreciate Wassil's teachings on purity and I argued once too often with him on the perils of the underworld. As soon as Wassil had persuaded my mother to revoke the vow she'd made on my birthday, I was free to leave the monastery, but I can see now how much of the Reversionist worldview came with me on my travels, more than I realised at the time.

"By First Summer's Day 614 I'd been back in the Third Army for six months. I stood much higher in the marshal's estimation than he did in mine. That he drank and gambled bored me because I had to sit with him and steer him home at dawn and nurse his hangover the next morning and coax him to do his paperwork. The Reversionist in me despised him for shirking his duties and family responsibilities. The other, darker side of me revelled in the power I had over him and over officers senior to me who had to reach him through me... I really enjoyed that.

"Maybe I would have let things carry on if Filowet had not celebrated First Summer's Eve in the whorehouse... Even a man as bad as I was then can have standards. I despise men who get their pleasure from a woman's pain, and the girl the marshal hurt that night was no more than sixteen. He did it deliberately you understand. As I hauled him out into the street, I saw her and what he'd done to her, and I had to listen to him boast about his prowess. I almost drowned him in a puddle.

"Usually Donsgrat's First Summer's Day service is held in the square outside the abbey, but that year it was inside because of the rain. All the bigwigs of the town, the army officers of course, the councillors, the wealthiest businessmen, had to endure the anthems and the prayers and the abbot's sermon, which sounded word for word the same as I'd heard him preach while I was at cadet school. You can imagine how bored I was.

"Then I noticed the resemblance between the marshal and the statue of our renowned founder Woldymer Chrezdonow, the same lack of focus to the eyes maybe... Something got me thinking, 'What if?'

"There you have it Alfin, no politics, no ambition to make the empire better or stronger, just the intent to save another girl from a beating, combined with a meddlesome nature and a theoretical knowledge of mesmerism. I didn't have a clue about the monster that lurked inside Filowet's skull or that it would merge so easily with what I created outside. I didn't expect it, but I admit, I used it."

Shennikov was disconcerted when Filowet remained rapt in prayer after the Abbot's final blessing. The marshal was supposed to lead the worthy citizens of Donsgrat in procession to the door. When he did not move, they started to fidget. The manager of the Sillin-Wrecov Barge Company's Donsgrat office coughed significantly but did not quite dare to leave ahead of the army officers. Captain Zharalov was about to shake Filowet's arm until Shennikov hissed, "Leave him be!"

Such was the force of the lieutenant's command that his superior obeyed without hesitation. Zharalov organised the rest of the officers into the procession and slowly the great church emptied. The rain dripping through the leaks in the roof plopped into buckets.

Shennikov listened to the raindrops. After some minutes Filowet returned to normality. He hauled himself upright and saluted the statue before he announced, "I am reborn." He began to laugh.

Politely Shennikov laughed too, "Who are you reborn as?"

"As myself. Who else could I be?"

"Forgive my stupidity, but I'm still not sure... I mean I know you as commander in chief of the Third Army..."

"That's the body I've had to put up with. Such good qualities as he has come from my spirit."

"Woldymer Chrezdonow," Shennikov said with a small bow. "How wonderful that you have made yourself known. Do you wish to go to the First Summer's Day luncheon at the Imperial Hotel?"

"Luncheon? Waste of time." Filowet's boots clattered on the stone flags as he marched down the aisle and out into the rain-drenched square. More flustered than he wanted to show, Shennikov offered to deliver the guest of honour's apologies to the Imperial Hotel.

"If you must," Chrezdonow said with a faint Heartland accent that was not the Marshal's. "Meet me later at his house. Hurry."

2.

The annual First Summer's Day picnic in the park by the river had been cancelled because of the rain. The servants were still entitled to their day's holiday so Madame Filowet was alone indoors with three fretful sons. She had just banished the two elder boys to their rooms and was wiping the tears from Mhailo's cheeks when she heard the front door slam. She jumped in surprise and Mhailo wailed in renewed distress.

More exasperated than scared by the intrusion, she hurried to investigate. Looking over the banisters from the first floor landing, she thought for the briefest moment that a giant brandishing a huge sword stood in the hall. She was about to scream when the apparition diminished to the size of her husband, and in sharper tones than she usually dared to use, she demanded, "What are you doing here?"

Filowet gazed up at her with the eyes of a stranger. He removed his rain-sodden military cap, bowed to her and in the rolling accent of the Heartlands invited her to join him.

Even as she walked down the stairs, she knew that her husband had become more dangerous than ever and that she needed to humour him. As she reached the bottom step, Erwan clasped her hand and led her into the drawing room, where he fell to his knees like some gallant from romance.

'This is not happening,' she thought, 'this cannot be happening.'

His face level with her waist, he said with a fervour as foreign as his accent, "I swear I'll make him pay for every time he has hurt you. I'll be a kinder husband than he was, I promise."

Despite her resolve to placate him, she snatched her hand away from his and said, "Stop this nonsense. Please stop it."

He grabbed her as a counterweight to heave himself upright, then thrust his face into hers, "I've told you I'm a better man than he was. You should be grateful but you don't sound it. Say thank you like a good girl."

She closed her eyes so that she did not have to squint and stood mute. He shook her, "I gave you an order. Say thank you."

"I don't know who you are, I don't know who to thank."

The bell in the porch jangled. Erwan shoved her towards the door. At the sight of Lieutenant Shennikov, she said bitterly, "Why amn't I surprised to see you?"

"How is the marshal?"

"Something has got into him, as I'm sure you know."

"Something indeed. Woldymer Chrezdonow."

"Don't be ridiculous!"

"How about you let me in and give me a drink," Shennikov suggested. She stood aside to let him enter while from behind her, Filowet growled, "I'll not have alcohol served in this house."

"I was thinking of tea. Perhaps if Madame were to boil the kettle..."

Elyda escaped to the kitchen.

Repeating, "I'll not have alcohol in the house," the marshal gathered the decanters from the dining room and carried them to the scullery. One by one he upended them over the sink. Various ports and precious Mardestiniak brandies glugged and gurgled down the drain. He went down to the cellar to destroy the wines stored there.

In the kitchen, Shennikov found Elyda leaning against the range. She said, "I'm not going to pretend he's been a good or kind husband but I can see how he's changed. I don't just mean today. I mean since you came back to Donsgrat last year. *I* didn't enjoy it when he went on a drunken binge but he did. Nowadays he's not the same. He's desperate. He had joy and you've stolen it. He used to be Erwan Filowet, I don't know how you've done it, but you've turned him into Woldymer Chrezdonow." Breathless, barely coherent, she stopped.

From the cobbled yard at the back of the house they heard the smash of bottles. Shennikov said softly, "In your shoes, I wouldn't make such accusations. I wouldn't want me to retaliate."

"What do you mean retaliate?" She was suddenly cautious.

"Let me put it this way. Your youngest son hasn't inherited his looks from your husband has he?" The kettle started to whistle as it came to the boil. "Make the tea, and learn to live with your new man."

Later, Shennikov went to the sports field where the traditional First Summer's Day games were in progress despite the weather. In the smaller than usual crowd of spectators, Shennikov found Zharalov in the expansive phase of drunkenness. Full of bonhomie the captain ordered another bottle of fizzy wine and draped his arm round Shennikov's neck, asking with fumy breath, "What's the matter with our good leader? Been converted to the true faith has he?"

"In a manner of speaking," Shennikov said. "He's convinced he's the reincarnation of Woldymer Chrezdonow."

Zharalov was suddenly reflective. "They used to call him that during the Western War, the peasant boys particularly. My dad told me. I think in his heart of hearts Dad believed it too though he never committed himself. Erwan Filowet as Woldymer Chrezdonow. Well, well, well." He drained his glass and to the bottom of it he said, "The Most Holy knows the Empire needs a new Chrezdonow."

They talked far into the night, and somewhere they shifted from conditional to definite tenses.

3.

Very late in the evening of First Summer's Day, Mishka Sillin paid Bogan a visit. Unusually, the men invited Fahra to join them over their brandy and cigars.

"Here's to the end of a difficult day," Mishka said as he raised his glass in a toast. "Under instructions from His Imperial Majesty, I am required to ask you what you know of Elizvet Rokovsky's departure from this house this morning."

"I know nothing," Bogan said.

His cousin interpreted the intonation of the 'I' as he was meant to, and groaned, "Oh Fahra, you didn't did you?"

"All I did was cut her hair and stuff newspaper into the cook's old shoes. The last time I saw Elizvet she was limping down the drive in a maid's uniform. I didn't enquire where she meant to go so I wouldn't have to lie to you."

Mishka swirled the brandy round his glass. "I was ordered to ask you. I have asked you. That's one of my duties done. If I see her again I'll wring her pretty little neck, the grief she has caused. I have spent hours with the emperor today and whenever I tried to persuade him to focus upon last night's outrage in the port, he demanded why I haven't found his woman yet... Once upon a time I wanted this job. I thought I'd be able to handle him, I thought he'd listen to me. I used to blame my predecessor for not telling him the truth, but now I understand. The emperor does not want to hear it. Imperial Guards shoot children in the back. So what! Their parents should not have let them out on the streets. In short, the rioters got what they deserved... I don't know how much longer he can reign before he has to notice."

Meanwhile, Tenja was at the sort of First Summer's Day party Mishka Sillin did not approve of, where radical ideas were discussed and those condemned as deviant associated with others of similar proclivities. When she arrived, the mood was sombre. Rumours of the trouble in the port were already in circulation. A journalist, who always knew more than the *Imperial Gazette* would publish, claimed that the death toll was two hundred and eighty seven, which made it the bloodiest riot in recent history.

"There'll be worse riots before the end of the summer," someone commented gloomily.

The serious sad conversation was interrupted by the sculptor, "Tenja darling, what's this about the ball last night? You're such a bitch not to have told us the Rokovsky shouted at the emperor."

She fluttered her eyelashes at him, "Why should I when you pretend to despise gossip?"

A bald man, fattening in his middle years, gazed at the sculptor from the corner where he sat alone. When she had told as much of Elizvet's story as she was prepared to tell, Tenja approached the sad man. Someone caught her arm, and whispered, "Don't get involved with him. He's a ministry spy."

Tenja raised her voice, "I wish the ministry would put the effort it puts into its reports on me and my friends into prosecuting factory owners who kill their workers."

"I agree," the fat bald man protested. "I'm not a spy. In fact I'd lose my job if the minister knew I'd come here, but he's worth breaking the law for." He stared wistfully at the sculptor who blew him a kiss.

Tenja sat down beside the ministry man. "Don't get involved with him. He's a wonderful friend, an even better artist, and the meanest and cruellest of lovers."

The man said, "I'm content to admire from afar. I'll have to be. I daren't do more." He went quiet but Tenja could not be bothered to move from his side. His unprepossessing appearance could not mask his essential kindness. Suddenly he said, as though he had been thinking about it for a long time and had finally reached a conclusion, "The ministry has changed since Mishka Sillin took over. He's given me a new job. He calls me his watchdog."

"You're a spy after all," Tenja said.

He giggled, "I suppose I am. I spy on Marshal Filowet. The minister suspects he's fiddling the Third Army accounts."

"Tell me more," Tenja said, and so the clerk did. Her father was quite pleased when she passed on the information.

4.
To COL. A. NALLIKINO
REPORT HQ DONSGRAT IMMEDIATELY

Aleksandr Nallikino was not pleased by the sweaty fingerprints left on the note when he put it down on his desk. He had six hours in which to organise his deputies and to pack before the next eastbound train departed from Danillingrat. He did not expect to return.

For four and a half years as the emperor's most senior representative in a fast-growing industrial town, he had played many roles: lawmaker, policeman, politician, educator, businessman, judge. Placed in this almost impossible position by Nikolka's refusal to reform local government east of the Manahantjils, Nallikino was quite proud of his record. The one riot that had happened under his rule had been dispersed with the minimum use of force, and unlike those Imperial Guard idiots on First Summer's Eve, his troops had not fired directly into a mob. He had not accepted bribes, or lined his pockets with the profits from the army-controlled brewery, preferring to spend them on the welfare of his soldiers. He had kept the workers calm and productive, and he had worked hard to improve their conditions.

Born into the land- and peasant-owning classes, he was not a natural liberal. However, he accepted that workers, including his own men, were more productive if their basic needs - food, rest, clean and dry accommodation, the chance to let off steam occasionally at dances or sports - were met, and if their craving for intoxicants was limited to mild beers. He had argued and cajoled and demonstrated with balance sheets to the more exploitative of the industrialists the advantages of treating their workers like humans, not like animals.

He wished that his peers elsewhere in the Don basin were as scrupulous. Unfortunately most of them abused their authority. In the absence of legislation, local law was whatever they said it was, and they took bribes from distillers of hard liquors, from builders, from anyone who needed the authorities to look the other way. In such places, the workforce was volatile and bloody riots happened all too frequently during the heat of summer. Up to 614, such uprisings had been spontaneous reactions to employers' stupidity and greed, but like the wisest of his colleagues, Nallikino feared that soon the workers of one town would join with those in another to plan strikes and protests. As soon as the workers united, the whole line of towns that had mushroomed beside the railway from Manahantjil Summit to sleepy old Donsgrat would explode out of the Third Army's control. He hoped that the emperor would realise the seriousness of the situation and take appropriate action on the basis that change had to come from the top before it was forced from below, but he doubted both Nikolka's will and capacity.

Only on the train from Danillingrat to Donsgrat did Nallikino allow himself time to reflect on the likely reason for his sudden recall: his affair with his commander's wife. Rather than dwell on the past when they met in delight and parted in sadness, he imagined possible futures. Perhaps they would never meet again, perhaps they would face disgrace together, he jobless and she without her children. He railed against the unfairness of the matrimonial laws, which expected a married woman to tolerate her husband's behaviour whatever he did, but deprived her of her children and such wealth as she had brought to the marriage if she was found to have taken comfort in another man's bed.

In nervous anticipation of his interview with the cuckolded husband, Nallikino hardly slept.

The meeting was not as expected. Without mention of Elyda, it lasted less than two minutes.

Filowet said, "Some of my staff think I'm making a mistake. They would think that. They want the honour I'm about to give you. Poor things, none of them had a chance of getting this job. They're not descended from Vano Nallikino. Show me his blood runs true. Serve me now as well as he served me in the past and I might make you a general too."

Confused by the content of Filowet's speech and by the strange new accent, Nallikino babbled, "I'll certainly do my best. What is it you want of me?"

"I want you to recruit ten thousand Heartlanders and have them battle trained by First Summer's Day next year."

Nallikino knew his history. His distant but direct ancestor Vano Nallikino had been born in the same village as Woldymer Chrezdonow in the same year. Fighting together in the battles that ravaged the Heartlands, Vano had dressed Woldymer's wounds, had been the first to hear of the vision granted by the Third Incarnation, had inspired volunteers from each of the warring villages to unite in pursuit of conquest north and east and west of the Heartlands, but Woldymer, not Vano, had led the army of ten thousand into unknown territory. Woldymer, not Vano, had taken the title of emperor.

Aleksandr Nallikino could not understand why Filowet wanted him to repeat Vano's exploits. For the first time in his career he queried an order. "Why?"

Filowet shouted, "You dare ask why? Because I order you to, that's why. Get to work, and remember I expect the same loyalty from you as your ancestor showed me. Your office is along the corridor."

Stunned, Nallikino reeled out of Filowet's room. In the corridor, he collided with one of his fellow officers. After the proper apologies, Cadet Master Sladkin said, "Congratulations on your new appointment. Are we not privileged that Chrezdonow is returned to us in these troubled times?"

The expression on Sladkin's face reminded Nallikino of peasant women kissing an icon of the Most Holy Incarnate. "We are?" he said.

"Of course," Sladkin snorted.

In Nallikino's opinion, it was nonsense. Death was more probably a full stop than a comma and as there were no such things as souls, they could not return to this world in new bodies. Soon he discovered that he was the only sceptic on the third floor. His fellow officers wore the same blissful expression as Sladkin and seemed convinced that the commander was Woldymer Chrezdonow reborn.

By the end of his first day back at Donsgrat HQ, Nallikino was a worried man, alone and already lonely in the opinion that a second Chrezdonow at the head of ten thousand Heartland recruits was not the solution to the Third Army's very real problems.

He walked from the barracks to his house wondering how his forebears would have reacted. Since Vano, each generation of male Nallikinos had served as officers, though none had reached such high rank as Vano and his son Igar. Most had been captains or majors, the odd colonel, recipients of orders as much as givers of orders. No doubt every single one of them had been ordered to do something stupid – think of his father Lyov and his uncle Stepano – and no doubt every single one of them had obeyed. Stepano's obedience had cost him his leg, Lyov's had cost him his life. Good and loyal and disciplined, any one of the ancestors would probably have gone to the Heartlands proudly, so why could he not follow the example of his uncle, his father, his great-great grandfather? Why did every fibre of his being want him to cry out 'this is pointless, crazy, wrong'?

A younger officer fell into step beside him, "Welcome back to Donsgrat, Colonel."

Without breaking his stride, Nallikino looked sidelong and said, "Thank you. I apologise, I forget your name."

"Shennikov, Voldimir Shennikov, captain."

Nallikino vaguely remembered the cockier of the two cadets who had attended the Marshal's inauguration.

Shennikov enquired, "Tell me if you will, how you find your new assignment."

Nallikino wanted to say that it was a waste of time, effort and money, but he opted for caution, "It's too soon to have opinion."

"That doesn't sound consistent with what I've heard of your character," Shennikov said softly. "I'm quite sure you have an opinion that is not favourable."

Unused to overt challenges to his rank, Nallikino stopped in the middle of the pavement, "Your manner is offensive."

"I am the marshal's eyes and ears. I forget sometimes I am not his mouth too," Shennikov inclined his head in mock humility.

"The marshal seems well able to speak for himself."

"Nevertheless, he relies on my advice. I would offer you some advice too. Understand that he is a changed man. Where he used to neglect his wife, he attends to her, not least because Woldymer Chrezdonow had four sons, and he has but two."

"Three," Nallikino corrected firmly.

"It's true three boys live under his roof."

Nallikino's fists were clenched. He had not felt such intense desire to thump somebody since cadet school where he had often yearned to break Cadet Master Sladkin's neck. He willed his fingers to uncurl, his arm muscles to relax.

Shennikov, aware of Nallikino's fury, chuckled quietly, "I'm sure we can count on you to do your job without complaint." He turned on his heel and strode back towards the barracks.

Nallikino was glad to reach the four-storied terraced house that his family had bought from the builder a couple of centuries earlier. The smell of roast chicken filled the hall. His housekeeper, a dressmaker who lived in the basement rent-free in exchange for keeping the rest of the house clean and aired, had been advised of his return, he supposed by Captain Shennikov, which did not improve his temper. He did not like to be beholden any more than he liked to be threatened.

Over the next few days Nallikino saw Elyda twice, but only from a distance. Both times he was staring out of the window of his third floor office and she was in the garden of the marshal's house playing with the youngest of her sons. Although he now wondered if he was indeed the father, Nallikino could not remember the lad's name. He did not spend much of his precious time with Elyda talking about her children.

"I have a son," he murmured aloud. He felt proud and frustrated. He longed to talk to her, but he did not dare to approach her. He was glad that she was still in Donsgrat.

Usually she spent the summer months with her parents on their estate near Danillingrat, and every spare evening he used to ride over there for dinner and often he would stay the night under her parents' roof. At first he had felt that he was betraying their hospitality every time he crept along the dark landings between his bedroom and hers, but very early one morning he had met her father. Embarrassment had turned to amazement when her father had punched him lightly on the arm, saying, "Glad you're showing my darling girl how a gentleman behaves." After breakfast, her mother had said, "We were fools to let her marry him... I suppose we were so flattered the great man was taking an interest in her, we didn't see past his reputation... Mind you take the best care of her you can." Thereafter the subject was never mentioned again.

He would miss those summer evenings, dinners as a welcome guest, almost a member of the family, strolls in the park, nights of passion and affection.

He had to wait to talk to Elyda until the evening before he left for the Heartlands. With a parcel of clothes in need of alterations under her arm, she knocked on the door of his house. She winced when he embraced her, then lifted her blouse to show him the bruises on her back.

"Erwan beat me because I am not pregnant. Woldymer Chrezdonow had four sons, so he must have four sons. According to him it is my fault I am not pregnant this month," she said in the flat listless voice in which she always spoke of her husband, almost as though she agreed that she was to blame.

Nallikino felt the desire to murder rise in him. He gripped his right hand in his left behind his back, and did not criticise Filowet, because criticism did not help Elyda.

"He says I must stay in Donsgrat until I'm pregnant so I don't know when I'll see next Mamma and Papa." She started to cry into her lover's shoulder and he held her as gently as he could.

They sat together in his small drawing room. She wanted to plan to meet again.

He said, "I leave tomorrow. I don't know how long I'll be away. He wants me to recruit ten thousand Heartlanders."

"This Chrezdonow nonsense!" Elyda leapt to her feet. "I blame that appalling man Shennikov."

"That appalling captain thinks we have a son."

She began to cry again. Of their many partings this was one of the more difficult.

5.

In olden days, the Heartlands were called the Settlement, because this area of low wooded hills and fertile valleys was colonised by the refugees who over a thousand years before had fled from religious persecution in their own country. From the Third Incarnation to the Tenth, the Settlers had lived peacefully and more or less happily in self-sufficient, self-governing villages. Those times before emperors, landlords or serfs resonated through the stories as idyllic.

Then came the Disruption, the civil war that shredded the peace of the Settlement. The Eleventh Incarnation withdrew to the north bank of the river Don to meditate in the wilderness and in the absence of His mediation, disputes erupted into fistfights and village fought village with knives and spades. Heartlander killed Heartlander until in the middle of a battle a young peasant called Woldymer was knocked unconscious and on waking had a vision of the Third Incarnation.

Once he and his ten thousand followers had set off on their conquests, the Settlers who stayed at home remembered how to resolve disagreements without violence. Over the years, the Eleventh Incarnation's hermitage on the north bank of the Don grew into Donsgrat abbey, and Woldymer bequeathed his growing empire to his son Nikolka the First, who in due course passed it on to his son Fyedor the First and Great. In the imperial year 86, Fyedor changed the name of the Settlement to the Heartlands and decreed that they keep their traditional egalitarian structures. The villages were run by councils of elders, advised by the local priests, and as Nallikino was discovering, by the local wise women.

In three villages already, the wise women had challenged him. Weather-beaten wrinkled peasants who dared to look him in the face because they were freeborn, they asked, "Is the empire at war with the Katorians or the K'firis again?"

"No," he replied.

"Is the war in the east then?"

"There isn't a war."

"Then why do you take our boys away from us?"

"Because the Third Army needs them."

The wise women were no more convinced by Nallikino's words than he was.

On his eighth day in the Heartlands, the air was fresh and sparkling. The thunderstorm that had ripped across the sky the night before had cleared the humidity, and the sun shone from cloudless blue. It ought to have been a good morning to be alive. Nallikino, at the head of the column of recruiters, glanced sourly over his shoulder at Captain Shennikov, who, oddly, appeared to be dozing.

The colonel pulled his horse to the side of the imperial highway and let the rest of the column jog past him. His soldiers looked impressive. He fell in at the rear alongside Sergeant Pridushkin, nicknamed Long Ears because he picked up every passing rumour and indulged in all the scams that made army life tolerable. Over their years of service, he and Nallikino had learned wary respect for each other.

Their horses trotted side by side for about a mile. Nallikino broke the silence by asking, "What do you think of all this?"

"It's beautiful, sir."

"I mean what do you think of what we are doing?"

"Since when did the army pay me to think sir?" Pridushkin's grin showed a gap in his front teeth. "Seriously, I think the same as what you do. I can't see us drilling savvy into these kids along with proper marching order. They'll be no bloody use to the Third Army, so what we're doing tearing them from their mammies' skirts is stupid as well as cruel. But you could make it easier on their mammies and pappies, you could tell them you're a Nallikino, and tell them Chrezdonow himself wants their sons."

"You think I should lie to them?"

"Yes sir, I do sir. It's rubbish, but it's rubbish as'll ease their hearts. Trust me, they'll cry with pride as well as grief watching their boys march away to serve the great Woldymer."

Before Nallikino could thank him, Pridushkin continued more quietly, "I'm not sure what the marshal plans for them but I reckon it's something to do with the Okhpat goldfields. While you was in Danillingrat I got sent up there a couple of times on the supply trains. Horrible place Okhpat is, marshes and swamps and insects that like nothing so much as human blood. Drain you dry they do. Conditions for the miners are terrible... you wouldn't keep a pig in that filth... and just as bad for the Fourth Army lads who guard them. When the miners rebel, which they will, the guards will likely side with them. We both know the troubles will come and it's my guess they'll start in the Okhpat, and I'll tell you something else, these Heartlanders don't have no chance up in the marshes. They're too soft and a year isn't enough to toughen them up."

Pridushkin slowed his horse so that he and Nallikino dropped five or six lengths behind the last of the troopers, and whispered, "What's more, there's that Captain Shennikov. Don't trust him no further than you can throw him. He's been heard talking about the Okhpat goldfields like he's involved with the supply trains. It's Captain Khren's job, always has been, ever since they opened the railway into the goldfields. You have to ask yourself why Shennikov's sticking his nose in."

"Do I indeed," Nallikino said noncommittally, before he nudged his horse to a canter to overtake the rest of the men. He was at the front as they swept from the imperial highway down the track that led to the village that was that morning's destination.

They were expected. The recruiters could rely on the Heartlanders to pass the news from one place to the next. The local minister had thirty-three men aged between eighteen and twenty-four lined up in front of the whitewashed chapel. Their parents and siblings stood close to them, watching the soldiers with a mixture of curiosity and resentment. Nallikino decided to give them a speech about the return of Chrezdonow and was astonished to see smiles on the peasant faces.

"Praise be," someone in the crowd said, and others repeated it. "Praise be, Chrezdonow walks among us again."

Shennikov was cross. "They didn't need to know about Chrezdonow, so why did you tell them?"

"To make it easier for them."

"They're peasants. They're used to hardship."

The start of an argument was interrupted by the local minister who told them, "One boy's not here. He's still laid out on his bed after an accident this morning."

"An accident?" Shennikov sneered. "I'll go and investigate this so-called accident."

Irritated by Shennikov's keenness, Nallikino said, "You check the fitness of the men here, and I'll visit the chap who's injured."

"I think you should check the men while I do the visiting."

Nallikino thought of himself as a practical man, not given to fancy, yet when he looked into the captain's eyes, he saw a will to control that appalled him and the words 'soul eater' sprang into his mind. Although he did not believe in the existence of souls, Nallikino was not prepared to feed the captain's hunger, so he beckoned to the elders, "Take me to the injured lad."

Two of the elders guided Nallikino a little way along the wide main street, then down a narrower alley that led past the cowsheds almost to the edge of the village. They pointed to a cottage that stood apart from the others, its garden a riot of colour, as if the inhabitants cultivated flowers for the joy of them as well as the uses.

An old woman, with forearms like hams folded round her stomach, did not so much sit as lean backwards on a bench by the eaved door. Inwardly, Nallikino groaned in recognition of a wise woman. Outwardly, he gave her a polite good morning.

"Good morning to you too, young man. What a fine uniform you wear. Shame 'bout the mud you got on your boots coming through the puddles. You've dirtied them for nothing 'cos you can't come in."

Nallikino suddenly realised that the elders who had accompanied him had anticipated this confrontation. Before he could decide on his tactics, the old woman shouted, "There's nothing for you two to gawp at. Clear off the pair of you."

"Come on Maria," one grumbled but she waved them away, and reluctantly they plodded back towards the main street.

"It's my duty to see the youngster who's supposed to have had an accident this morning," Nallikino said quietly.

"Duty!" Maria sniffed. "Pigs' tails and trotters to your duty. You hate this duty of yours."

"Whether I like it or not is irrelevant. It is my duty to decide if the boy is fit for the army."

"Doctor are you as well as army man? Tough. You can't see Nikolas, not while the kam is with him. It's the kam who'll decide on his fitness, not you…"

Maria's voice faded, as Nallikino's attention poured from the present into the past.

Himself, head high to his uncle's desk. His treble voice asking, "Uncle Stepano, what's a kam?"

Stepano's reply, "A kam is Father Kazimir, Morya the cook and the Wicked Emperor rolled into one," was scary because Father Kazimir and Morya were ogres present in his life and the Wicked Emperor of story was worse.

On another occasion, Stepano added more information based on his studies of the local tribe, the Kohantsi, "A kam does magic, bad magic, that works because the tribals are convinced it works. If you don't believe bad magic works, it doesn't. That's why the kams don't have any power over us."

The boy Aleksandr eight years old, maybe nine, out of the house before the servants woke and off on an adventure of his own. The morning mist beside the river. The path overgrown by grasses as tall as he was. The shock when the tribal reared up in front of him. The smell of the man - sweat and rotten fish and foul breath as he snarled and cursed. Little Aleksandr rooted to the ground, too afraid to run for home until the kam had gone. Scared Aleksandr who did not dare to tell anyone what had happened, but who watched his mother every day and when she fell ill prayed to the Most Holy to make her well again. Sorrowful Aleksandr who did not pray again after she died as the kam had predicted she would.

"Don't you drift off on a journey too!" Maria hauled herself off the bench and waddled down the path to the garden gate. She flapped her hand under his nose. He jumped and apologised.

"Have kams got something on you then that there's at least one in your past and one in your present?" she asked, then added slyly, "If you want to know if there's kams in your future, I can read your palm for you. Kolli's da taught him and me both. Kolli does palms for lots of gentlemen at the horse fair every year, aye and some ladies too. Stuck here in the village I don't get much of a chance to practise, strangers don't pass this way, and the folk round here reckon I know too much about them since I saw most of them in their skins when they got born and I'll see some of them in their skins again when they die... Go on, let me see if there's kams in your future."

"What if you can see the fate of the ten thousand in my hand?"

"Didn't you hear what I said? Those boys lined up by the chapel into this world, I helped them into this world... Let's just say I know the ones you take are dead to us the moment they leave us. Nothing in your hand will shock me." Nevertheless, when she lifted his palms close enough to her eyes to see the lines, she shivered and muttered, "May the Most Holy protect and guide you!"

"What did you see? Was it war? Was it death?"

"Of course death. Death can't shock me... It's the kams. There's at least two, maybe three in your future and they stand at the forks in your life road. It's like you have choices and when you choose what to do or not do, I pray you let the Most Holy guide you... You ask Him, are you an officer or are you a man? If the officer chooses the path, you've done your precious duty. If the man chooses it will cost the officer dear, but the man's choices are the right ones."

"Which do you think I am, the officer or the man?"

"I'm just an old peasant woman, what do I know of your world?"

"More than you're pretending."

She smiled her sly smile, "I'll say this then. Most men think with their balls and don't use their brains. You're different. You've got the balls, and a son to prove it, for all you're not a married man, but you're ruled by your head. At the moment, you're going round and round in your head when in this instance you need to let your balls do the thinking. Well, perhaps not your balls. Your gut. Belly over brain. You'll be a no good soldier, and a real fine man."

The colours of the rain-battered flowers in the garden suddenly seemed very bright. Nallikino kissed Maria's wrinkled cheek.

"I'll try to be a man," he said.

When the kam emerged form the cottage, Nallikino recognised him. They had often discussed the merits of golden horses at the annual fair in Donsgrat. Heretofore he had never perceived any special powers in the wizened tribal.

After Kolli had explained the nature of Nikolas's illness and shown him the unconscious youth, Nallikino agreed not to recruit him into the army.

Nikolas's stepmother was livid. "You've got to take him to be a soldier. I'm not having him go off with a kam, great-uncle or no."

As patiently as possible, the colonel suggested, "Imagine he has a rifle in his hand when he goes into another trance."

"He won't," the stepmother snapped.

"Kolli says he might unless he learns to control himself. I value Kolli's opinion. I can't risk the lives of other soldiers. I won't recruit him." He walked away before the stepmother could protest further. Maria who had observed the whole exchange called after Nallikino as he strode through the mud back to the village square, "Good on the man."

"Don't tell me you couldn't spot a malingerer when you saw one," Shennikov jeered the next time that he and Nallikino were alone. The colonel forced himself to count to ten, to open his clenched fists and tensed shoulders before he dared to reply, "Because you have in your hands the good name of the woman I... a woman I hold in high esteem, you think you can behave as rudely as you like. I suggest you do not push me past the point of recklessness."

6.

To the end of her days Tenja insisted that her sighting of Shennikov at the station was more than chance or coincidence, although she stopped short of calling it fate or predestination. Moments after her return to the capital from summer holidays in the country, she glimpsed him on the far side of the concourse. Insofar as she could hurry through the crowd of the passengers who had just disembarked from the train, she hurried after him and emerged into the street just in time to see him climb into a cab drawn by a stocky dun pony. Amidst the usual western reds, the so-called golden horse was a distinctive creature. Watching it set off in the direction of the Third Ring, rather than the Fifth where his parents lived, Tenja wondered what on earth Voldimir Shennikov was up to.

Traffic was so heavy that the cab she hired could not keep pace with his. For old times' sake she asked her driver to drop her by the statue of Fyedor the Great.

"What brings him here do you think? And why was he wearing civilian clothes when last I saw of him he was a novice monk?" she demanded, but neither the bronze emperor nor the proud stallion condescended to reply. She walked the rest of the way home.

In the Nobles' Avenue she met the cab drawn by the dun pony coming the other way, and flagged it down so that she could ask the driver where he had dropped his last passenger.

"At the monastery," was the reply. "Odd that. He weren't no priest. No dress, see, and a proper tip, not a blessing, which is all them crows give."

Tenja gave him a quarter crown.

She walked past her house to the bridge between the Second and First Rings, pretending that she wanted to look at the view across the Olnish. She was not waiting for anyone.

Eventually three civilians emerged from the monastery gate and strolled down the road. Awareness of his companions was pushed from Tenja's mind as Shennikov approached. The years disappeared. She forgot the end and remembered only the perfection of their affair.

He bowed very low to her. Neither of them spoke, because words were limited, trivial. Tenja felt that in his company she was more than she could be apart from him, as if he was her completion. Her head swam.

A few seconds lasted forever. He said, regretfully she thought, "I must go. I have a train to catch."

Through the woolliness that passed for her intelligence Tenja could not think of the obvious questions. She wailed like a little girl, "Don't go! Please."

He did not embrace her. Standing back from her, he repeated, "I must go... You always have had the best of me."

Too flustered to speak, Tenja watched him leave, his companions in step behind him. She took the little path down to a hidden beach and for a long time sat on a rock while the waves danced in the sunshine. As her emotions settled, curiosity reasserted itself, strongly enough to impel her on a rare journey into the underworld.

"Why did Voldimir visit the monastery today?" she enquired of her guide. Balanced on three legs to scratch one of his ears with the fourth, the wolf ignored her.

"Does Voldimir exist in your world?" She was exasperated when he finished scratching and stood ready and eager to play. She asked about another former lover, and was told more than she wanted to hear, which proved that the wolf's deafness was selective.

"Is it possible for someone to hide in the mesh of the web or to fall through it?" she asked in bewilderment.

"Of course not," the wolf replied. "Everything that was or is has a scent."

"Except the one I want," Tenja muttered as he saw or heard some small movement in the tundra snow and dashed off to investigate.

A similar scene was repeated in the upper world, where her guide to the realm of the spirits spoke very fondly of the Shennikov of a decade earlier, "He's the twin who should have been born with you, but wasn't."

"So that's why I feel unfinished without him," Tenja said. "Where is he now?"

The guide behaved as though Tenja had not added the question. "You can't expect lovers to give you that sense of completion. Only your twin can provide it."

"Tell me where he is now," Tenja shouted. It was useless. Her guide did not respond, not even to her rudeness.

Tenja knocked softly on her mother's bedroom door. Fahra was brushing her long hair. It shone gold and silver in the candlelight that she preferred to the newfangled gas lamps in the rest of the house. Sometimes Tenja wished that she had inherited that fair straight hair and pale skin. Tonight she did not notice.

"How can someone very much alive in this world disappear from the sight of my guides?" she demanded, abrupt because she was worried.

Fahra put the brush down and looked at her mirror. A twin self looked back. "Ah," she said, "We've waited a long time for his return."

"You might have, I haven't... Tell me how he's managed to make himself invisible."

"I don't know. The Miacharnay do not try to hide. I don't believe the monks on the esoteric path do either. Perhaps it's a technique used by some of the other peoples. The Shoshanu maybe. After all, Maro and Nilhri walked a hundred miles and more along the Goroki ridge without anyone seeing them."

"I don't mean unnoticed in this world. I mean cut out of the web like he never existed."

Fahra picked up her hairbrush. "I'm sorry I can't help."

Tenja might have left the enigma unresolved but for her father's request that she visit his office. There she was introduced to Bogan's most valued informant, a dapper man called Ygar who worked as head steward on the Donsgrat express.

Bogan said to his daughter, "Your mother tells me you have an interest in Voldimir Shennikov. Listen to Ygar and tell me if you've any clue what your friend is up to."

"He's hardly my friend."

"Your mother implied he used to be more than that."

Ygar cleared his throat, "Before you get into the kind of discussion fathers are better off not having with grown-up daughters..." He began to describe the journeys of Captain Shennikov and Major

Zharalov since the rumours that Filowet was the reincarnation of Woldymer Chrezdonow had begun to circulate around Donsgrat.

First, the pair had travelled from Donsgrat to the Nilentin capital where they had stayed two days before returning home. On both trips they had remained in their compartment, and on their rare forays along the corridors they wore civilian suits. They next came to Ygar's attention on a trip to the imperial capital when they flaunted the red and gold of the Third Army uniform to such effect that their boisterousness offended an elderly baroness, who complained to the stewards at tedious length.

On their return journey to Donsgrat, Shennikov and Zharalov had ten crates of extra luggage, which they stored in a locked passenger compartment. Equipped with the key to every door on the train, Ygar investigated the crates, and greatly to his alarm discovered that they contained rifles of the Western War vintage.

Donsgrat's stationmaster Galiskin confirmed that all ten crates had travelled to the Okhpat goldfields on the next supply train, and that Major Zharalov and half a dozen Third Army men had joined the regular Fourth Army soldiers for the trip. Meanwhile Shennikov had been busy in the Heartlands.

The night prior to this meeting, Ygar had been astonished to spot Shennikov here in the capital. "You ever been in that restaurant at the back of the station? The food's almost as good as the prices. That's where he was, arguing with two men. Course I spied on them, saw the two unknowns get aboard the slow train to Arbitsk. Third class coach. Not that they were poor, for all they wore second-hand suits and walked like their shoes hurt, they were only pretending. They had too much life in their eyes to have lived poor," Ygar said.

Tenja mentioned the two companions Shennikov had acquired from the monastery, but her descriptions were too nondescript for Ygar to be sure that they were the men he had seen.

Finally, Tenja asked, "What do you think is going on?"

"I don't know," Bogan replied gloomily. "I can't see minions like Zharalov or your Shennikov travelling all over the place without their commander's permission any more than I can figure out why it's in the interests of Erwan Filowet to ferment trouble in the goldfields."

"What does the Minister think?"

"Take your pick. One or all of the following. That the transport of rifles on a passenger train, though peculiar, is the army's business, not mine. That if I am concerned, I should talk to the junior minister for the army, which I won't bother with, as I think the wretched man is an unimaginative pen-pushing martinet and he thinks I'm too nice to my employees. That perhaps my spies give me too much information. That His Imperial Majesty does not care whether Marshal Filowet is the reincarnation of the first Chrezdonow or not, so long as he keeps the peace east of the Manahantjils, and that if he needs to add ten thousand Heartlanders to the Third Army he's welcome to, provided that he doesn't expect the Treasury to pay for them... In other words, don't bother him when he has to cope with the emperor's broken heart and the never-ending drift of peasants away from the land."

"You're both really worried aren't you?" Tenja looked from her father to Ygar.

"The more so when you tell me uncle Wassil's involved," her father replied.

Ygar said, "Last time he had ten thousand Heartlanders at his back, Woldymer Chrezdonow conquered an empire. You've got to wonder what exactly he's planning to do this time."

Tenja decided to find out. She went back to her wolf and through patient questioning discovered that he could detail Shennikov's career up to the spring of 610. At that point Brother Voldimir left the church of his own volition and shortly afterwards disappeared from the web.

Thinking that perhaps his next teacher had taught him how to disappear she ordered the wolf to tell her the present whereabouts of Konstanti Rylov.

7.

When Tenja told her parents that she was going to the Heartlands in pursuit of information about Shennikov, her mother gave her kind messages to pass to "that nice Major Nallikino."

Tenja caught the next train to Donsgrat.

Going towards the man without whom she was less than whole, going away, further and further away, from loving him, she tried not to think too much about him. West of the Manahantjils, the land basked in the warm autumn sunshine. Gazing out of the windows she looked for visible signs of change.

Theoretically she already knew about the changes in the rural economy, because her radical friends organised lectures during the winters. With academic impersonality, the speakers informed the small select audience about the shift from agriculture on the western plains to the new and growing industries of the east, about depopulation, about new fashions in farming. As a member of the high nobility, Tenja was well placed to observe some of the changes, as old landed families had to service high mortgages out of diminishing incomes or – the greatest shame – to divide and sell property.

As a teacher in the Fifth Ring, she could see how fast patterns of life were evolving there too. When Dora Sillin opened the school, the locals scoffed. As they expected their children to stay in the social class into which they had been born, they could not see the point of education. Then self-employed craftsmen began to discover that their handmade items could not compete with factory products. Many lost their businesses and had to choose between unskilled labour for low wages or starvation. Bitter and resentful, they pushed their sons into school for the chance to move out of the Fifth Ring. One of Dora's first pupils was now a teacher, another was training to be a doctor and several more had entered government service. The academics called the process by which the people Tenja knew lost and gained, gained and lost, *social mobility*. The words struck her as dry.

Through the compartment window, she saw deserted villages, where the roofs of empty cottages sagged and doors hung askew on rusty hinges, and ungrazed meadows and untilled fields where grasses and flowers overtopped dilapidated fences. Passing mile after mile after mile of neglected farmland that had been and could again be rich and productive, she could not help feeling guilty. The railways had changed the lives of millions of people, and not all the changes were beneficial or easy to accept.

She had supper brought to her compartment, and ate while she gazed at the passing countryside. Gradually the colours turned from greens to golds to pinks to greys when the evening sun slid under the horizon. She watched the land until it was too dark to see.

On the descent down the eastern side of the Manahantjil hills in the morning, Tenja began to see evidence of industrialization. Centuries earlier, the uplands had been home to the Elantsim people who lived off their herds of sheep. Sheep still grazed the moors, but steam powered woollen mills had replaced most of the original handloom weavers even before the railway arrived. The stark brick mills were hard and angular amidst the rounded hills and wide valleys.

Then the moors turned to forest that was torn and gashed by open cast mines and spoil tips from the deep shafts. Geological quirks meant that the bedrock below the trees was layered with seams of coal, semi-precious stones and other minerals previously of little value, now in demand for one industrial use or another. At Khila a pretty woman with rings on every finger and bracelets up both arms boarded the train to sell gemstones and jewellery to the passengers in the lounge car. Several of the officers bought trinkets for their wives or daughters.

On the long dreary ride from Khila to Donsgrat, Tenja saw signs of human activity whenever she was awake. Along the left side of the track, trees and undergrowth had been cut back to allow for the erection of poles and wires for the new Sillin-Vrekov Telegraph Company. Day and night, the train stopped at least once an hour at a new town where the air reeked of smoke and chemicals, or at one or other of the private stations built by landowners whose forebears had fought the Kohantsi and carved estates out of virgin forest.

Much as she remembered it, the old town of Donsgrat nestled between the river and the sheer chalky cliff. One new factory sat in solitude on the western outskirts, and in place of the open fields on the south bank of the Don stood a small town of green canvas tents to shelter the ten thousand Heartland recruits. Shortly before the train slipped into the station, Tenja noticed that the abbey, which dominated the town from its elevated position below the cliff, was encased in scaffolding.

Stationmaster Galiskin who waited on the platform to greet the arrivals from the first class coaches, was a friend from Tenja's childhood. Along with extra bulk, he had gained in self-importance since their last meeting. Delighted to see her, he assured her that he would do everything he could to make her stay in the town pleasant. She gave him an invitation to deliver personally to Major Nallikino.

"It's Colonel Nallikino these days," Galiskin corrected.

Tenja smiled, "My mother will be pleased to hear of his promotion. She suggested that I invite him to dinner."

Tenja occupied the Imperial Suite at the Imperial Hotel, which as the owner's daughter she was bound to do, though she found the bedroom draughty. The staff were attentive to her needs and by the dawn of the next morning they had provided a guide, horses and everything else necessary for an expedition to where Father Konstanti lived in the Heartlands.

8.

Not a natural horsewoman, Tenja appreciated the stolidness of her mount. Her guide, a cheerful man in his fifties, said, "His hide may not be golden but his heart is." They jogged for miles along the highway that ran from the Donsgrat ferry to the tax halls at Zwemco lake.

The few locals they passed on the road were briskly cheerful. Tenja did not cherish fond illusions about country life. Peasants were not picturesque. They worked hard in all weathers and were totally dependent upon the fruits of their labours. In bad seasons, when the frosts damaged the blossoms on the trees, when the rains flooded the fields, when the droughts parched the seedlings, they went hungry, and where their owners were uncharitable, they died of starvation. The tribulations of their lives did not make them better or nobler than anyone else, though some of Tenja's city-bred friends would have it so. Nonetheless, the Heartlanders had an openness and a dignity that warmed her heart.

As the shadows lengthened on that sunny autumn afternoon, they reached the Zwemco lake. Tenja's thigh muscles wobbled when she dismounted and tried to walk towards the man. He was so absorbed in the task of mending his nets that he seemed oblivious of her arrival. At a polite distance, she stopped and said, "Good day Father."

With a long sigh, he replied without looking at her, "He warned me you'd come to bother me Countess Sillin-Vrekov. He told me to expect you in the spring. You are a little ahead of yourself."

Tenja stepped back, her stomach suddenly hollow. Carefully the hermit rolled and picked up his net, rose easily to his feet and turned to her. He reeked of fish, and his chin was stained red by the blackberries he had recently eaten. "First you will see the paintings. They are after all the draw for most of my visitors." His smile revealed blackened stumps of teeth.

She followed him along the lakeshore and when they rounded the headland she was astonished to see the strange construction that was his gallery. Built on stilts, it lent out over the waters of the lake. She clambered after him up the ladder, and was required to wait by the door until he had lit the candle below each of the twenty-three portraits. Then she was allowed to look, while he went down to the shack in which he cooked and slept.

Simple, strong, the portraits were great art, and they were more than art, because each was imbued with the spirit of the person it depicted. Tenja was shifted to a place that touched the other worlds while she remained firmly rooted in the ordinary one. As she moved slowly round the room from the First Incarnation to the Twenty-Third, she felt in her head and in her solar plexus that the circle of her life turned.

Father Konstanti returned with two mugs of tea and invited her to be seated. In the absence of chairs or cushions, she was obliged to sit on bare boards. She chose to position herself beneath the portrait of the Third Incarnation, one of only three lives for which the Most Holy had chosen a woman's skin.

The hermit waved his hands at the paintings. "These are the penance for my misdeeds, the only penance which the Most Holy demanded of me, and no penance because in the making of them I came to know Him a little better. The more I know Him the more I love Him. Despite the fact that Father Wassil severed me, He still speaks to me sometimes. At His will, not mine. I speak to you today only to accord with His will. I do not want to dwell on the past. He tells me I must. It is another step on my road to forgiveness, He says...

"To begin at my beginning, I am Heartland born and bred. My father worked at the tax halls, which is why I had enough education to read the lists of produce and to do the weights and measures and simple mathematics needed to follow in his footsteps, and that's why I quickly got made corporal, then sergeant, last time the recruitment officers took young men from the Heartlands.

"The history books tell you seventy thousand Heartlanders were wiped out in less than three months on the Goroki ridge. It's not quite true. Not all of us died. I did not die. I wanted to, but the Most Holy didn't let me. Once He'd sunk His teeth into my soul He didn't let go. When I tried to get myself killed, He made the bullets swerve away from me. Men to my left were blown to smithereens: men to my right were blasted to bits. I was unscathed. I was called lucky by a lieutenant, two hours later he was dead. I was called blessed by a major, within a day he died screaming for his mother.

"Madness by day, madness by night too because He invaded my dreams. 'I'm waiting for you. Come to Me,' He said. At last I couldn't stand it any longer. 'All right, you bastard, you win,' I told Him. I deserted the trench and I walked away from the front line and on along the Goroki ridge. Nobody stopped me. Nobody challenged me, until that awful little bird attacked me and luckily for me, two kams appeared and drove it off. One was the Miacharnay, your uncle, and the other was the Shoshanu, Nilhri, who gave almost the last drop of his life strength to deliver the guardian's message. With the little he had left, he dictated what he could remember of his tradition before it died with him... I was his scribe... My notebooks came to the Monastery of the Most Holy with me.

"At the gate, I was refused entry until a messenger came running from the Most Holy's office, saying, 'The Most Holy wants to see this man immediately.' How can I describe that first meeting with the Most Holy?"

"They say He is greatly changed," Tenja said gently.

Father Konstanti was vehement, "Only the outer shell has changed. Only the outer shell can change. The core of Him is unchanging and eternal. He set my feet upon the Esoteric Path, which annoyed Father Wassil because I wasn't well read and found those early days of book learning a struggle. Father Wassil never thought me worthy. It took me many years of hating him to realise how his obstructions had strengthened me, but apart from how I felt about Wassil I walked the path as straight and true as I could. Until I met Brother Voldimir."

For the first time, Father Konstanti met Tenja's eyes and held her gaze. "I do not need to remind you how beautiful he was. He came to me as my student and I loved him in all the ways one man can love another, bar one, and I wanted to love him like that too. Despite the army and the monastic life, I was ignorant because nobody, not a woman, not a man, had aroused in me the feeling that Voldimir did. Intellectually I knew of the forbidden love, but I did not, could not apply my intellect to my feeling. I could not deny him. When he asked me about Shoshanu customs to compare them with what he had learned of Miacharnay tradition, I told him without asking how he had discovered Miacharnay secrets. He was of course using your love as he used mine and like you I gave him what he wanted, except I stopped short of the final sin. In the end when he offered me his body in exchange to the key to the underworld, I found the determination to deny him."

Tenja's cheeks burned with shame. An expression of triumph flashed across Konstanti's face. He seemed to listen for a moment, then, almost as embarrassed as she was, he continued, "Actually my first denial was not effective. One day he stood close to me and he ... caressed my face, my back, kissed my mouth. Desire almost consumed me. The Most Holy insists that I confess this. We are the same you and I. We wanted to love him every way one person can love another. The truth is we still do."

Tenja bowed her head. Her heart and her breathing were fast.

"The rest is quickly told. Neither of us gave him the key to the Below. I confessed to Wassil how but not why Voldimir had tempted me, and was severed and dismissed. I went to a small hermitage on the edge of the tundra where I painted these portraits. Then the Most Holy let me come home. For years that was the whole story....

"A few weeks ago Voldimir came to tell me Marshal Filowet was the reincarnation of Woldymer Chrezdonow. When I said nonsense, he laughed. Like music his laughter was... He is as beautiful as he ever was..."

Her voice raspy, Tenja interrupted Konstanti's silence to ask, "Did he tell you what the marshal plans to do as Chrezdonow reborn?"

Konstanti nodded his head in approval, "I asked him the same thing. He refused to tell me because he did not expect me to lie when you came here with your meddlesome questions. He gave me a message for you. I am to beg you not to interfere. For the love that he has for you, please leave him to do as he must. When his task is finished he will be free to be with you, which is his heart's desire, and his and your destiny. According to him."

9.

In defiance of convention, Tenja received her dinner guest Colonel Aleksandr Nallikino in the privacy of her suite at the hotel. She ordered candles rather than light the gas lamps because she wanted to create a particular atmosphere. If she appeared seductive, so much the better: she wanted her guest to relax, to trust, to confide.

While the servants were present, Colonel Nallikino showed easy social skills. He was well presented, good looking, politely attentive, almost flirtatious, not at all the provincial bore she had dreaded, and she easily responded in kind. They sat on either side of the log fire, sipping aperitifs, chatting brightly while the hotel staff finished the preparations for dinner. After Tenja had dismissed the servants, she was gratified by the quiver - anticipation? excitement? – that passed through the colonel's body, but then he behaved as though the waiters had taken his vitality with them. Through the entrees, through the fish course, through the main course, his conversation was stilted, awkward. Whenever Tenja tried to lead him towards Shennikov, Filowet, the current situation, he skittered and sidestepped like a shy young horse, and she had to rein in her irritation.

At last, he laid his knife and fork on his plate and pushed them aside. His glass was empty. He reached over to the sideboard for the fresh bottle of Mardestiniak brandy, and poured himself a generous measure. In breach of perfect manners, he did not offer her any. She bit her lower lip, to remind herself to let him take his time.

With a rueful smile he raised the glass to her in silent toast, drank the contents in one, and banged the glass down on the polished table more forcefully than he meant to. "It's more difficult than I thought it would be," he said. "I came to meet you with every intention of telling you exactly what is happening here in Donsgrat but I find the traitor's role distasteful... When you look at me Countess, what do you see?"

"Well," she began, slowly, a small signal of possibility.

"That's not quite what I meant," he responded gently. "Looking at you, I see a most attractive woman, but also and at this moment more importantly, I see the same quality that the Countess your mother has, that the abbot has, that a certain Que-Que horse dealer has ..."

"Like them I walk the worlds. I am a kam," Tenja said.

"As a kam, do you see me as an officer of the Third Army or as a man?" He held his breath while she answered a little too flippantly, "Since they do not recruit women into the Third or any other Army, you must be a man before you can be an officer."

"I appreciate the obviousness," he said dryly. He poured more brandy, two glasses this time, and handed one to her. Then he told everything he knew and everything he thought and almost everything he felt about Filowet's emergence as Chrezdonow and the recruitment of the ten thousand Heartlanders, and because she was aware how difficult it was for him to go against his code as an officer and to betray so many secrets, she had not the heart to tell him that she already knew most of what he was telling her, and more besides, such as the relocation of ten crates of obsolescent rifles.

The colonel's loathing for the whole business shone crystal clear. "I lie awake at night and I fantasise about how and where and when I could end it. You have no idea how much I want to kill Erwan Filowet. He is a brute and a bully, and sober as Chrezdonow he is more of a monster than he was as Filowet the drunk. I don't point the gun at him. I don't pull the trigger. I can't. I tell myself I can't blacken my family name. The truth is my motives are not clean." The appeal in his expression asked a slightly different question, 'You don't think I'm a coward do you?'

Very carefully, Tenja said, "I think I understand... When my mother suggested I talk with you, she also expressed a concern for Madame Filowet. I am to pass on a message. Madame Filowet's friends matter now more than before."

Nallikino drained the last drops from his second glass. While he concentrated on pouring the next one, he said, "Please thank Countess Fahra for her thoughtfulness, assure her that I remain Madame Filowet's true friend. Which is of course the reason why I cannot kill her husband. Assassination – the grand gesture for a noble cause – is one thing, murder quite another."

"I understand, perhaps better than you think." She inhaled deeply, "You see my involvement is also personal. I used to know Captain Shennikov rather well."

"I think I remember, you danced with him at that ball didn't you?"

"And saw him several times during his noviciate. Four years ago he left the monastery and disappeared... I asked you to dine with me tonight because I hoped you might be able to tell me where he went and what he did after he left the church."

"I regret I can't. I only know he came back to the army about a year ago. I can't be more precise because I was in Danillingrat."

"Would you be able to look at his records?"

"Not easily. I'm not part of the charmed circle. Filowet uses me because of my name. Nallikinos served the real Chrezdonow and his son and grandson... Mention of my ancestors reminds me. I have to loan you something." He stood up from the table and searched in the pocket of his greatcoat which had been hung on the back of the door. He placed a slim wooden box on his side of the table, before he continued, "As to why I'm not trusted... Shennikov knows of my involvement with Madame Filowet. He hasn't told the marshal yet. He may have been a friend of yours but he is a nasty piece of work..."

"I know... However much I want to believe he is capable of goodness, I keep discovering new twists to his nastiness." She rose from her chair and winced when she used muscles that were still sore after her ride to the Heartlands.

"I suppose we're all a mixture of good and bad," Nallikino said to Tenja's back. She hobbled into the bedroom and returned with a piece of paper to show her guest.

It was a quick pencil sketch of Shennikov's head and shoulders, done by Father Konstanti a few weeks earlier. "Better you have it as a reminder of his beauty than I drool over it," the hermit had said as he offered her the picture.

Tenja said as she let Nallikino see the portrait, "Every time I look at it I try to see the nastiness. It's hidden from me."

"But it is there," Nallikino said, his voice high with alarm. His finger shook as he pointed at the smudge on the left side of Shennikov's chest. "He's a shadow heart."

Tenja started to tremble, her body able to accept what her mind refused to comprehend, and she repeated stupidly, "A shadow heart?"

"Among the Kohantsi, there are two sorts of kams, the so-called pale hearts, usually women, who work spiteful kinds of magic, and the so-called shadow hearts, usually men, who work seriously nasty kinds of magic. That's as much as I know. My uncle Stepano is the real scholar – corresponds with experts on other tribes from all over the empire, General Lasaryk, Professor Chrezdonow... You're shaking! Sit down... Let me get you another drink. I didn't realise how talk of shadow hearts would upset you." With a hand under her elbow to steady her, he helped her to one of the armchairs by the fire before he busied himself, pouring her another brandy, and putting fresh logs on the fire. The little wooden box stayed unnoticed amidst the empty plates on the table.

Tenja demanded abruptly, "Can these shadow hearts cut themselves out of the web?"

Nallikino who was squatting on his heels in front of the fire, turned to look at her, concern and incomprehension in his expression.

"Uncle Stepano's the expert, not me." He stabbed so viciously at a log with the poker that it crumbled with a sudden flare of light. "If it's mean and destructive, I'm sure a shadow heart can do it."

"He's Settler through and through, he can't possibly be any kind of kam," Tenja announced.

Nallikino lent the poker against the corner of the fireplace and said with quiet authority, "He may be as Settler as I am, but he is a shadow heart."

Tenja said in a small voice, "I just don't want to admit he's a kam because I don't want to have to go where knowing will take me."

"And where might that be?"

Tenja was quiet for a while before she replied. She stared at the candles through her glass. "The ancestors call Voldimir my twin even though he's not my parents' son. He believes he and I are destined to be together when this, whatever this is, is all over. At least, that's what he told Father Konstanti, who told me. Perhaps it's a clever ploy to divert me. To play on my affections so I won't try to oppose him ... I don't actually love him, but the Most Holy knows I'm so mixed up with him that I can't imagine loving anyone else... The truth is, I so hate what he's doing that I need to find out how he's doing it in order to fight him on his ground. Because fight him I will."

"Sounds like you need to talk to my uncle," Nallikino said, "I'll write an introduction for you. I'm sure he'll be delighted to meet you."

"Thank you. I'd like to meet him too. But I must also talk to a shadow heart."

"My dear girl! You can't! It's far too dangerous!" Nallikino protested. Subjected to Tenja's glare, most men would have backed down and apologised, but this one had the courage and concern to persist, "The Kohantsi may not be the force they were when my forebears fought them, but you mustn't underrate them."

10.

Three days later, Tenja stood alone on the edge of the forest east of Donsgrat. The train that had brought her disappeared into the distance. She wished that she had stayed on it for the next fifteen miles to the Nallikino family's private station. She should have asked for Stepano's advice first, she really should. Now that she needed practical support in the ordinary world, none was available.

From their sanctuary in the realm of spirits, the ancestors had encouraged her to confront their old enemy and boasted that she was the equal to three shadow hearts, but as she hesitated on the edge of Kohantsi territory, her mind was filled not by the stories of

Miacharnay successes but by the shorter sadder tales of losses and defeats.

Reluctantly she hoisted her pack on to her back and walked along the railway line parallel to the trees, not daring to enter the forest. "It's like getting into a cold bath,' she told herself, remembering how good she felt once she had warmed and dried herself.

When she came to a track made by deer where they crossed the railway to drink in the river, she muttered a prayer that the Most Holy and her guides protect her, then followed the line of hoof prints away from the Don.

Trees blocked the wide vistas that she, like most Miacharnay, preferred. She felt enclosed, almost trapped. She could not help seeing in the shapes of lichens, of fungi, of the branches, the monsters of childhood nightmares. To break their hold on her imagination she sang silly happy peasant songs. Her voice was small among the oppressive, malevolent conifers that were imbued with a spirit not natural to them. Her body sensed a vibration too low to be heard with her ears, which she tried to ignore. When it grew too insistent, she paused in her walk and took the endless stair down into the Underworld. Her wolf guide told her, "It's how the forest spreads the news of your presence."

"Does that mean the kams know I'm here?" she asked in alarm.

"If they don't, they will soon."

The deer track did not lead anywhere in particular. It merged with other tracks and separated again, and at each crossroads, she had to decide which way to go. Tempted to head back to the comparative safety of the railway and the river, she forced herself go deeper into the forest. Progress was slow. Deer were shorter than she was. Her hair, her sleeves, her pack snagged on low-hanging branches. She was scratched and cross and nervous. She stopped for a rest, drinking from the water bottle that she carried in her pack. The sky that she could not properly see through the foliage had clouded over and a heavy shower began. Wet as well as nervous and sore, she plodded on.

Faced by yet another fork in the deer path Tenja stopped. She saw, or thought she saw, a white owl ghosting across one of the possible tracks. Unsure whether the owl was friend, foe or simply disturbed from its roost, she chose its path.

Due to the cloud cover, twilight came early. In the rain, she erected the small tent that she had purchased in Donsgrat, ate and drank from her supplies, and tried to sleep. For the first time she was in the wilds at night on her own, and she was uncomfortable at every level of her being. At last she slid into dreams where her wolf warmed and comforted her.

By morning, the rain had stopped. After she had hefted her pack on to her stiff back and started to tramp through the sodden undergrowth, she pretended that the wolf followed her because it made her feel braver. Perhaps it was not pretence, perhaps she sensed a real and reassuring presence. Twice during the morning she glimpsed the white owl glide between trees ahead of her. The third time she saw it, she decided that it offered trustworthy guidance, and following it brought her in the middle of the afternoon to a path well trodden by human feet. The owl settled on a branch over her head as if to bid her farewell. As thanks for its help, she bowed to it before she set off in the footsteps of the Kohantsi.

Forewarned of her arrival, about forty people, mostly women and small children, waited for her in a clearing. Their appearance appalled her. Although she had seen poor folk in city slums and peasants weak from hunger at the end of spring, never had she seen such miserable specimens as those who stood defensively in front of their shacks. She walked towards them with her hands open and empty, to let them see that she was unarmed. Nevertheless, they shrank from her, the littlest children hiding behind their mothers' filthy skirts. She halted.

Youngsters, especially those who lived in the outer rings of the capital, usually crowded round her. Less inhibited than the offspring of the nobility, they cheekily demanded sweets that she carried in her pockets. She reached into her pack for the toffees she had bought in Donsgrat before she realised that these miserable brats would not know what they were.

The older children and the grown women glanced anxiously over their shoulders at the newest and largest of the huts. When the door opened, they dropped to their knees and touched their foreheads to the ground. Not even the emperor had such power that his people lay in the dirt for him. Despite trepidation about what might emerge, Tenja stood proud and straight.

The woman who came out of the hut had the sharp features of a weasel. She clapped her hands for her people to rise awkwardly to their feet. Tenja exhaled in relief: the imperious manner and the fierce gestures and muttered incantations hid a pale heart, whose spell was no more than a minor disturbance in the air. Tenja stood as nonchalantly as possible while it dispersed harmlessly. The scent of wolf was suddenly strong.

Perplexed by the spell's failure, the pale heart peered past Tenja, then jumped backwards, apparently able to see something more than the path, forest litter and trees that Tenja saw. Instead of threatening, the pale heart now fawned. She invited Tenja to stay for the night in one of the huts, and with reluctance Tenja accepted the invitation. They both knew that their interaction was only a prelude.

Towards sundown, the pale heart strode purposefully into the forest with something tucked under her arm. Watching her go, Tenja hoped that the other members of the tribe might relax in her absence, but they did not. Tense and impervious to her gestures of friendliness, they did not offer her a share of their food. She devoured more of the rations from her pack. The hours dragged until bedtime, when Tenja was invited to sleep in the most tumbledown of the huts. She had not noticed the pale heart's return.

Tenja did not think that she had fallen asleep until she was woken by the owl's hoot. Her head ached and her clothes were damp. The owl hooted again as if to prove that it called to her. Picking up the coat that she had folded inside out for her pillow, she stepped over sleeping stinking bodies to reach the hut door.

The night air was deliciously cool and clean after the foetid interior. She inhaled gratefully though her heartbeat thumped painfully inside her skull. Spectral in the pre-dawn light, the owl peered at her intently from the ridge of the hut's roof. When it lifted into the air she accepted its invitation to follow.

Flying slightly above head height, the owl led her for almost a mile along a little-used trail through the forest until she heard the faint whimper of a young creature in distress. Her first thought was of a fawn or cub caught in a gin trap. The cry was repeated and Tenja was suddenly certain it came from a human throat. When the owl chose a branch to land on, she knew to search the ground beneath it. Scrabbling in the leaf mould round the tree trunk she touched something damp and chill.

She scooped the soggy bundle up from the damp ground, cradled it in one arm under her coat, chafed tiny hands, chanted to hold the life within it. Deliberately dumped amidst the dead leaves, the baby had survived the night only because it had been mild for the time of year. Tenja tried very hard to suppress the rage that roiled in the pit of her stomach. She longed to scream, 'How could you?' as she remembered the parcel that the pale heart had carried and the purpose with which the woman had moved. In response to the anger, the baby squirmed and screamed feebly. Tenja shushed it and apologised and concentrated on a calming chant as she walked back to the Kohantsi camp.

Outside the hut she paused to invoke the help of all the friendly and supportive powers she could think of, the Most Holy in all

Incarnations, her mother's ancestors, her guides, before she yanked open the door. Light, which might have been the righteousness of her fury, blazed around her and terrified the dozen or so occupants of the hut as they woke from their slumbers. One of the women gazed longingly at the baby in Tenja's arms but did not dare to reach for it.

"What kind of people are you that you let this happen?" Tenja demanded. The baby grizzled, she rocked it. "Not you," she crooned, "You're innocent."

The pale heart came up behind Tenja and said, "Take it back. It is his."

Despite the pain that hammered inside her head, Tenja said, "If he wants it, he must take it from me."

The pale heart inhaled sharply, "You stand against him, you are fool. First he eat it, second he eat you."

"He can try," Tenja retorted. "Meanwhile, the baby needs dry cloths and food."

The mother did not dare to touch her child, but she fetched water, which Tenja dribbled into the baby's mouth, and chewed up morsels of food, which Tenja fed to the child, and provided a dry cloth and a handful of moss, which Tenja inexpertly wrapped around the little girl's bottom. Inwardly Tenja seethed.

The pale heart kam watched, her lips twisted into a sneer, "He come here soon."

11.

He did not arrive soon. The baby required two more small feeds and fresh clumps of moss before he sauntered out of the forest.

The shadow heart was fatter, sleeker than the rest of the Kohantsi who grovelled before him. He did not acknowledge their prostrations, for he was intent upon his victims, who waited where weak sunlight fell on the middle of the clearing. The baby lay asleep on Tenja's lap.

With apparent unconcern, the shadow heart kam ambled over the grass towards her, but he halted precisely where Tenja intended that he should, outside the protective ring of golden light that she had imagined around her.

"Give," he ordered.

"No."

"You defy me?"

"Yes."

The shadow heart waved his fingers in the air and spoke a spell. A black cat appeared at his feet, ready to pounce. To Tenja's eyes, its spitting hostility was so comic that she laughed aloud. Affronted, the cat backed delicately away. The shadow heart aimed a kick at it. It vanished. Tenja had time to wonder whether the cat had had real substance, before another of the kam's creatures launched an attack on her.

A black falcon plummeted out of the clear sky, but veered sharply away before it could tear at Tenja's eyes. As she caught the stench of singed feathers, it occurred to her that the gold light around her was fire hot.

She was tempted to taunt him over the failure of his proxies, but as she felt him gather power, she could tell that his attack had barely begun. She braced herself to resist but was unprepared for what happened.

Outside her circle of protection, blackness oozed out of the ground, rose into the air like smoke to obscure everything else. For a moment she was an autumn leaf, a tiny bubble, afloat on a dark river, until to her horror, she plunged over an edge. Once more she had that awful vertiginous sensation of falling. She fell for a long time or no time through black nothingness. She might have screamed the last of her resistance, or she might not, because her awareness was in shreds.

Across the distance inside, something whispered, "Be not afraid."

A fragment of Tenja's consciousness noticed the quaint construction: "Be not," rather than "Don't be." It helped her to gather some of the threads of herself from the void and to rework them into a form able to inhabit the ordinary world.

The ground beneath her was steady, the grass was green, the sky above was blue, but her ring of gold light lay in tatters.

Where her protection had burned, this dark new circle chilled. The baby in Tenja's arms yelled as loudly as her small lungs allowed, and in the act of shielding the child's eyes from the sight of the ghosts, Tenja found the courage to chant. The notes were robbed of their warmth by the spirits of the dead and she could feel the brightness of her life and the baby's slipping into their unquenchable bleakness.

Her attempts to pray caused the shadow heart to laugh harshly, "Your holy man no hear you."

"But I hear her," a familiar voice said jauntily. Amidst the blackness of the dead Tenja saw the flash of red. Resplendent in his uniform, Shennikov thrust past the shades to tower over her. The desperate hope that rose in her died before it was properly born, as he suggested, "You could give him the baby you know. It would be much easier all round."

"Whose side are you on?"

"That's a tricky question. I beg you, don't make me choose... You see, dear as you are to me, I am also one of them. The only reason they don't bother me now is because they know the time will come when I am as they are. They'll wait until my successor kills me as their successors killed them... Hadn't you realised that the shadow passes from one kam to the next through murder? You should have done some basic research before you came here."

"Yes," she agreed. "I should have but it doesn't matter because you have told me each of these was a murderer who was murdered in his turn." She dared to look up at the dark grey faces around her. They fed on her terror and her revulsion, but beneath their hate they hungered for some other nourishment. She searched Shennikov's face for a clue. He tried to appear bland but because he had once loved her, he was unable to hide.

Her smile was almost radiant.

Uncertainly, he said, "You've nothing to grin about! I can't help you. I'm one of them and you're going to become like me, you poor stupid idiot. You're going to have to kill this kam and take his shadow into you before he kills you."

"Not necessarily. I can see past your malice, and theirs."

She started a new chant. The previous one, the one that had failed, had been intended to drive them away, but this one offered them something. At first, her voice quavered, then as she realised that she was also singing to restore herself, it grew stronger. Her song brought back the last of the threads that had been scattered in the void and made her whole.

And the whole of her was calm. The ghosts no longer frightened her. She forgot that the shadow heart was there, she forgot that Shennikov was there. She inhaled peace, exhaled peace, she was peace and the shades of the shadow hearts kams had to partake of it or leave.

They were proud and ferocious, and they were bound by the shadow heart's command. They raged against the contradictions, they crowded in on Tenja, pressed against her, but they no longer had the power to terrify. Heedless of their fury, she sang the song that offered them release from their torment. In the end they rejected their chance to rest and refused to obey the shadow heart, who continued to flick useless fingers and shout impotent spells, until the last of the spirits had drifted away.

"There's hope for me yet." Shennikov sounded almost embarrassed before he vanished, extinguished as abruptly as the flame of a snuffed candle.

Abandoned by his lineage, the Kohantsi kam trudged across the clearing.

"Stop!" Tenja called. She stood up and hoisted the baby on to her hip. The shadow heart stopped. "You do not have my permission to go," she said with the firmness that she had acquired at the front of a classroom. "You owe me your life."

"Kill me," the shadow heart said wearily.

"I do not want your death, or your shadow. I want your knowledge. Show me how you made your creatures manifest in this world."

The shadow heart's eyes widened, "You know. You call wolf and you call owl."

"I didn't. Show me."

When she copied the spell that the shadow heart demonstrated, it brought the wolf to her side. She was more careful with the rest of the spells that she forced from the shadow heart, practising the Kohantsi words and gestures separately. As she learned how to summon her guides into the ordinary world, how to hide among the threads of the web as though she had never existed, how to work all manner of incantations that corrupted and harmed and spoiled, the peace that had filled her drained out of her, and filth seeped in. By the end of the lesson, she felt that she would never be properly clean again. The shadow might not have reached her heart, but it had surely contaminated her mind.

"Leave me," she barked.

"Where I go?" he whined.

"I don't care."

He shuffled away. He seemed thinner. The Kohantsi women came out of their huts to jeer at him. Somebody threw a stone that hit his head. He did not retaliate. Crowing women bent to pick up more stones. Tenja screamed, "NO!" as she saw the glint of sunlight on the metal of a blade.

The pale heart kam stabbed the vanquished shadow heart in the back. He pitched forward. The pale heart stood astride him while he coughed out the last of his life. After she had pulled her knife out of the body, she brandished it at the women and children around her, as if to say, "See how I have got rid of him for you. See how I look after you." She kicked the body.

Clutching the little girl, Tenja dropped to her knees and was sick. She wiped her mouth on her handkerchief. The aftertaste was vile. The baby's mother crossed the grass and held out her arms to her child, but Tenja did not let go. For the first time, she understood why Elizvet Rokovsky had ended her affair with the emperor for the chance to have a child.

"She'll be better off with me," Tenja said to the mother, then added for the baby, "I'm going to take you away from this, give you a good life, yes I am." The baby stopped grizzling and smiled up at her, while the mother stood shocked, open-mouthed. "I'll pay you for her if you want." Tenja wilfully misunderstood the woman's expression.

The mother screeched, "Give. GIVE."

The pale heart who had voluntarily taken the shadow into her, ran to them. Panting, she said to Tenja, "You give baby and I no fight."

Tenja did not release the baby. "She'll be happier with me and rich, richer than you can imagine."

"You no give baby, I fight." The pale heart waved her fingers in the air and spoke the summoning spell. A white dove flew into the Ordinary World and landed on the kam's outstretched hand.

"See the kam's creature, see the kam's power," Tenja mocked. With a curse, the pale heart wrung the bird's neck and hurled the carcass to the ground. Her face was livid as she drew her knife.

Tenja could not stop staring at the shiny serrated blade, as more poison rose into her throat. "I can give her a better life than you can," she wheedled. "If she stays here, she's likely to be dead before she's three."

When the pale heart lunged at her, Tenja was too slow to move. The tip of the knife sliced through the fabric of her coat sleeve. Again the pale heart jabbed at her. Quicker this time, Tenja moved out of range. Unbidden, unexpected, her wolf seized the pale heart's wrist between his teeth without closing his jaw. His eyes were very yellow while advice that had the force of instruction passed from him to Tenja, "Leave the child and get away from here."

She glared at him, reminding him that she was changed, informing him that the baby's future in the ordinary world was none of his business. He growled, as a threat to release the pale heart's hand, "Go now."

"But I want a baby," Tenja wailed. The yearning was visceral.

"And perhaps one day you'll have one." Speaking as the voice of her conscience, the wolf was implacable. "But not this one."

Passing the baby into her mother's arms, Tenja backed away from the pale heart empty-handed. The tribals watched her go in silence.

She was over a mile away when she realised that she had left her pack in the hut where she had slept. She was hungry but more than she wanted to eat, she longed to wash the taste of vomit from her mouth, but she did not turn back to collect her belongings. Instead she continued to walk away from their encampment along a broad well-trodden trail. She hoped that she was headed in the direction of the railway, but without a map she could not be sure. She felt light-headed.

By dusk she was so feverish that she did not know where she was. She staggered along the path and did not notice when she emerged from the forest into open farmland.

She was found early the next morning by a peasant who took her in his cart to his master's house. Vavrja, wife of Lionid Nallikino and sister-by-marriage to Aleksandr, nursed her day and night for the best part of a week before the fever broke.

12.

Tenja stayed almost a month with the Nallikinos, longer than she needed to recover. They were what she thought a family should be, affectionate and hospitable and more cultured than most people who lived in such isolation, but also disciplined and practical. Lionid and Vavrja were the older brother and sister, their children the niece and nephew, that she had never had, while Stepano was a kind of replacement for her late uncle Maro.

Stepano reminded Tenja of a sparrow, bright, curious, lively. He swung around the house and garden on his crutches so nimbly that it was easy to forget that he was disabled. He explained to Tenja how his fascination with kams had started in the military hospital where his leg had been amputated. "Funny little chap stood behind my head and sang to me. That's all he did. He sang. Same tune over and over. D'you know what? That dull tune worked. I didn't feel a thing. I could hear the doc sawing away, but not a flicker of pain. He was Miacharnay. And a kam of course." When Tenja admitted that the kam had been her uncle Maro, Stepano seized her hand and pumped it up and down.

Stepano's study was the territory of a meticulous, ordered eccentric. The books stood in perfect alignment an inch back from the edge of their shelves. The labels by the objects in the glass display cases were handwritten in a beautiful clear script. He was passionately interested in the customs, past and present, of the tribes who lived within the imperial boundaries. He was, he tweaked his moustache with pride, the greatest living expert on the Kohantsi, and he was also very interested in the kams of the other tribes.

Little as Tenja wanted to talk about her experience in the forest, Stepano was a skilled interrogator. Polite, charming, he induced her to say more than she had meant to about everything except the spells that she had learnt. Of those, she refused to speak because every time she came near them, her eyes filled with tears.

Over dinner one evening, something in the manner of Tenja's reply to a question about Aleksandr encouraged Stepano to hint that a fondness existed between her and his nephew. Keen to disabuse him of this notion, Tenja implied that Aleksandr's heart was given elsewhere.

"Aleks is in love? Why have we not heard?" Vavrja said.

"Perhaps because the lady in question is married," Tenja replied carelessly.

Stepano narrowed his eyes. "A married woman indeed!"

"It's my mother's fault. She encouraged him to... to protect this lady from her husband, who mistreats her terribly," Tenja tried to make amends for her tactlessness.

Stepano peered at her over the top of his glasses. Severely, he snapped, "If your mother's encouragement is supposed to excuse Aleksandr's behaviour, it does not." He took a deep breath to steady himself. "Living where we do, next to the Kohantsi, we have to maintain the highest standards. If we fall below them, we are open to corruption. The shadow hearts never stop trying to corrupt us. These days they are no longer strong enough to fight us openly, so they seek to undermine us. Sometimes they succeed. They killed Aleks's mother. I can't blame my brother for falling in love with her, she was such a pretty girl, but he should have known she was too susceptible to live here. When the shadow hearts left tokens of their spells where she was bound to find them, she let them eat at her. I don't think it is mere coincidence that she died of cancer a year or two after the war.

"You may think it's a far cry from spells affecting Aleksandr's mother because she believed they could, to Aleks's involvement with a married woman, but both reveal a lack of moral fibre that enemies can exploit. Do you see?"

Tenja did see, because she had acquired enough of the shadow heart mentality to enjoy the manipulation and destruction of a weak personality. Stepano made her realise that, however much she yearned to be part of a normal family, she could not remain any longer under the Nallikinos' roof.

She returned to Donsgrat on the next westbound train.

13.

The first visitor to Tenja's suite at the Imperial Hotel was the manager. Apologetically, he presented her with a rectangular box, "My staff cleared this from your dinner table along with the crockery."

Tenja received the box from his hand, but dropped it as if it had scorched her skin. The manager bent to pick it up as though he had been the one who had let it fall.

"Put it on the mantelpiece," Tenja ordered. Of the peremptory tone in her voice she thought, 'This is not like me.'

The manager did as she required, bowed and left. When she bathed, she wanted to cleanse more than her body.

Her second visitor blew into the room like a gale before her hair was dry. It hung down her back loose and uncombed.

In a loud voice, Shennikov berated her, "You stupid woman! What did you think you were doing?"

"I was getting even with you."

"You didn't kill him did you?" He looked her up and down. "Most Holy be thanked you weren't that stupid." He checked her again looking around rather than at her. "You've taken some of the shadow."

"A bit."

"Too much. Any is too much. I wish you hadn't."

"Of course you wish I hadn't. You don't want opposition."

"Is that what you think I am? Your opponent?" He appeared confused. "I'm the one who rescued you, remember."

"You arrived at precisely the right moment, I admit. But you didn't exactly rescue me."

"Who summoned the owl and the wolf? Me."

"I appreciate that."

"At least you're showing the start of gratitude."

"Thank you."

"A hug would be better thanks than words."

She did not encourage him to wrap her in his arms, nor did she resist when he did, and immediately she felt that she had come home, that this was the only place she wanted to be. She was his, he was hers. For the briefest instant, she was fully herself and more than herself.

And she hated him for the reminder that she had any need for him. She pushed hard with the palms of her hands against his chest.

"I don't want to see you again."

"You will though. We cannot escape each other." He tugged at his uniform jacket to straighten it. "I wish I were free of you as much as you want to be rid of me."

"We're even in that case."

They were like two cats, with flat ears and spiteful hisses. They both began to giggle, and they grabbed at each other for support while they laughed until tears rolled down their cheeks.

Careful not to meet his eyes in case she started to laugh again, Tenja asked, "By the way how did you manage to vanish?"

"Because I wasn't actually there. What you saw was just a sending."

"How do you do that?"

"I'm not going to tell you. I have to keep some tricks up my sleeve."

"Give me a clue."

"It's not a Kohantsi technique. Nor is it Miacharnay."

She was suddenly very angry. "Go away. Leave me alone."

"You'll have to watch your temper," he warned. "Anger is one of the ways the shadow works, but not the most effective." He saluted, and said, "Goodbye my love and good luck."

The room seemed brighter after Shennikov departed. It was also emptier. Tenja scribbled a quick note to Aleksandr Nallikino and said to a member of the hotel staff, "Deliver this to the colonel." Again she heard the curtness of her tone, but she did not bother to apologise.

In the morning the servant brought her the return message from Aleksandr. It was polite but brief. Unfortunately he was too busy to spare the time to meet her before she left Donsgrat. He appreciated news of his family and was glad that they had been of assistance to her. Finally he hoped that she would make use of the contents of the box if and when the right moment arrived.

She picked the box up with the fire tongs and positioned it in the middle of the floor. She viewed it from every possible angle. She considered whether to open it, but the box almost glowered at her. Either it possessed of a will of its own or she had an overactive imagination. She made one of the chambermaids pack the box into a suitcase.

When she arrived home, her mother surveyed her before she embraced her and said, "Your adventures have hurt you. Please try not to inflict your hurts on the rest of us."

"Easier said than done," Tenja confessed, "I've already been horrid to several people, including a couple of women on the train. Silly as they were, they didn't deserve the tongue lashing they got."

"Breathe before you speak, that's my advice. If you can't breathe, try to think instead."

"At least I've found out how and where Voldimir Shennikov hid when I hunted him in the other worlds."

"Well done. Did you also find out what Marshal Filowet plans to do with his ten thousand new soldiers? Your father's more worried than he lets on."

Tenja shook her head.

She was too tired that night to journey into the other worlds in search of the Marshal's plans. As soon as she reached the realm of the spirits the next morning, the ancestors shied away from her. She was so upset by their rejection that she hurried back to the ordinary world to consult with her mother, who said sadly, "They've already complained to me. They think you've gone over to the enemy."

"You don't agree with them do you?"

Fahra sighed, "I understand how it looks to them."

"You do agree with them."

"Of course I don't. I know my own daughter."

Tenja went back to the school where she taught. The children hung back like the Kohantsi brats. Dora said, "They're cross with you for deserting them. Don't let them upset you."

Tenja sat on the high stool behind her desk and glowered at her pupils. When the whole class was slow to respond, she rapped the ruler on the top of her desk. The children reacted fearfully, and Tenja discovered that she enjoyed being able to frighten them.

At the end of the week, as the children ran from the school gates, shouting and whooping in celebration of their release, Dora called Tenja into her office. "I've had a mother complain about you. First time ever. I don't believe her of course."

Halfway through the second week, Dora again called Tenja to her office. "I walked past your classroom this afternoon and I heard you shouting. What's the matter Tenja dear? It's not like you to yell."

The next time she saw fit to discuss Tenja's treatment of her class, Dora said, "I don't know what happened while you were away but you've changed, and not for the better. I'd like you to consider your position here."

"You can't sack me. The school belongs to me, remember."

Dora's anger was needle sharp, "You're the main investor, not the headmistress. Give me a month and I'll repay every single crown you put in. In the meantime I don't want to see you within the school bounds."

Tenja walked out of the gates with her head held high, but within a few steps her temper cooled and she wondered why she had behaved so badly. She loved teaching, she loved the children, she loved Dora. She headed for the sculptor's studio.

He was building a small armature out of match-thin slivers of wood and did not want to be interrupted. Tenja sat in a corner feeling very small. When the armature was complete, the sculptor knelt in front of her chair and reached for her hands, "Tell uncle what's the matter."

"I'm turning into a monster," she said.

"You're darker than you used to be," he agreed. "And much more interesting." He turned her face towards the light and studied it. "Now you're ready to be cast in bronze."

14.

The sculptor escorted her to a party where she let a well-known art dealer approach her because he reminded her of Shennikov, but when he bent his head to kiss her, she recoiled. He held her shoulders, pushed her against the wall. "Don't pretend you don't want it."

"Not with a conman like you."

"Nothing's ever been proved."

"Nevertheless you reek of guilt." She slid under his arm and went in search of the sculptor. He was as ready to leave as she was.

The night was so cold that they could see their breath. They walked briskly arm in arm partly for warmth, partly because they were both uneasy, though neither of them could name the source of their disquiet. In the stairwell of the sculptor's tenement block, they were surprised by the bald clerk from the Ministry of the Interior. He gushed exclusively to the sculptor, "Praise be to the Most Holy that you're safe! I looked for you everywhere I could think of and when I didn't find you, I thought the worst."

"What's happening?" Tenja asked to bait him.

"Imperial Guards are searching the premises of known radicals."

"Why?" she asked.

"The Minister doesn't have to explain to the likes of me why he sends out the soldiers," the clerk replied, "But I guess they're looking for Yosip Klun."

"Who's he?"

"Who's Yosip Klun?" the clerk echoed derisively. "I thought your father told you everything."

They heard the regular tramp of boots on the cobbles outside.

"Quick!" hissed the sculptor, pushing Tenja and the clerk together as though they were illicit lovers with nowhere else to go, before he hid as best he could in the gloom under the stairs. They hardly breathed while they listened to the soldiers approach, then exhaled noisily when they passed.

As soon as he was sure that the guards were gone, the sculptor re-emerged from the shadows, "We were lucky."

"Not so much lucky as well-connected," said the clerk.

The three of them climbed the four flights of stairs to the sculptor's apartment where the clerk told what he knew.

During the three weeks that it had taken for the story of Yosip Klun to reach the capital and to filter through the ranks of ministry officials, it had probably been embellished, but the incontrovertible facts were these: a man described variously as bearded and as clean shaven, as young and as middle-aged, as a priest and as a soldier - here Tenja thought savagely of a man who had been both - had led a gang of Okhpat miners in the deliberate derailment of an armoured train. Treasury officials investigating the non-arrival of their gold had tracked the train back to the Okhpati Spur where they had found the remains of thirty-four bodies - the twenty-six soldiers and four railmen that they expected, plus four miners. Some of the dead had been killed by the derailment, the rest of the corpses were riddled by bullet holes. The rebels had been ruthless, but not quite ruthless enough. Two wounded miners were found alive in a hut some ten miles from the scene. According to information extracted from these two, the rebel leader Yosip Klun intended to contact his supporters in the capital, which explained the Imperial Guards' search.

At the end of the clerk's story, the sculptor took his hands and squeezed them gently, "Thank you. I really am grateful."

That night Tenja and the sculptor lay together in his bed, anxious friends in need of comfort. She stared up at the cracks in the ceiling; in the candlelight, odd beasts stalked across the dingy plaster.

"We've talked so often about the need for change, about revolution, but now it's here, I don't like it. I don't like violence," the sculptor murmured.

"Worse than violence, murder," Tenja said crisply. "And I do not believe it's real revolution. I don't think for one minute it was the miners' idea to steal the gold."

"You see Voldimir Shennikov's hand in everything."

In the morning, Tenja called on her father at his office. She was too angry to care that she was still wearing yesterday's party clothes. To defuse her obvious annoyance, Bogan was flippant, "I'm glad to see you weren't arrested last night."

"You could have warned me," she shouted.

"No I couldn't. I promised not to, in exchange for your safety."

"Oh," said Tenja, chastened. "Mishka Sillin doesn't really think I'd anything to do with the gold theft does he?"

"Poor Mishka doesn't know what to think. His spies lose track of you for the best part of a month and then you reappear from a little place called Nallikino that is suspiciously close to where my train was wrecked. Given your radical sympathies, the minister has cause to suspect that you were involved in the robbery. Of course he hopes you weren't."

"And what do you suspect?"

Bogan's smile was tight, "You don't need to snarl at me. I've never thought that coincidence is evidence. However, you must be careful. A man I believed to be loyal to the railways and to me personally takes money from my cousin's department too. I admit I am disappointed in him, and in the manager of the Imperial Hotel, who has told my cousin as well as me about the visitors to your suite."

"One of whom moved ten crates of rifles into the Okhpat marshes."

Bogan fiddled with the ornaments on his highly polished desk. "Ygar and Vano Galiskin both saw Captain Shennikov with those wretched crates, but their testimony counts for nothing with Mishka. He prefers to trust the written word. He has documents which show that the rifles were acquired by one Yosip Klun."

Tenja said the surname in chorus with her father, who raised one eyebrow in question. She explained, "The name was whispered around the Fifth Ring last night. Occasionally information trickles out of the ministry. I don't suppose the mysterious Klun was found."

"Not so far as I've heard. Several students and a couple of printers were arrested for possession of forbidden literature." Bogan rose from his chair and walked over to the window. "Yosip Klun will never be found because he's only an alias... I wish I knew what Filowet and his sidekicks are up to. They've killed four of my people besides those poor soldiers, and I do not like it."

The students were sentenced to three years' imprisonment, while the printers each received five years' hard labour. Their supporters were dismayed. In the immediate aftermath of the trial, they were noisy in their protests against the sentences, but ineffective. The minister was not inclined to leniency. Most of the radicals retreated. They stopped meeting, and writing, and they spoke in favour of the rebels only in whispers, if indeed they spoke for them at all. Most were like the sculptor, theoretically certain of the need for change, but unable to condone the violence.

When Tenja tried to explain why the rebellion in the goldfields was the cynical exploitation of the workers' desperation, not a true expression of working class resolve, nobody wanted to listen. Her parents agreed so there was little point in rehearsing the arguments with them. Dora Sillin, who would probably have agreed, was not talking to her. The few radicals brave enough to gather had lost trust in the sculptor because he had not faced the terror of the midnight knock on the door or the indignity of a search by the Imperial Guard.

So it was that Tenja spent most of the winter at the sculptor's studio, modelling for him or losing herself in a book or a daydream while he worked. Sometimes in the evenings, the clerk, who was an accomplished violinist, played music for them. Occasionally, Tenja helped her mother with patients, but when she sang she heard the chants as shrill and off-key. She continued to struggle with the old issue: to concentrate on healing individuals, especially when most of them were sick because of their habits, felt like a waste of time and effort when the whole structure of the empire was unhealthy. She avoided the other worlds altogether, too hurt by the ancestors' rebuff to risk the same from her beloved wolf.

15.

For the emperor, who had barely recovered from the loss of his love, the loss of his gold ranked as a second assault upon his person. Hurt and angry, Nikolka turned to the church for comfort. Father Wassil willingly provided Antoni Marmasy as the new court chaplain.

Mishka Sillin complained to Bogan and Fahra, "I don't know whether to cry or to laugh. Antoni Marmasy indeed! By blood one of us, by inclination one of Wassil's, a Reversionist who will have the emperor pray over every decision I want him to make. Another excuse for prevarication and inaction. I despair of the man, I really do."

Through Mishka and from his private sources, Bogan gleaned snippets of information from the Okhpat, none of them good for the government. The stolen gold could not be found. Yosip Klun was sighted in Leyarsk, the region's main town, on a date that coincided with one of Shennikov's absences from Donsgrat. In addition to Klun, the Fourth Army failed to catch two men, alleged to be renegade priests, who were preaching sedition to the scattered communities of free miners throughout the Okhpat.

The year turned and in the spring of 615, more bad news reached the capital. The gold mines in the Okhpat had been seized by rebels, and as far as the authorities could tell from thousands of miles away, at some of the mines, the guards and the convict labourers had cooperated. Rough justice ruled as old scores were settled and mine administrators were imprisoned or executed. Work came to a halt.

Ygar informed Bogan that Major Zharalov and Captain Shennikov had visited the capital of Nilens again. Once more Bogan tried to persuade his cousin to investigate their activities but Mishka shrugged his shoulders, "You can say what you like in criticism of the Fourth Army, but not the Third Army. Oh no, not the Third. You see, Marshal Filowet has a plan to save us."

"What plan is this?" Bogan enquired, trying to appear less interested than he was.

Mishka shrugged again, "We will be told in due course. In the meantime, Father Wassil tells Father Antoni who tells the Emperor who tells me we must not worry, for all will be well... I might as well invite Wassil and Antoni to attend council meetings the pair of them have so much influence these days. I confess I'm not immune. Sometimes I want to do what Father Wassil suggests, because it seems easiest to let the man destined to clean up nasty messes clean up this one, but I can't, because you have me half convinced that Filowet and his minions incited the miners to revolt in the first place."

When the spring thaw permitted train travel along the Okhpati Spur, General Aksalov, commander in chief of the Fourth Army, ordered a detachment of troops of proven loyalty to repossess the railhead. The first of the trains upon which the soldiers travelled was derailed less than a mile from the previous ambush. When the driver and the fireman emerged groggily from the wreckage, they were led to safety by a couple of well-armed youths.

"Yosip Klun told us to look out for you 'cos you're workers like our dads," one of the lads explained.

"What's this Yosip Klun like? Is he brave like they say?" asked the driver.

"Is he as good looking? I've heard he's handsomer than me," added the fireman. In their innocent enthusiasm for their hero, the youths gave descriptions of Yosip Klun that matched Shennikov's.

When this item of information reached Bogan many days after the actual event, he decided to discuss it directly with the Emperor.

To demonstrate his newfound piety, Nikolka helped the monks and nuns at the soup kitchen in the outermost ring. Once a week he donned the brown habit of a work brother and joined the procession that went on foot from the monastery to the seventh ring. The work was probably as distasteful to him as it had been to Tenja on the one occasion that she had volunteered, but he was more tenacious.

One afternoon Bogan threaded his way through the line of nuns, monks, novices and work brothers to reach the emperor's side.

"Your Imperial Majesty," Bogan said quietly with the slightest inclination of his head to serve as a bow.

"Brother Nik in our present surroundings," Nikolka hissed irritably, before he dismissed as fabrication and nonsense the idea that Third Army personnel had persuaded the gold miners to rebel.

The rest of the procession filed round and past him, while Bogan stood in the middle of the street. Rarely in his life had he felt so deflated, so defeated.

16.

The weather warmed, the evenings lengthened, First Summer's Eve approached. Tenja longed for something to happen. Her days were dull but her nights were broken by bad dreams. Boredom turned to dread.

One afternoon, she felt so tormented that she could not bear to be confined indoors. She spent hours on the small beach below the monastery, watching the tide ebb. The huge bulk of the building behind her was oppressive. She felt small by comparison.

Flow like the river, no need to resist, relax. Instructions slipped into her mind. *Let what will happen, happen.*

"No," she said to the insinuating voice inside her head. She thought she saw Father Wassil's lean hawk-like face. He smiled and for the third time, the world before her eyes shimmered, started to dissolve. She pressed her hands to her eyelids as the ground beneath her feet seemed to melt. She whimpered until a different voice, deeper and calmer, called her back from the edge.

She sat on a sun-warmed rock until her breathing slowed to normal, not quite sure what had happened to her. She was, she realised, very thirsty. Maybe dehydration produced strange effects in brain matter. Something inside quivered with laughter.

As soon as she reached home, she drank two glassfuls of water. The strangeness of the afternoon would not leave her. She sat in the summerhouse close to where the lawns met the high tide mark until the sun set and the warmth of the day faded. She shivered. It was time to go indoors. She rose and stretched because she had been sitting too long.

The small hairs on the back of her neck prickled, and the air was suddenly, briefly, thick with the smell of earth. The fabric of the web ripped as something from the underworld burst into this world. Tenja caught something of its raw energy as it surged into the city. It was very angry. It was also heading towards her.

She wanted to stay where she was, hidden and safe. She did not want to confront a monster that had been called into her world to hunt her. She could feel the hunger with which it searched for her, and part of her responded to it. Though she could not name it, she knew it, and knew that she loved it almost as much she feared it. She forced lead heavy legs to move over the gardens, through the great wrought iron gates.

Out in the avenue, she heard screams long before the clatter of hooves and the rumble of wheels drowned all other sounds. As he wrestled with four crazed horses, the coachman yelled curses but she could not distinguish his words in the cacophony of sound. She flattened herself against the wall as the coach cannoned into the kerb, swayed alarmingly towards her and away. She saw the passengers clinging to each other, open-mouthed in horror. The horses were past her, the carriage was past her. Quaking with fear, she walked into the middle of the road to meet the cause of the terror.

It rounded the curve in the road, three times the height of a man, a swirl of colours that spun and twisted in a vertical column as it rushed towards her. She saw, but did not have time to interpret, the layers of brick reds, grass greens, stone greys, and drab browns that oscillated around the still centre, and the flecks of turquoise, pinks, sky blue and gold that danced close to the core.

It enveloped her, flooded her so that she could no longer tell quite where she ended and it began. It was around her, and in her, and the fiercer her struggle to free herself became, the tighter its stranglehold grew. She could hardly breathe for the stink of sewage and smoke and the grit that filled her mouth and nostrils, but she had to, and its sickness churned in her stomach.

Just as it dwarfed her physically, its huge emotions swept over her like a breaking wave. The anger that she felt was not merely her response to invasion, but the colossal blind rage that carried the creature forward, that threatened to destroy whatever stood in its path, and under the fury lay a depth of despair that could break a human heart. She plunged down the spiral of pain and surged up in the swirl of rage, even as she tried to fight her way to the edge of the grey brown fog, and she would have surrendered the last vestige of her humanity but for the shouts from the periphery of her hearing.

"Go into it. Into the middle." This was not the calm wisdom that had broken Father Wassil's spell in the afternoon. The man who shouted sounded desperate, but he managed to reach what remained of Tenja's will.

Through the seethe of emotions, the whirl of colour, the thickness and the heat of the dust, she could vaguely see the clear crystal core. In the midst of crazy activity, it was motionless and apparently calm. She wanted to reach out for it, but something about it pushed her back to the outermost layer, where she was choking.

"You must go to the middle," the man yelled.

To force her way towards the creature's centre was akin to wading through a mesh of cobwebs that stuck to her hair, her clothes, her skin. The smell grew worse. Despite the shallowness of her breaths, acrid chemicals stung her nose and throat. Half-blinded by the tears that streamed from her eyes, she clawed open a path to its heart.

With a sudden shift she tumbled into a different layer where the air was cleaner, and new colours, the redness of brick and the occasional flash of flower blues, yellows and pinks, mingled with the stone greys and wood browns. Though the crystal glowed more clearly, it did not seem to pacify the emotions present here, which seemed both more controlled and more dangerous. The rage was turned inward. At this level the being hated everything that danced in the brightness of pink and gold and sky blue and the dazzle of marble white between it and its heart, yet when Tenja broke through into the highly coloured layer, the hate was directed outwards. The creature was at war with itself.

She could quite understand why it defended the spaciousness and the lightness near its centre from encroachment by the dense nastiness of the outer skins. The interplay of colours enthralled her. Like a kitten chasing leaves on the autumn breeze, she tried to catch one of the strands of gold that spun past her, and in the joy of the dance she forgot her purpose.

A third time, she heard the thin despairing shout from beyond the limits of the creature, "Don't stop! Go to the middle!"

With difficulty she pulled her attention away from the elusive twist of gold light and turned to the centre of the being. It was so clear that at first she thought it was a mirror. For a moment, she saw the creature as an underworld version of herself where its rage and misery, its self-hatred and its beauty were her moods exaggerated and magnified, and she understood why she had both feared and loved it.

She thought of love and the core seemed to shimmer. When she stared into it she realised how arrogant she had been to think that a being so huge could possibly be an other world counterpart of a puny human. This creature contained the patterns of the city: each of its levels was one of the rings. With the Monastery of the Most Holy Incarnate at its centre, it was no wonder that the crystal absorbed the passions from the outer rings yet remained clear and still. In front of it, focussed on it to the exclusion of all else, she asked from her heart directly to the being's heart how best she could help it.

She then noticed a tiny black speck that marred the perfection, and once she had seen it, it grew to be all she could see. The corruption that was Father Wassil's intention spread like an ink spill over paper.

Shocked, beaten, Tenja fell away from the centre and landed so heavily on her knees in the gravelled avenue that she scraped the skin. The grit of the outer layers blocked her nose so that she coughed. The creature brought into the ordinary world at Father Wassil's call, was heavy on her shoulders. Furious, it pounded at her back, hungry for something she could not name, that she could not give.

"Get off," she yelped because she was hurt and angry too.

The man called from the side of the avenue, "Send it back where it came from."

"Does it want to go home?" Tenja asked incredulously.

The being answered by loosening its hold. On her knees in the road, she muttered a shadow heart spell to open a doorway from this world to the one below. With a hiss that might have been gratitude or relief, the being poured through it and was gone.

Tenja spat grit from her mouth.

An elderly gentleman said, "Well done. Especially if that was the first time you've met one of those."

She held out her hand and the man pulled her to her feet. She winced as the barked skin on her knees stung. "I guess it's something to do with the city."

"Quite right, it is."

"I'd still be stuck on the edge if I hadn't heard you tell me to go to its centre." As she spoke she knew that she would not have lasted long on the edge. She would in all probability have choked to death. The thought chilled her.

From further along the avenue, they heard worried shouts and splashes.

"It sounds as though the Baranovs' coach has met with an accident," the old gentleman said.

"I don't think I can cope with any more," Tenja said.

"Let's get you home." He helped her to the gates of her house and up the drive. At the front door, they were met by both Fahra and Bogan.

"What in the Most Holy's name was that?" Bogan demanded. He had seen the dance of unearthly lights above the garden wall.

"The guardian of this city. Fortunately, as guardians go, it is a small one, and quite young. Your daughter has sent it back where it belongs. She was very brave."

"I couldn't have done it without you," Tenja repeated and with a nervous giggle added, "And I don't even know who you are."

"Pavel Chrezdonow," the old gentleman said with a slight bow.

Bogan held out his hand, "I've heard of you of course. Delighted to make your acquaintance."

"The pleasure is mutual," Pavel replied, particularly pleased to meet Fahra. "I should like to call on you tomorrow if I may."

Fahra was gracious as they arranged a time, but when the door was closed behind him, she turned to Bogan with a worried frown on her face, "Isn't he the one they call the storm crow because he only appears in times of crisis?"

Despite a long sleep and a hot bath, Tenja still felt fragile when Pavel Chrezdonow arrived. Unless she kept a tight rein on her thoughts, they drifted back to the black stain spreading across the clean crystal. Each time she saw it was as horrible as the first.

Pavel Chrezdonow looked to be in his seventies. His hair was silver, his face was lined, but his spine was ramrod straight. He steepled his forefingers thoughtfully before he asked Tenja about what had happened the previous evening. She gasped as she once more saw the blackness corrupt the purity of the crystal. Pavel Chrezdonow lent forward in his chair, "Tell me."

"Didn't you see it yourself? Not it, him. Father Wassil. He spoilt the guardian's heart."

"Ah," said Pavel leaning back again. "I wonder how you have upset him."

"I hate what he and his nephew are doing or about to do," she replied vehemently. "I'd stop them if I could. If I was privy to their plans."

"Ah," Pavel repeated. "I can understand why you might want to put a spanner in their works, and they in yours."

He drank the last of the tea and traced the S-V monogram on the side of the fine porcelain cup. "One of Seb's flourishes I presume. A remarkable man, your great-grandfather. He loved flamboyance. Marshal Filowet is also flamboyant. You must be very clear about your motives if you carry your opposition to him into action."

He gazed up at the ceiling as if to lessen the intrusive nature of his next question, "Are you sure you know better than Father Wassil and the marshal what serves the needs of the Empire?"

Tenja felt that her brain was fizzing. "Are you suggesting they're right?"

"I cannot share my opinion with you. If indeed I have an opinion. Perhaps I have already stepped too far into action by sharing knowledge with you... One branch of the Chrezdonow family rules: the other branch, my branch, observes, and at points of transition offers information and suggestions from our store of knowledge, historical, anthropological, esoteric. Usually we confine our advice to our fellow Chrezdonows, and sometimes, not always unfortunately, they are wise enough to listen. I tried to tell Fyedor the Third about... about the... call them guardians if you will, for they protect our boundaries and the places we hold most dear. I tried to tell Fyedor about Mu-Mumis, but he was old and experienced and I was not so young as you but new to the court and green and easily dismissed. A million deaths later, he was ready to hear your father's description of the small red bird that was Mu-Mumis in a reduced form. That first experience made me cautious about mentioning the existence of guardians and about the timing of my interventions. Too cautious perhaps."

"Surely, there's no question!"

Pavel lowered his gaze from the ceiling and watched Tenja while he said, "You are a kam of the Miacharnay, a people who value harmony above conflict and you are also a woman of child-bearing years. On both counts, you are inclined to think that the Western War was a dreadful waste of lives.

"It was also more than that. Because of the war, your father was permitted to build his railways. Because of the experiences that many now senior priests had during the war, the church draws a clearer, harsher distinction between good and evil than it used to. The empire changed more in the years of the Western War than it had in the previous century, and the processes begun then continue to this day. We are still trying to catch up with what these changes mean for us as individuals, as aristocrats, as men and indeed as women. Father Wassil and his nephew have their interpretation, I have my interpretation and you have yours.

"This is why I say to you before you intervene, be sure of your motives."

Throughout his speech he observed her reactions in such an impersonal manner that she felt that she was little more than an interesting specimen. Hotly she burst out, "My motives are pure as snow compared to theirs. Theirs were born out of the shadow."

"The Kohantsi shadow. Ever it has been a menace," Pavel said unmoved by her passion. "I gather that you survived a confrontation with no worse effect than a high fever."

"I wish the fever had been the worst of its effects," Tenja admitted. "What I said a moment ago, about my motives... I was wrong. Once I might have been as pure as snow. Not any more. Not since I fought the shadow heart."

"You see why you must examine your motives. It is too easy to become what we oppose."

Tenja escorted him to the hall where the doorman gave him his hat, gloves and cane. Chrezdonow kissed her hand with old-fashioned courtesy and murmured, "I've so enjoyed my visit."

She watched him walk along the wide sweep of the drive. Near the gate, Pavel bowed politely to a man on horseback clad in the imperial livery. Tenja was annoyed to recognise the rider as Count Istven Boiyenabsty. She went outside to meet him.

Too formal to smile, he handed her an envelope of thick expensive paper, on which her name, but not her title, was written in black ink. She was loath to take it from Count Istven's hand. He brandished it under her nose. "His Imperial Majesty wrote in his own hand. You must read it."

"What have I done that concerns the emperor?"

Count Istven, the perfect courtier, seldom allowed himself to be surprised, but the naïveté of Tenja's question astonished him. "The Baranovs died because their horses were spooked by a demon. Your demon. And you wonder why the emperor is concerned. Could it be because the empress's mother was a Baranov or because it's against church law to consort with demons? Read and obey the emperor's instructions." He yanked on the reins with unnecessary force and wheeled the horse round, while Tenja held the unopened letter in trembling hands.

She went back into the house in a daze. "Why didn't you tell me about the Baranovs?" she asked her mother.

"What about the Baranovs?" Fahra's voice was high. The elderly count and his younger wife had not been close friends or patients, but they had always treated her kindly.

The emperor's letter remained unread until Bogan came home. It was a terse command for Tenja and her parents to attend a special ceremony of purification at the monastery chapel on First Summer's Day. Bogan, who was due to send the inaugural messages along his telegraph lines at the same time, had to delegate the task to one of his Sillin cousins.

17.

In the afternoon of First Summer's Eve, Colonel Aleksandr Nallikino met the abbot of Donsgrat to discuss plans for the next morning's service and special parade. In the square around them, cheerful workmen raised the awning above the dais, positioned flower tubs, hung banners from the lampposts. Their enthusiasm depressed Nallikino.

The old abbey was still encased in scaffolding, despite the abbot's assurance that the roof was now watertight. On impulse at the end of his meeting, Nallikino went inside to confront the statue of Woldymer Chrezdonow, as if it were responsible for the craziness of the last year. Every surface of the black stone figure was covered in fine dust which somehow accentuated the resemblance between Chrezdonow's features and Filowet's.

Two nuns, armed with brushes and dusters, approached. One said affectionately, "Woldymer has to be clean for his big day tomorrow."

The next morning, thousands of people packed the square to hear officially what had been bruited around the town unofficially for months. During the First Summer's Day service, they were reverential if perhaps a little impatient towards the end of the abbot's specially written sermon. Standing under the sun with two hundred representatives selected from the ten thousand Heartlanders, Nallikino was proud that not one of them fidgeted. They were good boys. Their drill was flawless, their presentation smart, their bearing in front of the crowds dignified. In their innocence, they had no inkling of the future that loomed darkly ahead of them.

The abbot dispensed his final blessing, and retired to the back of the dais, and nothing happened for so long that the crowd started to ask, "What's going on? Where is he?"

At the precise moment before anticipation changed to angry disappointment, Filowet rode into the square. His mount, a nervy golden stallion, was led by Shennikov. Horse, rider and acting groom reached the empty space in front of the dais, and turned to face the throng. With a flourish, the marshal drew his sword and brandished it above his head in deliberate imitation of the statue's pose. Applause for this piece of theatre was almost deafening. The stallion's eyes rolled and foam splattered his mouth and neck.

Filowet waited for quiet before he began to speak, "In the name of the Most Holy Incarnate I declare that I am Woldymer Chrezdonow reborn." The stallion was encouraged to rear, which sent another wave of thunderous applause around the crowd. "Long ago it was foretold that Chrezdonow would return in the hour of the Empire's greatest need. In the Western War he was looked for, and many were disappointed by his apparent absence. But unbeknownst to all, he was there to serve the empire he created, the empire he loves.

"Once more, we live in dark times. The threat is constant, yet invidious. These days it lies within our borders. Throughout the empire, decent people live in fear, the fear that the scum of the cities will turn on us, will rob us of our possessions, will burn our homes, will rape our women and murder our children.

"On account of the darkness Chrezdonow can now be revealed. I return to liberate you, to protect you and law-abiding folk like you. Fear not, I say. With ten thousand Heartlanders at my back, I issue a challenge to the rioters and the looters, the revolutionists and the scum. To those miserable wretches I say, come back to the church of your forefathers, submit to soldierly discipline, take your proper places in imperial society. Or face your destruction.

"I shall not rest until our beloved empire is cleansed. In the name of the Most Holy and in the name of Emperor Nikolka the Sixth, I vow to restore faith, purity and harmony to our great land."

The crowd erupted. Nallikino scanned the faces of the dignitaries on the dais, who stood to applaud with scarcely less restraint than the ordinary people. And Elyda stood with them. Her face was a tight mask.

This was the nearest that Nallikino had been to her for months, he longed to be much nearer. She turned towards him, and when he saw a new scar on her cheek, he was seized by an insane urge to draw his gun, to assassinate the marshal, because mad dogs must be destroyed. He had his hand on his holster, from where it moved involuntarily to the grip of his revolver. He was all set to avenge the hurts inflicted on his beloved by her monstrous husband until he noticed her children. At that moment he did not care about Kiril or Grischa, knowing from summers at their grandparents, that they were replicas of their father. They were cheering boisterously. The littlest one was a different matter. Terrified by the thunderous noise Mhailo cowered behind his mother, and the sight of him rendered Nallikino impotent. 'Uncle Aleks' could not bring himself to add to the boy's terror by executing 'Papa.'

The colonel signalled to the drummers. Time to march. The applause slowly died as the drums rolled and Filowet lived to enjoy the next appointment on his busy schedule.

18.

On First Summer's morning, the Sillin-Vrekovs travelled the short distance to the monastery in their own carriage. None of them spoke. Bogan was irritable because he had to attend church instead of the ceremony to mark the launch of the telegraph service. By the bridge, he and Tenja, who sat on the left hand side, peered over the broken railings to the wreckage of the Baranovs' coach on the river shore.

They were the first visitors to arrive at the circular chapel. In the gloom of the interior, Tenja chose to sit at the end of a row of seats halfway between the door and the round marble platform in the centre that served as the altar. Her mother and father sat silently in the row behind her. In threes and fours, blue-robed monks and nuns filed in. Eventually, the emperor, the empress, the crown prince,

Istven Boiyenabsty and the imperial chaplain were shown to front row seats on the opposite side of the chapel to the Sillin-Vrekovs.

The congregation rose to their feet as Father Wassil walked up the aisle to his place on the dais. He bowed to the emperor, and was starting to speak when the west door was dragged wide open. As rusty hinges squealed, daylight poured into the dimness.

The Most Holy Incarnate's bath chair was pushed up the aisle by a moon-faced work brother. The Most Holy's white robe was spotted with paint and stained by His breakfast of boiled or poached egg. He was humming a tune to which Tenja knew some rather coarse words. From His chair, He deliberately winked up at her, as if to say that He knew the same version of the song.

Father Wassil did not try to conceal his annoyance, demanding over the Most Holy's head, "What is *He* doing here?"

With a resigned shrug of his shoulders, the brown-robed work brother replied, "You know how He is when He wants something." He manoeuvred the chair expertly over the lip of the dais. The Most Holy grinned like a cheerful idiot.

Father Wassil resumed his speech. "Despite the extraordinary circumstances in which we find ourselves, let us not forget that today is First Summer's Day. The choir will sing the anthem *In Praise of Summer*."

The congregation stood while the choir sang. Perceptions heightened by nervousness, Tenja watched how the Most Holy Incarnate conducted the four-part harmony. What looked like a child's game was actually perfect. She was acutely aware not only of the amusement beneath the stained robe, but also the intelligence.

At the end of the anthem, Father Wassil intoned the seasonal prayers, while the congregation remained standing. He motioned them to sit, and he moved to a place on the dais behind the Most Holy from which he could see both the emperor and the Sillin-Wrecovs.

"Last night a demon rampaged across our beloved city, a monster summoned from Below by that woman." Wassil pointed to Tenja.

The Most Holy rolled His head back to squint up at Wassil, "By whom?"

The finger that had been pointing at Tenja dropped.

The Most Holy Incarnate stood up. The monks and nuns gasped. He walked unaided round the marble circle and He looked deep into the eyes of His congregation. Of the religious, only His attendant did not turn away from His assessment. Brother Porfyor nodded in approval, a parent encouraging a toddler. The emperor preferred to cover his face with his hands rather than witness the miracle, but all the Sillin-Vrekovs sat up straight, eager to see what happened next.

The Most Holy came full circle back to Father Wassil. The tall fastidious monk towered over the grubby old man, but in their wordless exchange it was Wassil who conceded by kneeling at the Most Holy's feet.

The Twenty-Third Incarnation beckoned to the librarian Father Boriko, "If you please, lead us through the rest of the service for the morning of First Summer's Day."

"Forgive me, I ... I do not have the liturgy by heart," Father Boriko spluttered, but he did manage to say the right prayers in more or less the right order, and to preach a coherent if brief sermon on the significance of summer in the church year. He rushed through the final prayers, then looked to the Most Holy for guidance. The whole congregation was expectant.

"Thank you," said the Most Holy. "Henceforth you will act as head of My Church."

"Are you sure?" Boriko was flustered. "Others are far above me in the order of precedence, and besides, what of Father Wassil?"

"What indeed?" the Most Holy said grimly. "Wassil, tell them what you have done."

With as much dignity as stiff muscles allowed, Father Wassil rose to his feet. "I have done nothing but protect and further the interests of the Church."

"Is that how you salve your conscience?"

"I do not wish to discuss this in public."

"You leave Me with no other option. How often have you heard My voice in the privacy of your thoughts and prayers, and how often have you ignored it?"

Father Wassil hung his head. Fahra thought gleefully that he resembled Tenja in her adolescent argumentative phase, obstinately unable to admit to wrongdoing

"Since you are reluctant to answer Me, here is another question. What happened the night before last?"

"A demon from Below erupted into the city. It shattered the statue of Fyedor the First, and terrified everyone and everything that saw it. Two night watchmen from the Ministry of the Interior who tried to intercept it were killed. The Baranovs' coach horses bolted, and unfortunately the count, the countess and their driver died in an accident."

"You think the bare facts will suffice?"

"You asked what happened."

The monks and nuns who were accustomed to obey Father Wassil's every word were confused, perhaps horrified, by his truculence, but they did not want the drama to end. The emperor appeared to find the scene distasteful, while Fahra and Tenja were frankly enjoying Wassil's humiliation.

"How did it happen? How did the demon come to the city?" the Most Holy enquired. Wassil was silent so long that the Most Holy had to add, "Do you still seek to blame to someone else?"

The most quick-witted of His audience understood. Someone muttered, "No. It cannot be."

"Do you deny that you summoned a being from its rightful abode Below?"

"I do not deny it because I cannot deny it." Wassil was loud, unexpectedly passionate. The hiss of indrawn breath was audible everywhere in the chapel. Chairs scraped on the floor as monks drew back from Wassil physically as well as mentally.

"Where did you learn how to summon it?"

"I read some notes on the practices of the Shoshanu people."

"A partial truth is better than an outright lie... Do you repent?"

After a long silence, Wassil muttered, "I do not, because the people must be brought back to the true faith, and that woman..." Again the finger was pointed at Tenja.

"No, Wassil, you may not accuse her," the Most Holy interrupted. In the air above Wassil's head, He made a sudden cut that Fahra and Tenja experienced as a knife that severed Wassil's connection to the Above. They winced because of the pain of it, and the finality. Damaged, hurt, but courageous, Wassil stayed on his feet.

The Most Holy said, "The Church forbids contact with the beings who reside Below. Rightly are such taboos imposed. I do not revoke them. As those who met the guardian of this city can testify, beings of its ilk are powerful, and their powers can be used, purposefully or thoughtlessly, to harm and to destroy. Therefore I say, let no man summon a guardian or any other being into this world from Below." The Most Holy revolved in order to face everyone present, to impress upon them the importance of His order. He stood in front of Tenja much longer than He stood before the emperor. "I encourage the walkers on both the exoteric and the esoteric paths to remember that their paths must not point downwards, nor must they climb upwards: they must remain precisely balanced between Below and Above."

His attention returned to Wassil. He said with sad gentleness, "You will leave the monastery immediately and for as long as you live you may not return."

Wassil crumpled prostrate at the Most Holy's feet. At the back of the church some of the novices stood up to get a better look. Nobody expected to hear him plead, but he did, "Don't make me leave. This place has been my life. I have done what I have done because of love."

"I send you away because you think love motivated you."

"Please."

The Most Holy was implacable, "Go away and stop thinking. Examine your heart. Find where your love truly is."

Gracelessly, Wassil struggled to his feet, and shuffled to the door. It banged shut behind him.

At the emperor's side, the imperial chaplain stood up. "Forgive me, Majesty," Father Antoni said with a bow to Nikolka. "I cannot let Father Wassil go alone. It is not right." Walking as fast as dignity allowed, he followed Wassil out of the church.

Members of the congregation exhaled their long-held breath.

The Most Holy complained to Brother Porfyor, "I'm hungry. I want My lunch."

"It's too early for lunch," Porfyor said as he negotiated the wheelchair off the dais. "But if You're really hungry I'm sure I can rustle up a snack. You've had a very busy morning."

Tenja sat as though glued to her seat. The chatter of the monks and nuns around her was no more meaningful to her than the twitter of birds. Before her arrival, she had screwed up her courage to face public humiliation and some kind of punishment, only to be rescued by the Most Holy. Relief, gratitude, puzzlement filled her heart. She did not notice that Pavel Chrezdonow and his son Shantor were watching her intently. Shantor was about to introduce himself and to comfort her or congratulate her, whichever she needed, but was prevented from so doing by Bogan, who hugged her and led her away.

19.

CHREZ-DO-NOW.CHREZ-DO-NOW. The Heartlanders, Nallikino at their head, marched down the street that led from the square to the Imperial Hotel where Filowet was due to lunch. CHREZ-DO-NOW. The people chanted and clapped in rhythm, and their noise bounced off buildings, became a wall of sound that assaulted the whole body and drowned the music of the military band. Infatuated women stepped off the kerb trying to reach the marshal as if his touch were precious. Without Shennikov's restraining hand on the bridle, the golden stallion sidled and pranced and kicked out with his hind hooves. Nallikino cursed Shennikov for his absence, and pushed the Heartlanders forward, so that they flanked horse and rider and protected the women from harm. The soldiers lost the rhythm and the style of their march: they almost waltzed to the three beats CHREZ-do-now, CHREZ-do-now. Bathed in adulation, Filowet did not seem to mind that the parade had turned into a shambolic dance.

Nallikino and the Heartlanders delivered him safely to the courtyard of the hotel where the directors of the barge company, hosts for the lunch, hailed their guest of honour as enthusiastically as the general populace had. The Heartlanders remained at attention to receive the carriages that had brought the other official guests: the abbot, the mayor, the chief revenue collector, the senior medical officer, the rest of the men who controlled local affairs, and used the lunch as an excuse to discuss business while their wives and children picnicked in the park. With the exception of the abbot, who was thoughtful, the guests looked and behaved like a team who had just won a match

The last carriage contained Filowet's older sons Kiril and Grischa. They seemed upset as they descended from it, so like the adopted uncle he was, Nallikino went over to comfort them.

"He went funny half-way here." Nine year old Kiril, lower lip quivering, pointed into the coach where their chaperon Shennikov sat, upright, rigid, oblivious to his surroundings.

"I'll look after him. He'll be back to his usual self soon," Nallikino assured them. "Go and get your lunch before the grown-ups scoff the lot."

Reassured, Kiril and Grischa trotted off to the dining room, and as discreetly as possible Nallikino detailed two porters to carry the captain into the hotel through a back door.

"Don't care for the look of him," one porter commented, as they laid Shennikov on a bed in an upstairs room. "Better get the doctor to him quick."

"Yes, fetch the doctor." Nallikino seized the chance to be alone with Shennikov whose symptoms reminded him of the Heartland lad's trance. For the second time within an hour, the colonel had murder in mind. Again his hand rested on the butt of his revolver.

Why did he hesitate? Because he feared arrest, trial, punishment, capital punishment? Did his life matter if he could end Shennikov's? Why did he delay? Because the room filled with sunlight was too pretty, too innocent to be the scene of heinous crime? Because shooting was not the most efficient method. The shot would resound inside the hotel, and outside where two hundred Heartlanders lounged about the stable-yard, swigging watered beer and munching bread and cheese.

'Don't shoot him, smother him. The doctor will assume the patient just stopped breathing,' he thought, but he did not pull the pillow from under Shennikov's head. Colonels do not murder captains.

"I pray the man not the officer makes the choices though they will cost the soldier dear." Old Maria had said that. Prayers ought to be answered, whatever the price. The colonel might think that he should not kill a captain, the man had to, in order to end a gross misuse of power.

Shennikov groaned, rolled over on to his side so that his head rested on only one corner of the pillow. Nallikino tugged at it a little too hard. Shennikov grabbed at his wrists, kicked out at his legs. Nallikino managed to twist away from the handgrip, but the captain's boots sent him sprawling against the wall.

"You traitor!" Shennikov yelled, "I saw you in the square. I heard your thoughts." More dangerous than the accusation was the gun that Shennikov, kneeling on the bed, pointed at Nallikino.

The door burst open. The doctor and the two porters behind him were appalled.

"Give me that," the doctor ordered, in possession of the authority that Nallikino had just lost. Shennikov laid his revolver across the doctor's open palm, saying to Nallikino, "You're finished, if not the way I want you finished."

The doctor cut across him, "Get a grip on yourself!"

"The colonel is a traitor to Marshal Filowet," Shennikov declared.

The doctor growled, "The colonel is your superior. You must not threaten him physically or verbally."

Nallikino lent against the wall, his thoughts in distinct layers:

Shennikov tried to kill me: outrage.
The doctor's timing is perfect: gratitude.
Shennikov tells the truth and is not believed: irony.
Play on the doctor's automatic response to hierarchy: cunning.

Watching Shennikov for aggressive intent, Nallikino said, "The captain has of course committed a serious offence which must be judged by the commander-in-chief. I am loath, however, to spoil the marshal's special day by informing him of this ugly incident straight away."

"Hypocrite," Shennikov muttered, while the doctor praised Nallikino's forbearance and waxed lyrical about Chrezdonow's rebirth. "Chrezdonow will save us," he concluded, his eyes misty.

"I'm sure he will. Meanwhile, there is the captain."

"Lock him up until the marshal is free to deal with him," the doctor advised.

"Might there be a better solution? After all, he has tried to harm me, might he not try to harm himself?"

"I doubt it. Throw him into a cell."

"If he's deluded, wouldn't it be kinder to sedate him until morning?" Nallikino persisted.

"No!" said Shennikov. "I must see the marshal. Now." He stood up from the bed. "Can't you see through the colonel's game, doctor? He's the traitor, he wants me sedated so he can escape. The marshal will listen to me, I guarantee it."

Once again the doctor did not accept the truth, "I'll sedate you so no-one has to listen to any more ridiculous accusations."

The doctor did not have to force the medicine down Shennikov's throat. The captain drank it willingly, raising the glass in mock toast to Nallikino, "Until we meet again, traitor."

The doctor shook his head, "Definitely deluded. The dose will keep him quiet for twelve to fifteen hours."

The doctor departed with Nallikino's thanks. As soon as his victim was deeply asleep, Nallikino locked the bedroom door, and headed downstairs to the stable-yard.

The Heartlanders were jovial. He regarded them with affection, unwilling to abandon them, but he had to. If he did not, he was truly finished. He strolled over to Major Zharalov to whom he was overdue to pass command of Filowet's escort. "As you are aware, Major, Captain Shennikov was taken ill. The doctor has sedated him. He'll sleep until morning... Oh and here's the key to his room."

Inside Filowet's circle of confidants, Zharalov eyed Nallikino suspiciously, but correct responses to seniors were ingrained in him too. Together they ran through the marshal's programme for the rest of the day.

3 pm	leave Imperial Hotel
3.15 pm	open telegraph office & send inaugural telegraph
3.40 pm	leave telegraph office
4 pm	arrive at sports field
5.30 pm	present trophies
6.15 pm	refreshments
8 pm	fireworks display
9 pm	dinner in the officers' mess

"See you in the mess tonight," Nallikino said to Zharalov at the end of his last duty as an officer of the Third Army. He left the Imperial Hotel.

In the streets of Donsgrat an officer alone on foot was a surrogate for the marshal, an approachable surrogate. Nallikino was slapped on the back, shaken by the hand, applauded. His smile fixed, he received the plaudits while inwardly he seethed.

At his house, he changed out of his uniform and out of habit, hung it in the wardrobe. He decided not to leave an explanatory note for his housekeeper. He pocketed all the cash he could find - a few banknotes, three or four coins - and some portable valuables, stole his revolver from the army, and set off to walk back to the city centre in search of an ally who could facilitate his escape. In civilian clothes he was able to move faster.

At the Railway Workers' Hostel the doorman was snoozing with his napkin tucked under his chin. An empty plate rested upon his desk, along with a bottle and his feet. The doorbell woke him up. Spotting a gentleman through the glass, he tugged the napkin from his shirtfront and lurched to the door. The gentleman asked him to fetch the stationmaster from the railway workers' First Summer's Day party. The doorman did not argue with gentlemen.

Vano Galiskin was benignly unsober when he greeted Nallikino in the hall. "Why it's you, Colonel! Good afternoon to you. How can I assist the countess's friend? Wonderful woman, Countess Tenja. She's ... wonderful." Galiskin hiccoughed.

"It's vital I leave Donsgrat today."

"No trains till tomorrow. No boats till tomorrow. The only way out of town today is on foot, horse or human," Galiskin said. For an inebriated man, he was suddenly shrewd. "Because of this Chrezdonow rubbish?" he asked. Nallikino nodded.

Galiskin reeled away. Two minutes later, he reappeared. His hair was wet. His manner remained whimsical, "We railmen do not like the army. For all the army's our best customer, we really do not like the army at all."

"I rather think I'm not in the army any more."

"Then we must get you far away from it. The army doesn't let go of its men willingly unless it leaves them on the battlefield... I'm sure the countess would give you sanctuary in the capital."

"I don't want to put her at risk in any way."

"My cousin Arkady in Nadonnu could take you in. Find you a job too. He's an engineer on the river boats."

"Nadonnu sounds good."

"Give me a couple of hours and I'll have the Nadonnu Special ready."

Nallikino waited under the sycamore tree that dominated the corner of the avenue near Filowet's house. He had already dared to ring the bell. The house was empty. Presumably Elyda was on her way back from the officers' wives picnic in Coronation Park. Surely she would arrive soon.

Two women, housemaids by their dress, meandered arm in arm along the avenue, raucously enjoying their holiday. Nallikino tried to be inconspicuous as though loitering in a wealthy district of the city was normal behaviour. Of course the housemaids noticed him and sized him up. Out of uniform, he was just an ordinary, possibly available, man. He felt suddenly vulnerable.

Vulnerable, as he had been when he stared into the dark round muzzle of Shennikov's gun. If Shennikov had flexed his trigger-finger, exit the soul Nallikino did not believe he had. He was sweaty. If the doctor had not arrived... He tried to tell himself that shock was a natural, acceptable reaction. He tried not to dwell upon what might have happened, because it had not happened. He was still alive.

Further along the avenue, the maids burst into guffaws of laughter.

He fretted. She could not have gone to the sports could she? She hated them. But if she was not at the sports where on earth was she? He was tempted to leave the shade of the tree, to look for her in more public places, but what if she did come home by a different route and he missed her. He stayed where he was and worried.

He was not a religious man. He prayed, 'Oh Most Holy, send her to me.'

The shadows cast by the tree lengthened. Galiskin's departure time for the Nadonnu Special approached.

Nallikino decided that prayer was useless. It made the inevitable disappointments harder to bear.

Throughout their affair, he had cursed the luck, and thanked the fate that had caused him to love another man's wife with a devotion that excluded easier, happier possibilities. He could not quite claim ten years of fidelity, but no-one had displaced Elyda from his heart. He could not leave her to the mercy of either her husband or Shennikov. He had to wait, as long as he possibly could.

Seconds ticked into minutes, the minutes added up to quarters of an hour, the quarters crept inexorably towards the deadline. And passed it.

Elyda half dragged, half cajoled her tired child along the avenue. He shouted, "Colonel Aleks! Mamma, it's Colonel Aleks!" Fatigue forgotten, the boy dashed to Nallikino who picked him up and whirled him round.

"Aleks?" Joy, uncertainty, concern mingled in Elyda's enunciation of his name.

"They're onto me," Nallikino explained, cryptic because of his son. "There's a train due to take me away from Donsgrat at six o'clock but I couldn't go without..."

"Saying goodbye?"

"No! Please, not goodbye. Come with me."

Elyda was still. Often in her fantasies Aleksandr asked her to elope. "Come with me." Magic words! But in her daydreams, her children had accompanied them into a golden future. "Grischa? Kiril?" she asked faintly.

Nallikino had not thought of them since lunchtime. He liked them. He knew their names but they were not his. He wanted only the one in his arms.

"It has to be your decision," he said gravely, and he swung his son around again so that he did not have to watch her decide.

Elyda's head swam. Aleksandr and Mhailo. Or Mhailo, Kiril and Grischa, minus Aleks, plus Erwan. Plus Shennikov. "I'll have to collect some of Mhailo's things."

"No time, I'm afraid. We'll have to hurry. The train's due to leave at six." Nallikino hugged Mhailo very tightly.

"I want to go home," the child announced.

"We're going on a train ride," his father said.

"I want to go home."

"Colonel Aleks will let you ride piggyback," his mother coaxed.

Hurrying through the back streets of Donsgrat, Elyda had no wish to turn back. Beyond doubt it was right to follow her lover, but the price to be paid for fulfilment of her heart's wish was one that she had never contemplated, the desertion of Kiril and Grischa. It hurt. Already it hurt and she felt that the pain would never entirely leave her.

At the freight yards, Vano Galiskin was rather surprised to see Madame Filowet and a child in Nallikino's company. A colleague from Danillingrat had whispered of a fondness between the colonel and the marshal's wife, but Vano had not expected fondness to lead to elopement.

"Anything to spite the army," he had said blithely to the doorman. The last two hours had been a glorious caper, but did "anything to spite the army" really include helping a disgraced colonel to run off with Madame Filowet?

Galiskin thought for a moment, noticed the resemblance between the colonel and the boy whose head lolled on his shoulder, and decided that he could not stop the departure of the Nadonnu Special even if it rendered his continuance as stationmaster unlikely.

"Sir, madam." He submerged his fears for his future under banter. "Your train awaits. The locomotive is I admit a trifle scruffy, it was in the yard for a repaint. I assure you it's in perfect working order. The carriage is equipped with every luxury, thanks to its owner, a beef baron. He won't begrudge the loan of it since he's in the capital trying to scrounge a title." Galiskin assisted the passengers to board and prattled on. "Unfortunately the attendants were too drunk to cater for you, and truth to tell I have reservations about the fireman. I'm sure he'll work the alcohol out of his system soon. The driver hasn't touched a drop of liquor all day, he'll be safe."

"I don't know how to thank you," Nallikino said awkwardly, because to offer Galiskin money would be offensive.

"I do," said Madame Filowet. She pressed something, a ring by the feel of it, into Galiskin's palm, folded his fingers over it.

Vano did not open his hand until he had waved the train out of the yard. She had given him a ring, set with diamonds of sufficient value to ease his fears about economic survival after his dismissal. He hoped that she would not regret her generosity. He knew Nadonnu for the rough difficult place it was.

20.

To preclude investigation into his personal life, the fat bald clerk strove to impress his superiors. He had been the first to volunteer for work on First Summer's Day collating the congratulatory telegraphs from all parts of the empire into a commemorative album for the emperor. Their content was trite, a play of variations on a theme: *The inhabitants of Backwaters welcome the inauguration of the nationwide telegraph service and pledge undying loyalty to His Imperial Majesty.* Although the emperor was unlikely to wade through the album from cover to cover unless he needed to bore himself to sleep, the messages required some sort of order.

Mid-afternoon, whoops of delight from the machine room down the corridor broke the tedium. Several colleagues bounded into the clerk's tiny office with another batch of messages, of which the top one was an abbreviated version of Filowet's address in Donsgrat's main square. Excitedly they read it aloud in chorus.

"It's official, praise be the Most Holy. Chrezdonow's back," one of the clerks said.

Practised in the arts of deceit, the clerk pretended to share in the jubilation. "This message will go right at the front," he declared.

He stuck the new page at the start of the album and picked up the next message. Someone had been careless. Someone had included a telegram for the personal attention of Mishka Sillin from General Aksalov at Fourth Army Headquarters in Kitak. It was not a piece of paper that ought to have landed on the clerk's desk, particularly after its text had been deciphered. He read it, and having read it, he copied it by hand.

He took the original and from the machine room door called to the head clerk, "Excuse me, sir... I don't think His Imperial Majesty will want to be bothered by this." The head clerk almost snatched the order from him.

Three-quarters of an hour later, he wished that he had not copied Aksalov's message. Too much knowledge was a burden, but if he could not forget it, he could at least share it in accord with the peasant saying that Granny had often quoted, "Loads get lighter the more men carry them." Granny had never been wrong.

When his shift ended, the clerk scoured the Fifth Ring in search of the sculptor.

Shortly before midnight, the sculptor read aloud, "General Aksalov's compliments to Count Mishka Sillin, by the appointment and favour of His Imperial Majesty Nikolka the Sixth, Minister of the Interior. The Minister is herewith requested to requisition rail and ferry transport for twelve thousand troops from Kitak to Leyarsk via Nadonnu and the Okhpati Spur, and for ten thousand five hundred troops from Donsgrat to Kitak."

"Do you think we should show this to Countess Tenja?"

"Absolutely," the sculptor agreed. "But not tonight."

21.

The consequences of the Nadonnu Special were not quite what Vano Galiskin expected. The morning after its departure, he suffered the worst hangover of his life: unsettled stomach, furred mouth, unquenchable thirst, skull–splitting headache. He shut himself away, ostensibly to attend to paperwork. His staff were careful not to disturb him. They were fragile too.

Just before lunch, Major Zharalov and Captain Shennikov burst noisily into his office. Vano had not expected to be called to account so quickly. His heart jumped.

"Good morning gentlemen. How may I be of assistance?"

"Yesterday," the captain began mildly. Galiskin braced himself. "Yesterday was a glorious day. Future generations will call those of us who witnessed it blessed. A pity the glory was marred. A traitor was unearthed, a traitor who deserves to be shot, a traitor who kidnapped an innocent child, a traitor who has thus far evaded justice. Treason and abduction are not crimes that anyone who holds a responsible job ought to be involved in."

"If I am involved, which I dispute, what are you going to do?"

"Nothing," said the major.

"Nothing except remember," said the captain. "You are a small cog in a big machine. Small cogs can easily be replaced. Count yourself fortunate that we need the big machine to be fully operational. Soon it will be stretched to capacity, so the replacement of small parts will have to wait. Come, Major Zharalov, our business is concluded."

"Not quite. The diamonds," said Zharalov. "Perhaps you aren't aware that diamonds are as individual as people. An expert can recognise where they were mined as well as who cut and set them. Fascinating isn't it?"

As soon as he had his office to himself again, Galiskin fumbled with the lock on the bottom drawer of his desk and at last extracted the brandy from the drawer. He did not bother with a glass, though he banged his teeth on the bottle's lip. He did not understand why his visitors had talked about diamonds. They could not possibly know that Madame Filowet had given him her ring, yet know they did. He drank another tot of brandy, before he locked the bottle safely in its drawer. He had to stay sober while he composed a letter of apology and explanation to his boss.

22.

The sculptor rarely visited the Nobles' Ring. He carried with him a small bronze of a horse in case anyone officious demanded to know why he was there. Tenja was surprised to see him and pleased until she read the message that the clerk had smuggled out of the Ministry.

"Ten thousand five hundred from Donsgrat to Kitak?" she queried.

"Ten thousand Heartlanders, plus five hundred officers, servants and cooks," the sculptor guessed. "It would be quicker and cheaper to send them to the Okhpat goldfields, a straight line instead of a dog leg."

"Chrezdonow and his ten thousand on the Nilentin border have a significance that Aksalov and the Fourth Army lack. Compared to that symbol, speed and cost are irrelevant."

"Who's the symbol for? Us or the Nilentins? I mean, why should the Nilentins remember six hundred years of our history? They were busy with a civil war in which Chrezdonow was a minor irritant."

"An irritant to whom they lost the vineyards at Mardestiniak only a century or so ago."

"Surely they aren't stupid enough to start another war for possession of a few grapevines and a symbol of the past are they?"

Mindful of Shennikov's travels to and from Nilens, Tenja replied, "I think they've been encouraged in their stupidity."

Bogan was two hours later than usual coming home from his office. He was not pleased to find his daughter waiting for him in the hall. He thrust the *Imperial Gazette* into her hand, "Read some of that. I need a large brandy before we start the serious discussion that you obviously want us to have."

The front page of the paper was devoted to the triumphant inauguration of the telegraph service and praised what it termed, *the innovatory technology we associate with the name Sillin-Vrekov*. The back page quoted some of the congratulatory messages. Inside, Tenja found an article from a contributor in Donsgrat that began, *Thanks to the technical marvel whereby words coded into electrical impulses travel along wires, you may read today your humble correspondent's report on yesterday's parade in the square in front of the newly repaired Donsgrat Abbey.*

With growing incredulity, Tenja read the full version of Marshal Filowet's speech. She joined her father in his study.

"The man's possessed," Bogan said. "And dangerous. And unstoppable now. The emperor will splutter and puff and do nothing while everyone who thinks he has something to lose will rally to Filowet's side." He drained his brandy. "And in the meantime I'm expected to suspend the normal timetable so the army can use my trains. For free, mark you. How dare I think of profit? I'm informed I have a patriotic duty to support General Aksalov and the Fourth Army in their attempt to end the gold miners' rebellion. I attempt to remind the council how it was orchestrated. Unfortunately I do not have documentary proof that Yosip Klun is an agent of Filowet's or that your friend Shennikov had secret discussions with representatives of a foreign power, and I'm told I must not allow an old enmity to prejudice my judgement."

He walked over to the window to look across the gardens to the river. With his back to Tenja he said, "They've won, my darling. Those bastards have won."

23.

"They hadn't of course," Van said cheerfully as Inika stretched.

"Don't give the end away," Pavl said crossly.

"There were no winners," Fyedora said. "Not in the conventional sense. You see, this is more the heroine's journey than the hero's. You boys might not have noticed but women do things differently." On that note, Fyedora swept from the room.

Before dinner, Pavl, Van and Inika walked to the monastery. In the dusky peace of the round chapel, Inika sat in silence and worried at the section of her grandmother's turbulent life with which she identified most closely. How well she understood that visceral need for a child! How hard it must have been for Tenja to leave that poor Kohantsi baby with her real mother!

Most of the time Inika managed to ignore the emptiness of her womb. She enjoyed her job, not so much the actual work, more the people she did it with. She enjoyed the sisterhood of her water polo team and the exercise. She enjoyed her social life, and if she and Van Morrison Smith often argued, well, nobody said marriage was meant to be easy, and of course the problem that underlay all the quarrels was her husband's reluctance to become a father versus her longing for a child. Weeks and months passed without resolution.

Tenja had had her babies in the end, the lucky woman. Or perhaps not so lucky, depending on who the father had been.

Walking back along Nobles' Avenue, Inika voiced her concerns, "Don't tell me Tenja and Shennikov..." She did not know quite how to finish.

"*We* won't tell you anything, Gran will," Van Nallikino said, while Pavl said with mock incredulity, "The empire trembles on the edge of war and you think about love!"

The Land Between Two Rivers

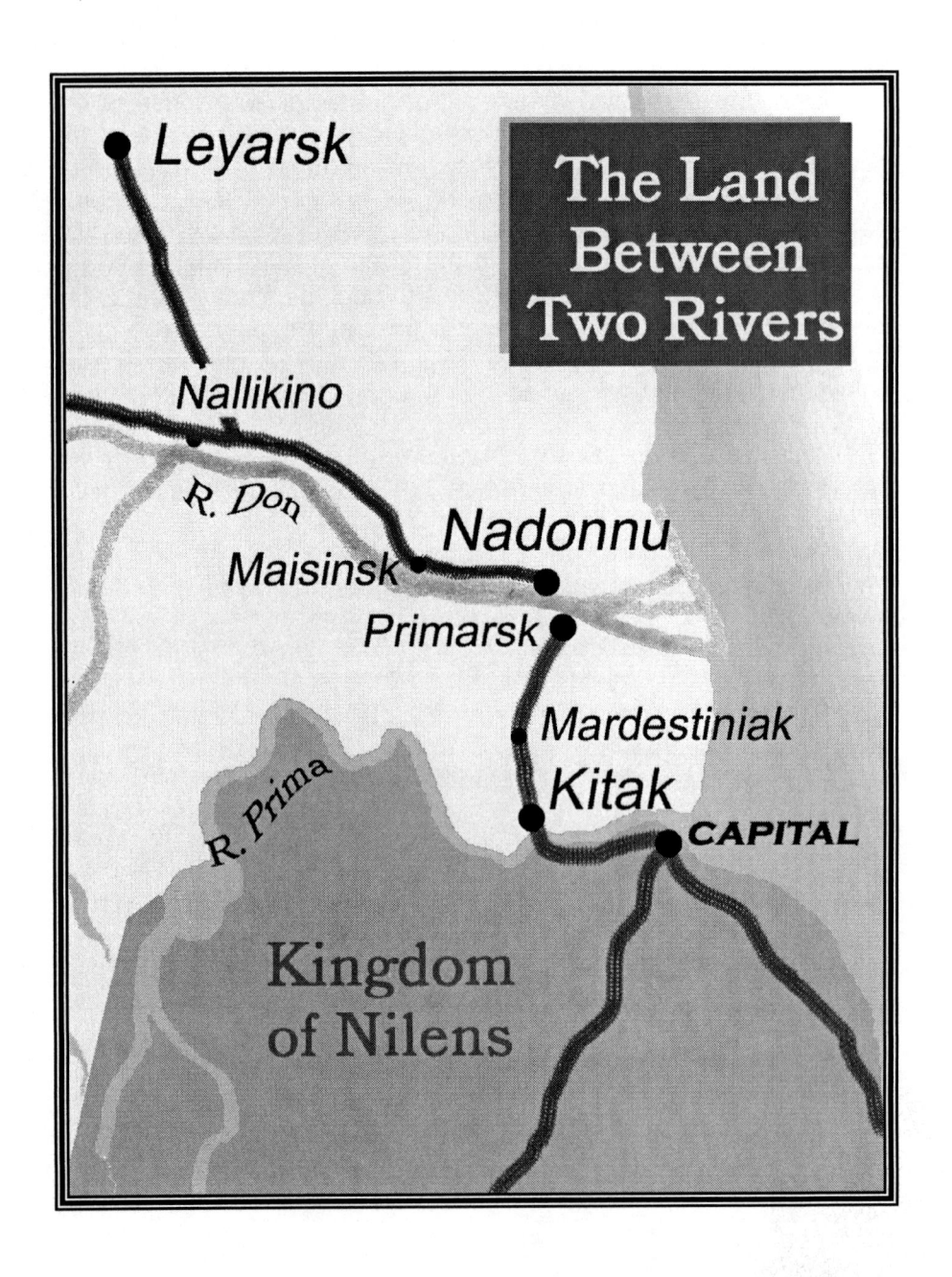

- Leyarsk
- Nallikino
- R. Don
- Maisinsk
- Nadonnu
- Primarsk
- Mardestiniak
- Kitak
- **CAPITAL**
- R. Prima
- Kingdom of Nilens

PART FOUR
THE POWER OF WATER
Imperial Year 615

1.

"In Nadonnu, you either develop a kind of robustness – our sense of humour is the best guide to what I mean – or you move on. Thing is, we're so far east there's nowhere left to move on to." Thus began Arkady Galiskin's introductory speech to the migrants who fetched up on his doorstep. "You'll have noticed Nadonnu's similarities to Donsgrat on your way from the station." Elyda giggled, because Nadonnu was as ugly as Donsgrat was picturesque. "Nadonnu has a station, like Donsgrat and a harbour, like Donsgrat. It's squashed between the river and the escarpment, like Donsgrat. All it lacks is the army."

"Fortunately," said Nallikino.

"Unlike Donsgrat, where everyone pries into everyone else's affairs – at least my cousin Vano does – locally it is the height of rudeness to ask newcomers why they are here, and for newcomers to volunteer explanations. You're judged on who you are, not who you were back west. Provided you behave by our rules, you'll be accepted. Protected too. If officials from outside ask about you, locals will deny any knowledge of you. But if criminals bring the old habits with them, Nadonnu justice is rough. Bodies are regularly fished out of the harbour, and if they're outsiders, no one bothers to investigate how they died. You'll do all right if you can take it for what it is and not expect it to be anything it isn't.

"Mind you, the climate's horrible: hot humid summers and cool wet winters, that are cold when the east wind blasts across the delta marshes."

"Nadonnu's not all bad," said Ana Galiskin. "It's not devoid of culture. There's the orchestra and the choir and one of the schoolmasters is an authority on the regional flora and fauna."

"He specialises in insects. We have lots of different sorts and most of them bite."

Ana swatted her husband with the newspaper, and added, "It's always easy to get work. What sort of work are you wanting?"

"Something as obscure as possible," Aleksandr replied.

"They always need stokers in the engine rooms on the ferries. It's a filthy job, long hours, poor conditions, worse pay. Ships are like the army, there's a strict pecking order and stokers are the lowest of the low. If obscurity really is important to you it's the best job available. Nobody recognises a stoker by his face, let alone by his name, just by the dirt on his hands and clothes. You can start as a stoker tomorrow if you want."

"Tomorrow it is," said Nallikino.

"Don't be so hasty." Ana was quite cross that Nallikino had not consulted Elyda. "If you work for the ferry company you can't stay with us. This is the company's house and it's against policy."

Elyda said, "I don't want to stay with you in any case." She wanted to shrink under the table. "I mean, I don't want to impose on you and I don't want to make your lives difficult. You see, we're bound to be traced to Nadonnu and I'd hate to repay your kindness by bringing reprisals down on you."

Ana offered gentle reassurance, "It's true what Arkady told you. No one gives outsiders information."

"One of the men who'll look for us could find us without assistance."

"He'd have to be a magician to do that," Arkady was jocular.

"He is," Elyda said. Ana frowned in disapproval.

The next day, Arkady took Aleksandr to the ferry company's office, and Ana introduced Elyda to a woman who rented out cheap accommodation. Thereafter, the Galiskins distanced themselves.

From the properties affordable, Elyda chose a cottage in the old quarter of Nadonnu known as the fisher town. With its view of the harbour, the cottage was a romantic rather than a practical choice. Elyda, who had always had servants, had much to learn about practicalities.

Her teacher was the local matriarch, Dina. They met when Elyda tried to work the pump at the top of the street.

"Not like that dearie, like this!" Despite hands twisted by arthritis, Dina filled Elyda's pails and her own with water. "Boil it afore you let your laddie drink it," Dina advised as they carried their buckets down the street together. Dina, who lived next door, soon seemed to prefer Elyda's cottage to her own.

"Not like that dearie," echoed like a chorus as Elyda attempted to scrub a floor, lay a fire, wash the pots. Nobody of Dina's class would have dared to address Madame Filowet as "dearie" but Madame Filowet had ceased to exist, her place taken by Elyda who needed advice and help so much that she had to accept the caustic manner with which it was given.

With his mother, Mhailo was by turns clingy and truculent, with his father, sullen. With Dina's granddaughter Tita, he beamed and giggled and played as though he did not miss his brothers or the routines of his old home.

"What did your ma teach you when you were Tita's age?" Dina demanded when Elyda's stew boiled dry.

Through gritted teeth Elyda replied, "Reading, writing, drawing, painting, music."

"They'll put a meal in your man's belly," Dina cackled.

"And sewing too." Elyda showed her the piece of cloth that she had embroidered with some threads left by a previous tenant.

"That's a bit more like it. You could sell work that neat to the posher folk round here. Maybe you'd get enough to pay someone to cook for you, so your man'd get to eat something decent once in a while. He ain't going to get much of a meal tonight."

Despite the scorn, Dina was fond of Elyda and because Dina, the arbiter of the street's opinion, liked her, the other women tolerated her, although they were jealous too. "The child's four and her and her man are still love-birds. How's she managed to keep him when she can't feed him proper?" they grumbled at the pump and Dina remarked coarsely about bedsprings.

2.

The next time Vano Galiskin saw Shennikov, the captain was in the queue at the ticket office. Told later that Shennikov's destination was the Nilentin capital via Nadonnu, Galiskin muttered a prayer for Nallikino and Madame Filowet.

The stationmaster was learning why he was regarded as indispensable. The regular timetable had been disrupted by the army's requisition of most of the rolling stock, but every passenger train that did reach Donsgrat was packed. Men of all classes except the lowest, of all ages from tall fourteen year olds who claimed to be eighteen to grandfathers of sixty-five who claimed to be fifty, of all degrees of physical fitness, flocked into town, eager to enlist under Chrezdonow's banner.

The army established a preliminary assessment centre where they rejected the majority of would-be soldiers, then refused to accept any responsibility for the discards. Disconsolate men hung around the station until places were available on homebound trains, and while they waited, they required food, water and adequate sanitation. In addition to all his other duties, Galiskin had to become their welfare officer.

3.

When stories of Filowet's announcement began to circulate in Nadonnu, the inhabitants of fisher town were not interested. They had their own problems.

On the evening that Elyda burnt the stew, the crew of one boat had to cut the nets that had snagged on an underwater obstacle. The following morning, a fisherman died of blood poisoning. The day after, another man was drowned. Two days later, a freak wave sank a boat with the loss of all hands.

"She brought the bad luck," one of the women snarled after Elyda had drawn her water from the pump.

"Nonsense!" said Dina sharply.

That evening the dog came. Several women saw trailing behind Nallikino like a shadow, although he was oblivious to it. Far from the usual type of mongrel that scavenged around the harbour and cringed from passers-by, this animal was an aristocrat that did not flinch.

Elyda and Aleksandr were unaware of the dog's existence until it began to howl in the middle of the moonlit night. They heard Dina fling the contents of her chamber pot at it from her upstairs window. Watching it lope away, Elyda asked Nallikino whether the creature reminded him of anyone.

"No. Should it?"

"Yes. Shennikov."

"It's a dog."

"It's his dog."

Aleksandr knew better than to rationalise or argue.

Against Elyda's wishes, he set off for work as usual in the morning. Elyda acted brave until minutes after leaving to play with Tita and her friends, Mhailo came back, bawling because the other children had shunned him. Dina found mother and son in tears, hugging each other.

Dina began kindly, "You're a good woman. Useless goes without saying. At bottom a good woman...

"Fact remains, nobody'd seen that dog afore you came. It's the last straw. Bad luck that dog is and you brought it. Eight men and a set of nets we've lost since you moved in. Up to now I've done my best to ward you. I can't do it any more. That dog weren't natural. Cases that aren't natural I always sends to Alsim."

"From Nadonnu there aren't many places to go," Elyda muttered.

"Silly girl! Alsim's not a place, he's a man. There's hardly a woman in this street who hasn't snuck off to Alsim at one time or another, and some of them have to go to his wife Hekenah but she's another story. Alsim's Nilenish and he's a magician. You must go to him and you mustn't come back. No matter what he says to you, you must not come back."

Elyda struggled along narrow pitted streets carrying the things she had acquired in a variety of bags, while her guide Tita skipped ahead with Mhailo. The day was so humid that sweat trickled down Elyda's face and back.

They turned right at a junction, and the terrace of houses ended abruptly. Ahead lay open ground crisscrossed by litter-strewn paths where the tall grass was already yellowed by the summer sun and the scrubby trees lent away from the east winds of winter. Tita pointed to a cluster of red roofs about a mile away and said, "Alsim lives over there." She ruffled Mhailo's hair, "See you sometime kid." Before Elyda could complain, Tita was walking back along the street.

Elyda rearranged her load so that she could link one finger with her son's small hand. Mhailo grizzled but somehow she managed to pull him along the path that led to the roofs.

The track dipped into a hollow, where willow trees fringed a dirty pond. A man stood under one of the trees, a man unlike anyone Elyda had seen before. If the shape of his face and the tones of his skin suggested that he was not of Settler stock, the style of his clothes confirmed it, for he wore a bright multi-coloured striped waistcoat over a long loose shirt and baggy pantaloons. Smiling politely he asked, "Were you looking for me by any chance? I am called Alsim."

Elyda dumped her bags on the ground. "How did you know?" she demanded.

"Last night I hunted a hunter."

"If you found it, why didn't you kill it?"

"I was not asked to, and besides, creatures that are not of this world do not die in this world. What I can do is offer you the protection of my house and village."

"We've nowhere else to go." Elyda was too upset to be gracious. Nevertheless, Alsim picked up her bags and invited her to follow him.

The red-tiled roofs of his village showed above the wall that curved away from Nadonnu. The main entrance, Alsim explained, faced the river. Mhailo screamed when he saw the carvings on the arch above the open gates. The garishly painted monsters with bulging eyes and slavering jaws and pointed white fangs scared his mother too.

"They are part of the protection that I offer you, the outward representation of powers which work on all perceivable levels," Alsim said. "The dog that stalked you for instance cannot see the carvings but it will sense their powers. It will not pass between them, whatever the compulsion of its master."

Elyda had to carry Mhailo under the arch.

Although she did not see much of the village because Alsim's house was close to the gate, her initial impressions were of spaciousness and good order. Alsim's wife Hekenah was calm and courteous. She greeted her guests as though she also expected them, and invited Mhailo to the kitchen for something good to eat, while Alsim showed Elyda into his sparsely furnished study.

The simplicity suggested artistry, not poverty. Each of the few objects – the low table, the chairs, the cabinet, the flower vase – was beautifully crafted and carefully positioned to create an atmosphere of harmony. In contrast to her surroundings, Elyda felt awkward and dishevelled: her hair was plastered to her forehead, her dress, the one that she had worn at the First Summer's Day parade, was stained and crumpled, her nerves were jangled.

"You are safe here," Alsim said.

"But Aleksandr isn't."

4.

Raised beside the Don, Nallikino liked boats of all sorts, the coracles in which he had learnt to row, the barges which traded along the river, the yachts which the wealthy raced on Lake Illin near Danillingrat, the dumpy steamers which chugged between Nadonnu and Primarsk. He quite liked the hard physical work required of him in the engine-room because it stopped him thinking. When he started to think, he worried about the hardships to which Elyda was subjected, about her husband, about the disgrace which he had brought on his family, about money, about the future, about Shennikov. Today particularly about Shennikov.

He heard irregularities in the engine's rhythm. The chief engineer cursed. Someone yelled, "Mind out!" Someone else punched Nallikino's arm knocking him sideways. He banged his head on the pressure gauge as he fell to the studded metal floor. At least he was not hit in the face by the scalding water that spurted from the burst valve.

He never did discover which of his work-mates had saved him. The engineer trod on his hand, growled, "Get out from under my feet." Nallikino escaped from the engine room on to the lower deck.

The ferry wallowed, barely able to make headway against the strong current. Its passengers fretted about the sluggish progress, but for one nonchalant civilian sitting apart from the rest who continued to read his book. Nallikino recognised the dog that sat at the man's knee before he recognised Shennikov. Nudged by the dog, Shennikov looked up from his book and raised his hand in a lazy salute.

Nallikino stumbled back below decks. He touched the wound on his scalp, saw the blood mixed with the grime on his fingers. He looked at his hands as though they did not belong to him. He decided that he was concussed because he had the headache to prove it and because he had imagined that with the salute Shennikov threatened him, 'Next time you won't be so lucky.'

The ferry toiled through the water to dock at Primarsk. From a porthole Nallikino watched the passengers disembark. He did not see Shennikov or the hound, nor did he find them when he searched the ferry during the voyage back to Nadonnu. Not only had he imagined the threat, he had imagined the man and the dog too.

At Nadonnu, Nallikino walked down the gangway and, in defiance of the third officer who demanded to know where he was going, continued to walk until he was out of the harbour.

A woman dressed in a white cotton shirt and trousers with a bright striped waistcoat, tapped him on his arm. "Excuse me, are you Aleksandr Nallikino?"

"Yes."

"I'm sorry you were hurt. Still, better a bump on the head than a scalded face."

Nallikino stared at her in astonishment. "Are you a kam or something?"

"Do I look like a tent dweller?" she asked crossly.

"Of the five kams I've met in my life, only two live in tents. Moreover, I was once told to expect to meet kams at the forks in my life path, and having just quit my job, I reckon I've probably reached another one of these forks. For myself I wouldn't mind but I have dependents."

"Madame Elyda and Mhailo." She giggled at the perplexed expression on Nallikino's face. "They are in my house where the dog and its master cannot harm them. I came here to invite you to take sanctuary with us."

"Why do you do this for us? You do not know us."

"We are mages. We recognise the ill workings of a shadow heart, and we can tell you do not have the resources to defeat him. You were lucky the first time you bested him. You had help this time. But next time?" She shrugged eloquently. "We cannot, will not, allow a shadow heart to hurt you or yours."

Hekenah and Alsim provided Elyda, Aleksandr and Mhailo with a house inside the Nilenish village, and with fresh foods and a kindly woman to cook for them. Alsim warned them not to stray outside the walls.

A few days of enforced leisure sufficed for Nallikino to recover from his head wound. Thereafter sanctuary became confinement and he was restless, impatient. Needing to provide for the woman he loved and for their son as a man should and to plan for the future, he did not want to depend indefinitely upon Alsim's charity. He tried to engage with the small things that filled their days, tried to pretend to Elyda that he was content, and when he made love with her in the night, he almost was.

After dinner on a sultry evening, Elyda set down her embroidery. "I cannot stand to see you caged like an animal in a zoo. One or both of us must talk to Alsim."

"I thought you were happy here... as happy as you can be in the circumstances." Nallikino was careful not to name the abandoned children.

"I am," Elyda replied. "It's as if I belong here, but you don't. We cannot carry on like this."

The cook watched over Mhailo while Aleksandr and Elyda went in search of Alsim. They found him at the harbour and he invited them to go fishing with him. The little skiff rocked as Elyda stepped into it, settled ominously low in the water when Aleksandr's weight was added. Alsim rowed out into the Don.

"You feel imprisoned... And frustrated. Elyda has discovered tranquillity in our society, but you are restless... Do not fret. The time for action approaches..." He lifted the oars from the water to let the boat drift with the current. "We Nilenish are a proud people. We mages are the proudest of the proud. We tend to treat Settlers as though you are stupid and ignorant, forgetting that you would not be quite so ignorant if we shared what we know." Apologetically he smiled. "I decided that information on which you were powerless to act would be bothersome to you, so I have not told you that since your accident four-fifths of the Fourth Army border guards have been withdrawn from the Nilentin frontier and sent north to recapture the gold mines. Their places in the border garrisons are taken by..."

Nallikino ended the sentence for him, "My Heartlanders."

"The last contingent passed through Nadonnu today. They are supposed to be dispersed to the various garrisons along the banks of the river you call the Prima and we call the Winding Serpent. For the time being they are camped at Kitak."

The little boat rocked as Nallikino shifted position too suddenly and the river water rippled red in the glow of the sunset. He asked quietly, "Do you expect the Nilentins to attack them?"

Alsim snorted almost derisively, "Look at the opposition! This ten thousand are even less experienced than the originals of six centuries ago."

"I did my best by them."

"Surely you knew all along they were only pawns in the shadow heart's game?" Alsim was not kind in his directness.

Nallikino focussed on the far bank of the Don. "I never guessed the game could get as dirty as deliberate sacrifice."

"Is there nothing you can do to stop it?" Elyda wailed.

"We cannot stand in the path of inevitability," Alsim said.

"But you're a mage. You must be able to do something!"

Alsim shook his head. "My task is to calm the Rushing Serpent. I do not interfere in the politics of this world unless they affect the spirit of the river."

Angrily, Elyda turned on Aleksandr, "Are you simply going to sit still and let it happen?"

Nallikino could not look at her. Alsim spoke in his defence, "He can't save them. He can waste his life trying, or he can wait in passive acceptance of the unacceptable."

"The familiar dilemma," Nallikino muttered. "The officer versus the man. One tries to warn the commander at Kitak, the other stays with his family."

The sun dipped below the horizon. The blood drained from the river as the short southern twilight began. Elyda was crying silently.

Alsim tensed. "He can't! He can't be that stupid!" Lowering the oars into the water he started to pull the skiff against the current. "The shadow heart," he explained, his speech jerky with the effort of rowing. "He has done... what only the rightful... king may do... He has summoned... the Winding Serpent... into this world."

5.

Aleksandr and Elyda slept fitfully, and were already up when Alsim visited them shortly after dawn. The mage was grey with fatigue. He said, "Most of the Most Holy's monks will have sensed what happened as clearly as every Nilenish mage has, but I expect our rulers will want hard facts that you are better placed to provide than they are."

"Is it safe for Aleks to leave the village?" Elyda asked.

"I doubt the shadow heart has spare energy to harass either of you," Alsim said. "I haven't enough left to help you either, but I think you'll find eyewitnesses."

Nallikino crossed to the south bank of the Don on the ferry. He noticed something strange about the crew but could not think what the oddness was. People seemed to be about their business as usual on a workday, and he knew better than to alarm them with talk of disaster.

At Primarsk, the stationmaster was fretful. The train due in from the south had not arrived. Nallikino asked him whether there had been any messages.

"The telegraph's not working," the stationmaster said. "Teething troubles, the telegraphist said, but I don't agree. I add no telegraph to no train to none of my Nilenish workers turning up for work to the stupidity of sending ten thousand Heartlanders to the banks of the Prima to the appearance of a military man - I've seen enough specimens of the type recently to spot another, even one dressed in the clothes of a poor man - and I come up with something more awful than I want to contemplate. Tell me I'm wrong if you can."

"I need incontrovertible facts before I can be definite."

"You'll be wanting to travel south... I can't risk a loco or a crew any further south than Mardestiniak. There's a turntable there, from before they finished the tunnel, so you can get back here in a hurry."

A comparatively short time later, Nallikino reached Mardestiniak. Alone in the carriage, he had not been able to keep memories of the Heartland boys out of his mind. He had turned them into men only for Filowet to waste them. Sad and angry, he stepped on to the platform of a pretty country station. It was crowded with Settler farmworkers who tried to climb into the empty carriage.

"Off with you!" the train guard roared. "We're turning round and heading back to Primarsk the second the gentleman's finished his business hereabouts."

With typical peasant resignation they got off the train and resumed their wait. There were no Nilenish among them.

Nallikino went through the white-painted gate on to the road that led up the Mardestiniak rise. Ahead of him the black mouth of the tunnel yawned: above it, the hillside was covered in orderly rows of vines hung with little clusters of the grapes destined to become the famed Mardestiniak brandy. Nallikino wondered whether this crop would grow to ripeness or whether it would be destroyed by fighting soldiers. A memorial to those who had died during the last war between the empire and the kingdom dominated the crest of the rise.

Nallikino climbed the hill and from beside the monument, he looked to the far horizon. Where he expected Kitak to be, he saw a dark smudge of smoke. He corrected himself, where Kitak had been. In front of him, and below, the road wound south between more vineyards and pastures and woodlands until it merged into the haze of distance. By contrast, the railway ran straight. He thought he saw movement on the tracks. He waited until he was sure before he hurried downhill.

"By all that's holy!" he exclaimed as he recognised the leader of the straggly line of men.

"What the fuck are you doing here sir?" Pridushkin asked.

"Looking for the likes of you, sergeant." Nallikino drew him apart from the rest of the soldiers, most of whom flopped to the ground, while the others stood staring vacantly at the railway tracks. "Tell me what happened."

Words did not come easily to Pridushkin at first, though by the end he was raging. "There was this girl see, the sort who looks innocent and isn't... We met up for a little outdoor frolic... I owe her my life, Most Holy bless her, but she scarpered when that thing lit up the sky and I lost her. Like a dragon out of a story it was, flaming wings... Sounds nuts sir but I swear I saw it and with it came the guns and she ran away and I lost her... I hope she's still alive, I tried to find her... Nearly got trampled by a Nilentin patrol. Nasty guttural talk they have, like savages. They are savages to do what they did. I got off lightly compared with some of these lads. Fourth Army lads they are. We've walked all night, we're knackered...

"Tell you what I reckon. Those Nilentin swine were waiting for us. Someone's got to tell the emperor the truth. We were set up sir. Fucking Marshal fucking Filowet and that bastard Shennikov, they set us up. Right from the beginning, you remember sir our little chat in the Heartlands, they set us up ... I'll kill them, I swear I will."

"You'll be behind me, Pridushkin, trust me on that one. Let's get these men to Mardestiniak."

Too exhausted to climb over the hill, the Fourth Army survivors joined hands and with hunched shoulders walked through the railway tunnel.

After Aleksandr left, Elyda sat in the garden nursing her cup of tea. She thought of the young men she had seen at the First Summer's Day parade, keen and proud under the sun, and she did not know who she hated most - her husband, Shennikov or the Nilentin soldiers. She knew she was not supposed to indulge in hatred. The church preached against it, but Dina had told her that the church had very little authority here at the empire's end.

She realised that ordinary folk, those who regarded religion as irrelevant and her husband as a hero, would blame the Nilentins, and perhaps their kinsfolk too. She did not want to wake Alsim and Hekenah so she went to call on Dina.

"You've a nerve showing your mug on my street. 'Specially this early of a morning, and looking so awful. You've been crying haven't you? Alsim kicked you out? You can't come crawling back here."

"Alsim has not kicked us out but I've come here on his behalf, his and Hekenah's, all the Nilenish in fact. They're going to need help and you're the best one to help them."

Dina was intrigued. She scanned the street: no one was watching so she invited Elyda into her tiny scullery.

"Spit it out girl! How can I help Alsim?"

"You know the Heartland soldiers who were sent to Kitak?"

"Can't say as I know them. About them yes. So what?"

"Last night Alsim had a vision. The Nilentin army has killed all the Heartlanders and the rest of the Fourth Army garrison."

"No!" cried Dina. "They can't be dead! Alsim must be wrong!"

"Is he ever wrong?"

"No, no he isn't. Never." Dina launched into a flood of invective against the Nilentins. Dead Heartlanders stirred her patriotism as living they had failed to.

When Dina's outrage had been fully, coarsely expressed, Elyda said, "I expect most people in Nadonnu will feel the same as you about the Nilentins."

"Naturally! They'll want revenge."

"And are they likely to take revenge on the nearest convenient target?"

"I get your drift. You're right. There's some as will blame our Nilenish ... My ma, she used to go to Alsim's grandpa when she had a spot of bother and he used to put her straight. There's not a woman on my street who hasn't been to Alsim or his wife. None of us would do Alsim any harm."

"What about your husbands and sons?"

"A different kettle of fish, they are. They don't like Nilentins, not even our Nilenish. Rivals in the fishing see. There's some as I can think of, hotheads who'll lash out first and think afterwards, if they think at all. It's not right."

"Can you stop them Dina?"

"Fat chance! They won't listen to me, why should they? They're men."

"If the women got together, could they make their men listen to reason? Tell them that if they go anywhere near the Nilenish, they'll refuse to cook with them or sleep with them?"

Dina was derisive, "And get themselves thumped? You've a lot to learn about our sort, dearie." Instinctively, Elyda fingered the scar on her cheek, a reflex which quick-eyed Dina did not miss. "On the other hand, you've already learnt some of it. Your Aleks did that to you did he?"

"Of course not. He couldn't, he'd never hurt me."

"Believe me, he could. All men are capable of hitting women when they're pissed or pissed off, just like they could all beat up our Nilenish because of those murdering demons over the border. It's not right though." Dina brooded for several minutes. "Tell you what dearie. Let's go visit Ksenja. See if she thinks the women in the district will stand together. It has to be all or none, mind you. I'm not having any of my women stick her neck out without hers doing the same. Not for Alsim, not for nobody."

Ksenja's many chins quivered when she heard of the Heartlanders' fate, but she was willing to differentiate between vicious Nilentins and kindly Nilenish. She was ready to agree to Elyda's plan, provided that Aksya, the third local matriarch, agreed too.

"This doesn't happen often, Dina and Ksenja together on my doorstep. You must want something pretty bad. And who is she?" Aksya did not rate Elyda very highly, but to impress her rivals, she served tea in her parlour. The room smelled musty.

Aksya's lament for the dead was prolonged: alone of the trio of matriarchs she mourned for the Fourth Army men as well as the Heartlanders. Despite her genuine grief, she exploited the situation for her advantage. Before she would involve her women, she demanded concessions from Dina and Ksenja on matters of long-standing dispute.

When Aksya announced, "I'm not giving in. That's the end of the whole daft scheme," Elyda shouted in righteous indignation, "You're the most selfish woman I've ever met! You'd let Alsim suffer rather than let Ksenja's cousin share your washing green. You should be ashamed of yourself!"

Dina cackled, "That's right dearie. You tell it straight. Forget the bargains. We owe it to Alsim to cooperate."

"Do we indeed?" Ksenja asked. "You're a fine one to talk about cooperation when you won't let your Tita out with my niece."

"I'll not have my Tita spoilt by that little tart."

"How dare you call my niece a tart!"

"Because she is. Not a day over fourteen and she spreads her legs for any man."

"Alsim can go hang. I'm not having my family insulted." Ksenja's departure was majestic. Dina apologised to Elyda, "Sorry, dearie. It had to be all or none and that bitch Ksenja's made sure it's none."

On her way back to the Nilenish colony, Elyda passed a forlorn-looking chapel. On impulse, she went in.

The lone priest reciting the noon service appeared surprised to have anyone in his congregation. Through a headache, Elyda intoned the prayers, and when they were finished, she stayed in the church. The priest came and sat beside her, too close for comfort.

"Tell me of your distress," he suggested, laying his arm along the back of her chair. She told him about the massacre at Kitak, then asked him to dissuade his flock from attacking the Nilenish in revenge. The priest withdrew his arm. "I won't intervene on behalf of those heathens. If the Most Holy sees fit to punish them, I'll bow down to Him in gratitude."

Her head pounding, Elyda stalked out of the Church. The bright sunlight dazzled her. She cannoned into someone.

"Mind where you're going," the woman was cross until she realised how upset Elyda was. "Here, you're crying. Did that old letch of a priest put his hand up your skirt?"

Elyda had wept most of the night, and having started to cry again because she was furious, she could not stop. The woman was solicitous, and Elyda found herself describing her abortive attempts to protect the Nilenish from reprisals.

The woman smiled. She had an ethereal beauty. "Hekenah saves me and my kind a lot of little problems. We're in her debt. We'll do what Dina won't. You go home and don't worry, and don't let Hekenah worry either."

The sun already hung low in the sky before Nallikino was able to escape from the meetings with Nadonnu's officials - the chief clerk, the judge, the captain of the local militia, two priests, and other greybeards whose precise function remained unclear – that were the consequence of the news he brought from Mardestiniak. He had composed the report that had been telegraphed to the capital under the chief clerk's signature, and he had seen to the survivors' welfare. He had wanted to retire at that point, but the civilians had asked, "What will the enemy do next?" and had refused to accept his answer, "Your guess is as good as mine." He had found himself closeted with the judge, the only official who had fought in the Western War, to devise the town's defensive strategy.

"The people in most immediate need of defence are the Nilenish," Nallikino had said.

"They can look after themselves," the judge had grunted. "They may have lived here forever and a day, but they're still Nilentin at heart. You've admitted yourself, they knew what was going to happen before it happened. I call that colluding with the enemy."

The captain of the militia had been blunter, "If the common folk want revenge off the Nilenish, I'll not stand in their way."

"It's your sworn duty to uphold the peace."

"What'll you do if I don't?" the militiaman had sneered. Nallikino had stared him down.

He hoped that the judge was right, but concern for the Nilenish was uppermost in his mind as he crossed the waste ground. To his annoyance, he found a group of women who had chosen to picnic close to the entrance arch. Something in the way they grinned at him told him how they earned their wages.

"Do you ladies realise you've chosen the most dangerous place in Nadonnu for your party," he called to them.

"Yes," they replied and, "We know what we're doing."

"Are you sure?" he asked.

"Perfectly."

"There aren't very many of you.

"There's enough. Watch."

So Nallikino watched from behind the arch. The sun set, and in the twilight, the fire on the far side of the river was clearly visible. He called to the picnickers and pointed across the Don, "That's the Nilenish quarter of Primarsk burning."

"Only because the girls over there are too chicken to protect their friends," one of the women replied.

They came in the dark, carrying torches, hardly a mob, just twenty drunk, aggressive men intent upon revenge and destruction. Then they noticed the skimpily dressed whores.

"Get out of the way Maryna. We don't want to burn you."

"Oh, you want to burn me Timo Mazli. You want to burn me with the heat of your passion." Mazli was proud and embarrassed to be singled out. "Come on Timo," Maryna continued, "Show me your heart is as big as your cock and go away from here."

"We all know how big your cock is," another woman said and the rest laughed. Timo was prouder and more embarrassed. "If you don't go away," the same woman continued, "We'll tell your wives and sweethearts you were here, and you don't them to find out how well we know you, do you?"

After more banter, the men retreated over the waste ground.

Eventually, more men arrived with more alcohol in their bloodstreams, and the exchanges between the sexes were more ugly. One man tried to lob his burning torch over the wall but was too drunk to aim true.

"Come out and fight," he yelled. "You're cowards to shelter behind women's skirts. Come and fight like real men." He grabbed one of the frailer girls by the hair and started to slap her. His mates dragged him off before Nallikino stepped out of the shadows.

"Here's the militia," Maryna shouted.

The constable in charge was gruff. He ordered the men to disperse or face arrest for disturbing the peace. The men griped, but obeyed. The constable ordered the prostitutes to leave too or face arrest for plying their trade in a public place. They packed up the remnants of their picnic and went home. Maryna blew Nallikino a farewell kiss.

"Will you be staying here?" he asked the constable.

"Yes sir. We're staying. The town clerk says they pays their taxes and their taxes pays our wages. We have to protect them."

At last Nallikino felt justified in going home. Alsim met him at his door, "I thank you for your efforts on our behalf. Our defences suffice to keep out unwanted individuals but they've never been tested by a mob. I thank you both."

"Both?"

"Both," Alsim confirmed. His voice was serious, but his eyes sparkled. "You brought the militia: Elyda brought the ladies."

6.

The days between First Summer's Day and the Nilentin invasion were fretful for Tenja and her mother. Bogan spent his waking hours at the office. Fahra's dreams were hectic but she forgot the details as soon as she awoke, until the night of the massacre at Kitak. What she thought was a nightmare turned out to be a vision of the rise of the Winding Serpent and of the slaughter.

The telegraph message sent from Nadonnu to the emperor and his council of ministers was a factual account of the invasion, and an outline of the measures taken to forestall each of the enemy's likely moves.

The following day, Aleksandr Nallikino sent a message to Bogan Sillin-Vrekov. Outrage crackled through every line and the last was a plea that Countess Tenja use her gifts wisely and soon.

Reading Nallikino's description of the Winding Serpent, Tenja relived her experience of its younger, weaker cousin. Her feelings for Shennikov, who had summoned the creature and loosed it into the ordinary world, hardened into a dark lump that she carried in the pit of her stomach. The last remnants of love, of gratitude, were scoured away, and she despised, reviled, hated him. In the most deeply hidden, most secret corner of her mind, she resolved to outdo him.

She could not shed tears for the Heartlanders.

The court, the church, the city mourned. The citizens demanded that the reborn hero extract blood for blood. The emperor felt obliged to declare war on the Kingdom of Nilens, but so little did he share the public's enthusiasm for the new Chrezdonow that he ordered Marshal Filowet to remain in Donsgrat until they could meet there face to face. The emperor and the council of ministers travelled east.

Where Nikolka went, Bogan had to follow. Much to Bogan's displeasure, his cousin had recommended his reinstatement to the post that he had held during the Western War because no one else had the necessary experience. The acting count marshal with responsibility for transport and distribution was accompanied on the journey east by Fahra, Tenja and Grigor the steward, who had charge of Nallikino's little wooden box.

The imperial train stopped at Manahantjil Summit. As soon as news of the disaster at Kitak reached the capital, Nikolka had sent for Pavel Chrezdonow. Without advice to give, Pavel had refused to leave his home at the foot of the Manahantjils. The emperor had insisted, and reluctantly Pavel had consented to travel to his nearest mainline station.

What was said during their short meeting was never revealed, but Pavel was still ruffled when he requested a restorative cup of green tea from the Sillin-Vrekovs. Tenja was pleased to provide one for him, and sensible enough not to engage him in conversation while he needed quiet.

Too soon, they heard the whistle that warned of the train's imminent departure. Hurriedly, Pavel picked up his cane and gloves, and stepped down on to the platform. Turning to face Tenja, he thanked her for her kindness. Then he added something, "On rare occasions, perhaps once or twice in a lifetime, one must throw caution to the wind and act without heed to causes or consequences."

At least that was what Tenja thought she heard him say. His actual words were lost in the clanks and wheezes of a huge locomotive starting to move forwards.

On arrival in Donsgrat, the emperor and senior councillors occupied the Imperial Hotel and ordered Filowet to report there immediately. The marshal arrived in his own time. Nikolka fumed while he waited.

Since he was not required for that meeting, Bogan was able to establish an office at the station, while Fahra, Tenja and Grigor travelled by cart to the cottage above the town that they had rented from the manager of the barge company. Glad of fresh air and exercise, Fahra and Tenja explored the beech woods around the house where the ground was tinder dry, streams were mere trickles and the leaves on the trees were curled and brown.

Fahra remarked, "I can already smell the rain on the wind."

"I can't," said Tenja.

"You spent too much of your youth indoors to develop your weather sense properly. Summers like this always end in severe storms."

Mother and daughter picked at the supper Grigor had prepared, then played silly card games while they waited for news.

Two a.m., the hour of dreams, came and went. At three, Fahra yawned and said, "Bogan won't bother to come here tonight." She went to bed.

Tenja stayed in the sitting room. The soft light cast by the lamp on the wood-panelled walls turned the room into a ship's cabin. She was on a boat, afloat on a calm empty sea, drifting in the emptiness.

Carriage wheels rumbled in the road. Tenja had the weird sensation of falling upwards into her body. Her lungs heaved as though she had been running and her skin felt hot because she had come back too fast from the place where nothing is, where everything is possible. She had brought back something more than a possibility.

Her father was home. She ought to have looked after him, for she had never seen him look so tired, so old, but instead she had to reassure him that she was perfectly well, just surprised by the sounds of his return.

Slumped into an armchair, he told her what he knew of the meeting. "Somehow Filowet convinced Nikolka that the slaughter of the Heartlanders was a necessary step along the road to renewal. Take the poor and dispossessed and troublesome from the slums for purification in war. They will die nobly for a noble cause. Their names will live forever... and the empire will be a better safer place for the rest of us. What rubbish! What utter rubbish!"

Tenja sat on the arm of her father's chair and lent into him, "I know how to stop the war before it starts. In theory, at any rate."

"If you can, you must."

"Even in defiance of the Most Holy Incarnate?"

Bogan rubbed his eyes with the heels of his palms, and sighed, "I wish... I don't know what I wish... Your mother is the expert in matters of the soul."

By the time Tenja woke in the morning, her father had already returned to his office at the station. She asked Grigor to show her the box. He took it from the breadbin and when he held it out to her, she was able to touch and hold it, to open it and to read the scroll it contained.

She carried both box and scroll outside to where her mother was sitting on the veranda. With a cup of tea forgotten on the boards beside her, Fahra was watching two little birds fly to and from their nest in the hedge.

"What have you got there?" Fahra asked.

"The spell that Fyedor the Great created to compel the Great White Mother and beings of her ilk to guard the borders of our country."

"Now I understand why your father says you have soul trouble. You think you can't use that spell because the Most Holy forbids the summoning of demons from Below." She squinted up at her daughter and grinned. "Do you remember what He actually said?"

"That nobody..."

"Wrong!"

"Wrong? How?"

"His actual words were 'Let no man and so on and so forth.'... You don't get it do you? 'Let no MAN...'"

"I did wonder at the time why He was staring at me." Tenja felt hollow inside. "I don't think I'm strong enough or wise enough."

Fahra raised the cup of cold tea to her lips and set it back in the saucer with a rattle. Her hand shook. "The White Bears tell us to sing truly. Only you know what your true song is."

Every detail of the sunlit garden appeared clear and vivid as adrenaline heightened Tenja's perceptions. "You saw the damage the capital's guardian did and you want me to set another loose?"

"When you met that being, you weren't expecting it, and you were not armed with this." Fahra tapped the box that lay on the veranda near her. "The least you can do is practise it. You aren't committed to performing it until you decide you are. Nobody can make you do this and nobody will know if you don't."

"Aleksandr Nallikino will know because he gave me the box. You and my father will know. And Pavel Chrezdonow."

"And none of us will think more or less of you whatever you do, because only you can sing your true song." Fahra took her cup and saucer back into the house.

Tenja dropped down the endless stair into the underworld. On the windswept tundra, she cuddled the wolf while he reminded her that a hunter does not stop a stride away from the throat of its prey.

"I'm not exactly on a hunt," Tenja said. The wolf wriggled free of her embrace and as he ran into the polar night he called, "Leap. Bite. Kill."

Inside the house, out of the sun and the breeze, Tenja opened Nallikino's box, and once more unrolled the fine vellum on which Fyedor the Great had written a few words of tremendous power. Tempting power. She thought of Shennikov who had raised just one being when she now possessed the ability to summon them all. At last she had more than he had. "Leap. Bite. Kill." Oh yes. She could have danced round the small room.

But her triumph song was not a true song. She could not summon the guardians simply to vanquish a rival, however loathsome he was. She decided to have a bath to cleanse her thoughts as well as her body.

The cottage lacked indoor plumbing. She asked Grigor to prepare the hipbath for her, and while he heated panfuls of water, she journeyed into the upper world.

The ancestors were distrustful of her. Nastily, they warned her on no account to involve the Great White Mother. One sneered, "Your Kohantsi friend should be enough."

"What do you mean?"

"Look at a map."

Among the books in the cottage she found an atlas. She turned to the pages that showed the empire east of the Manahantjils and understood what her ancestor meant.

She dissolved a handful of salt in the bath and washed her hair and her body as thoroughly as she could, imagining that she was cleaning her thoughts as well.

Dried and dressed, she went back into the garden where her mother was sitting in the shade.

"Would you like to be alone?" Fahra asked.

"I'd prefer you to watch. In case it's too much for me."

"Of course. The next question is where?"

"Somewhere in the woods. I'll know the place when I see it."

They set off in the opposite direction to the one they had taken the previous day, and their new path led them to yew trees so ancient that they had grown into a natural circle. Fahra touched one of the branches, "This place was sacred before the Settlers came. It's a good place."

Tenja paced slowly across the circle to find the spot where the energy was strongest. She looked up but could not see enough of the sky. "We have to find somewhere open. Somewhere a dragon can land."

They walked on until they came to the edge of the scarp where the trunks of felled trees lay among the new growth of grasses and flowering plants. The outskirts of Donsgrat lay at the foot of the cliff and the railway stretched to their left and right beside the shiny ribbon that was the river Don. On the southern horizon, the Heartlands merged with a bank of thick cloud.

"Here," Tenja said, savouring the wide view. She could now smell the distant rain. Rarely had she experienced such sweetness simply because she was alive. She let it course through her before she closed her eyes in prayer.

To the Most Holy Incarnate that she act in alignment with His will, to the Great White Father that He grant her icy clarity, to the Great White Mother that She grant her courage.

They remained aloof. Doubt seeped into her. Was she so tainted by the shadow that her deities repudiated her? So be it. If she were under the shadow, she would use it as best she could. She had memorised Fyedor's words and spoke them aloud to call her Kohantsi friend.

"Dominion I have over thee, Guardian of the Nilentin border. Dominion I have over thee. Thou shalt answer my call. Dominion I have over thee."

And nothing happened.

In the kitchen of the Nilenish house, Mhailo sat under the table while his mother measured ingredients and Hekenah translated the cook's instructions. This, rather than quarrels with his bigger brothers or the piggyback ride through Donsgrat or the special train or games with Tita, was his earliest memory: women's skirts and shoes and the smell of cut fruits and flour and the sudden alarm with which Hekenah yelped, "The snake dance has stopped," and the oddness that he could understand the Nilentin words but his mother could not until he translated for her.

Anxiously Tenja thought, 'It's no good. I've failed.' She was about to walk away when she saw her mother duck behind the closest tree trunk. Something fast and bright flamed across the sky and at the same moment something fluid, something sinuous invaded Tenja's mind. It was intent upon its freedom but she blocked its flight. Determined to break her, it wrapped itself around her and dragged her down into its depths, where she feared that she was drowning, airless, in the flow of browns, greens and blues.

She had to subdue it or die. She thought the words of command, found the breath to say them, for of course she was not drowning in the whirlpools of the Rushing Serpent, she was standing on sun baked earth, breathing in ordinary air.

"Thou art mine to command, Guardian of the Nilentin border. Thou art mine to command. I will thee to my will. Thou are mine to command." She heard splutters and gurgles and spat the taste of river water out of her mouth and held on to the fact that the ground was solid under the soles of her feet.

The spell was working. Sullen, resentful, the being ceased to fight her. She could see it wheeling in the sky above her, a shimmer of sapphire and emerald and bronze. It seemed to have four wings. Then she realised that two beings had answered her call, the Winding Serpent who was the guardian of the present border, and its mate the Rushing Serpent who had been the guardian of the border in Fyedor's time. She had not been precise.

She gazed up at them and realised that though they looked and felt similar, they had slight differences. One was overt in its resistance to her dominance, while the other waited, apparently quiescent, for her to relax her hold, for the chance to kill her.

The brightness dimmed. The beings became misty, wraith-like.

'Oh no, you don't escape from me so easily,' she thought yanking them back as though she were reeling in huge fish. She became aware of their tensions as they flickered between the worlds, present, absent, present again, torn between contradictory orders, hers to keep them here, and, she assumed, Shennikov's to send them back to the underworld. How dare he oppose her will! Wrath fuelled the third and final stage of the spell, where she formally bound the guardians to her bidding.

They shone like jewels, fully manifest in the ordinary world, hers not his. With their might at her disposal she revelled in the power that was limited solely by her imagination. She was a queen, an empress: she could have anything she wanted. She had but to command for the serpents to obey.

The Rushing Serpent seemed to encourage her vast ambition. It coiled and uncoiled across the sky, growing larger and darker on the nourishment she was feeding it. A strange sheep-like bleat somewhere close to her right ear warned that power was corruption.

She shrank back into her small skin. No longer empress of the world, she instructed the guardians to use all means at their disposal to prevent the war that Filowet had planned and to return to the underworld immediately upon completion of their task.

She watched them fly east until they were mere dots against the vast sky. Then they were gone, and she felt little and ordinary and lonely without them. Fahra took her in her arms, and she began to cry, as heavy cloud crossed the sun above them.

Bogan had pinned a huge map to the wall of Vano Galiskin's office, on which he had marked likely bottlenecks in the supply lines. A gust of wind through the open window spattered rain on to the linen map. With a mild curse, Bogan got up from his desk to close the window. This weather was not normal.

When he thought about his daughter's reluctance to defy the Most Holy Incarnate, he in his turn remembered exactly what He had said. Gleefully Bogan ripped the redundant map from the wall, tore his notes into shreds.

Raindrops drummed on the windowpanes. Bogan sobered. On a clean sheet of paper he listed his disposable assets, then wrote a series of short letters to his bankers and to the factors on his estates. He did not trust the emperor.

7.

Twelve hours out of Donsgrat, Marshal Filowet's train passed through the tiny village of Nallikino. When Colonel Viktor Zharalov read the sign, he made a bet with himself that he won before he had finished thinking of it. From the next compartment the marshal shouted, "Brandy. Get me a bottle of brandy."

Zharalov told Filowet's batman, "I'll take it to him. I've more chance of talking him out of it."

Showing the Mardestiniak label to the Marshal, he asked, "Are you sure sir? I mean, it's been a while."

Filowet growled, "Give me that bottle. It was *my* wife that traitor Nallikino stole, not *his*." The sudden absence of the Heartland accent jarred on Zharalov's ears. "Get another glass. I'm not drinking alone."

Zharalov found a second glass and slid cautiously into the seat opposite his commander's. On the table between them lay the final drafts of Filowet's plans. Even upside down Zharalov could read the ill-formed letters **W.Ch** at the foot of the top page. Alarm buzzed faintly.

Never before had he doubted or questioned. Primed by his father and by his friend Shennikov, he had accepted without analysis of the facts that Chrezdonow lived again in the Marshal. So far as Zharalov was concerned, talk of cleansing and purification was the rhetoric necessary to win popular support, and he ignored it to concentrate on practicalities and the chance offered by war to test his courage against his father's.

In negotiations with the Nilentins, Zharalov had played upon their opinion of him a typical boorish Settler. They did not try to conceal their conviction that they would win. "Consider the quality of your leadership," they had said.

"Emperor Nikolka the Sixth is no warrior," he had conceded, but the Nilentins had continued to smile condescendingly.

Divided from Filowet by a table and an emptying bottle, Zharalov began to understand why.

Beyond the window, the sky above the forest was darkened by grey clouds.

"He hates booze," Filowet said with a loud deliberate belch. "Well, I hate him. He claims credit for everything that goes right and punishes me for everything that goes awry, and I've had enough of him." He downed another large tot of spirit and refilled his glass and Zharalov's. "Come on man, drink up."

After months of abstinence, the alcohol brought Filowet to the confidential stage very quickly. "He was rude to the emperor you know, called him milksop and runtling. I could hardly keep a straight face. He's got a good sense of humour, I'll say that much for him... but he's a bully, and a coward. You wouldn't think it, given his reputation, but I'm telling you, he's a bully and a coward."

As the level in the bottle fell, Filowet replayed all three of the characters involved in the marshal's interview with the emperor.

The high-pitched voice was Nikolka's, "Nothing justifies the illegal supply of guns to the rebels, the incitement of rebellion, the collusion with an enemy, the murder – yes, murder - of several thousand unfortunates, not to mention connivance with that apostate cleric Wassil and evil creatures from Below."

The Heartland roll was Woldymer Chrezdonow's, "Yap, yap, yap! Remind him you've done it for him. That'll shut him up."

The normal narrative voice was Filowet's, describing how he had knelt at His Majesty's feet, drawn his ceremonial sword, and presented it, hilt first, to his overlord.

Chrezdonow: "Nice touch."

Filowet: "All I have done and will do is for you and for our beloved empire."

Nikolka: "Put it away. You are too like your uncle. He said he loved the church yet he broke its rules. Love indeed! Nothing he did benefited the church, and nothing you have done benefits me or my empire."

Filowet: "Desperate situations demand drastic remedies and you, sir, are too noble..."

Chrezdonow (interrupting): "Too feeble."

Filowet: "Too noble to have sacrificed the Heartlanders. I've taken upon myself the burdens necessary to unite a divided nation in a single cause."

Chrezdonow (irritated): "You're too humble. Besides what about me?"

Filowet: "Every move in my strategy has been guided by the hero whose soul resides within my heart, whose blood flows in your veins."

Chrezdonow (whispering): "Diluted to extinction, otherwise I'd have come back to him, not you."

Nikolka (petulant): "And does his strategy include replacing me upon the throne? Look at me when you answer."

Filowet: "Twice, once at my inception as Marshal of the Third Army and again now, I have pledged my loyalty to you by offering you my sword. If you do not trust me, sir, take my sword and cut off my head."

Chrezdonow: "Lucky for you he's too squeamish to do it."

Nikolka (pacing up and down the room): "Was your uncle's blasphemy part of the strategy?"

Filowet: "No."

Chrezdonow: "Dear uncle Wassil thought that one up by himself to disgrace Sillin-Vrekov's daughter and Sillin-Vrekov too. Stupid uncle Wassil, builder of his own downfall... Shall I tell you what that weak-kneed creature over by the window is thinking? He's thinking about me. He hates you because I'm alive in you and you were born common. He forgets I'm peasant born and proud of it."

Nikolka: "I have to admit I liked part of your speech, the part where you gave the looters and the anarchists the choice to submit to soldierly discipline or face their destruction. I liked that very much. You probably do not know that I visit the slums once a week to serve soup to the poor. I suppose a few of them are unfortunate but the majority are lazy and undisciplined. They disgust me. By all means, take them into the army, clean them, polish them, dress them in uniform, drill them, make them proud to be soldiers... But the fact remains, you have placed me in a quandary. I did not seek war with the Kingdom of Nilens and your methods appal me... However, I must accept that Chrezdonow chose to incarnate in you, and that he and you are more likely to bring the war to a speedy and victorious conclusion than General Aksalov. Therefore Aksalov must remain in the Okhpat while I appoint you commander of my combined armies on our southern frontier."

Chrezdonow: "Why couldn't he have said so in the first place?"

Filowet: "Thank you Your Imperial Majesty."

The scene was repeated three or four times until the bottle was empty and Filowet fell into a doze. Hard rain streamed on the outer side of the window. When eventually bladder pressure forced Zharalov to move, Filowet woke and said blearily, "Did I ever tell you how he came to me?"

"No sir, not in detail sir. I'll get us another bottle shall I sir?"

Zharalov took his time in the hopes that the marshal would fall asleep again. The ploy was unsuccessful and he had to listen to a second dialogue.

Filowet set the scene. "Let me tell you how it began. First Summer's Eve last year. It rained then like it's raining now. His statue saluted me you know. Not once but twice, just in case I hadn't seen it the first time."

Chrezdonow: "If you think you're special, it's because of me. I made you brave. You didn't think you did those daring deeds by yourself did you?"

Filowet: "Who are you that you condescend to me?"

Chrezdonow: "Who do you think I am?"

Filowet: "You sound rather like my father."

Chrezdonow: "Father of the empire more like."

Filowet: "You can't be!"

Chrezdonow: "I can 'cos I am, and I always have been. Think back to before you went on a raid. What did you feel?"

Filowet: "As if I was outside myself because something or someone greater than me had taken over. It..."

Chrezdonow: "You mean, he. Me."

Filowet: "He... you took away the fear. I never doubted I'd survive."

Chrezdonow: "I made sure you'd survive for the sake of our shared future. It's our sacred duty to make my empire great and proud again. Are you with me?"

Filowet: "I am. I am with you. I agree the empire is in a bit of a mess."

Chrezdonow: "And so are you. Before we can cleanse the empire, you must also be cleansed. You're a disgrace. You drink too much. You spend too much time and money on horses and cards. You waste your precious seed on whores. You must plough your wife's furrow, only hers you understand, and get another son. When you are sober, prudent and faithful, you will be a fit vessel for me. Together we can fulfil our destiny."

Filowet yawned. "He's very angry with me. He hates the booze you know. He says he'll make me pay, but I say to him, that when I see the name of the thief who stole my wife and kidnapped my child I think

I'm entitled to have a little drink..." Without bothering to refill his glass, he drank straight from the bottle and coughed and spluttered as the brandy burned his throat.

8.

Elyda was fretful. Dinnertime approached and she had not seen Aleksandr since before lunch. She did not know where he was. After running from the kitchen, Hekenah had not returned to explain, so Elyda could only guess that the weather was strange on account of the end of the snake dance. A mass of dark cloud had arrived from the west, and the temperature had dropped from hot to evening cool hours before sunset. She stared out of the window and watched the rain bounce off the cobbles. However much she hated getting her shoes wet, she needed to find out what was happening. Once again she left Mhailo with the cook and dashed up the street to Alsim's home. Brown water swirled along the gutters. Never had she seen a rainstorm quite like it.

She found Alsim on his knees with pieces of sailcloth spread on the floor around him. Wrapping up a vase, he smiled wryly, "I find I cannot let go of such beautiful objects. Perhaps in the attic they will remain undamaged. I'm sentimental and impractical in my wife's opinion. She is in the kitchen being sensible."

"No I'm not, I'm here," said Hekenah. "This may be difficult for you to understand, dearest Elyda, but you need to know. The Rushing Serpent and his beloved, the Winding Serpent, have been called into matter despite our efforts to hold them back. We cannot be certain precisely what they have been ordered to do, but they have brought the rain and if it continues, as we are sure it will, the rivers will burst their banks."

"You mean there'll be floods?"

"There will be floods."

"Your home will be wrecked, your garden ruined."

"Probably, but what do they matter?"

Elyda said, "You don't seem upset."

Hekenah explained, "Armies cannot fight over flooded ground."

At that point, they heard the street door open, and they went into the hall to greet a bedraggled Aleksandr. He emptied the water from his shoes into the plant pot while more dripped from his clothes to pool on the floor around him.

"Where were you?" Elyda asked.

"In Nadonnu, trying to persuade the elders to order the evacuation of the town," Aleksandr replied. "According to them, the five minutes

I've been here don't make me an expert on the Don's habits. Sure it's raining. Sure the river's rising. But flood? No, it won't flood. It's never flooded at this time of year." He pulled his sodden shirt over his head. Hekenah fetched him towels. As he dried his hair, he said, "I'm glad the war's going to be over before it's properly started, but a lot of people are going to suffer in the short term."

Physically exhausted, emotionally drained, Tenja slept for most of the afternoon. When she woke up, she was unable to keep still. She swayed gently back and forth, back and forth. At first, the movement was small, almost pleasant, but as time ticked by, the tide rose to turn the movements more vigorous, more compulsive. That she remained so closely linked to the guardians was a little scary. She tried to hold the tide down, but it coursed through her and she began to have visions of brown streams in spate, of rivers in place of roads and railways, and of lakes in place of fields.

Part of her was frightened and wanted everything to stop, while another part revelled in the power that raised and moved the waters.

At some point during the afternoon, Grigor had placed a jug of water on her dressing table. On impulse, she got off her bed and crossed her room so that she could dabble her fingers in the cool water. The sloshing sound enthralled her. She flapped her hand more roughly until little waves jumped over the neck of the container. Water that had slopped on the top of the table dripped down to the uncarpeted floor, but it was too tame to make enough of a mess and she lost interest. She craved violence, needed it in order to destroy. She sat on the edge of her bed, rocking to and fro, feeling the tide batter against anything that restricted its free flow and moving with terrible purpose.

As the night passed, the images were nastier - uprooted trees swirled downstream, upturned boats spun like tops and smashed against rocks, animals paddled with their forelegs in vain attempts to reach solid ground, people clung to roofs. Powerless to interfere, she had to witness scenes of viciousness and cruelty when the strong pushed the weak into the rising water. Unable to help, she watched scenes of heroism, as parents saved their children only to be washed away themselves. She saw tragedies and had to accept responsibility for each and every one of them, but when the floods reached the fortifications on the banks of the Prima, she rejoiced. Ancient cannon placed by Settlers and modern field guns brought by the Nilentin invaders were plucked from their positions and swept down river as lightly as twigs. Without remorse, she watched soldiers drown, for each one submerged beneath the filthy surging torrent was one more who could not kill.

After Zharalov's second escape, Filowet slept for hours. The colonel only woke him when circumstances demanded a decision, "Driver refuses to proceed, sir, floods, two feet deep and more. We'd be risking our necks to press on in weather like this. It's pissing down, never seen a storm like it in my life. We're presently a mile outside Maisink. The driver tells me there's a branch office of the Sillin-Vrekov Barge Company there. I recommend transfer to a barge as preferable to waiting for the floods to subside, especially since the barge can take us direct to Primarsk."

"Nadonnu. Must get to Nadonnu," Filowet insisted for reasons that Zharalov did not immediately understand.

"Nadonnu it is, sir. Via Maisink."

Easier said than done. The headlights from the locomotive showed them the start of the road that led down to the village on the far side of the flood. Filowet was travelling with a staff of five: it took their combined strength to help him down from the coach, and to carry him through the knee-deep puddles.

The road was no longer a road. It was a noisy stream coursing downhill in a headlong rush to meet the river. Twice Filowet skidded, dragging his minions into the mud with him. He bawled at them, blamed them because he was wet and filthy.

The rain poured.

At the rear of the party, Zharalov carried Filowet's plans in a heavy document case. He listened to the filthy language, beheld the spattered dirty appearance of his commander in the pre-dawn light, and his disillusionment was complete. When he slipped, he dropped the case and its contents spewed over the waterlogged ground. The ink ran. He shovelled a few of the sodden papers back into the case, and abandoned the rest because for the first and only time in his life he had an intuition. The plans would not be implemented.

In Maisink, the representative of the Sillin-Vrekov Barge Company refused to hire out a barge. He had to shout to make himself heard against the roar of the river, "The Don is hazardous at the best of times. In rain as heavy as this, the safety of passengers and crews cannot be guaranteed. Please return once the storm has passed, and we can review the situation. Meanwhile the hotel will provide adequate accommodation."

On the doorstep of the hotel a bearded ruffian approached the soldiers. For a substantial sum he was willing to ferry the soldiers to Nadonnu.

Filowet said, "Pay half now, the rest on arrival." He went straight down to the cabin and was asleep again before the barge's mooring ropes were loosed. He remained stretched out on the bunk for most of the wild voyage down the Don, but his staff were too busy to rest, and too frightened. The muscle power of the soldiers, the bargee and his mate was needed to hold the prow of the barge pointing downstream. Twice, terrifyingly, they lost control of the tiller. The barge was spun broadside to the force of the current, then back to front, and finally, miraculously, bow ahead. Water slopped over the gunwales.

Zharalov worked the pump. Up, down, up, down, up, down, rhythmic, crucial to survival. As fast as the bilges emptied, they refilled so the level of water remained constant. The rain did not stop. Up, down, up, down, past thought. The mate crawled forward to replace him. Zharalov swung his arms to ease his muscles, then inched aft along the slippery decks for a turn at the tiller. He wished that he, like Nallikino, had defected weeks ago.

Nallikino lost count of the number of times that he toiled up the scarp behind Nadonnu and back to the Nilenish village over the clods of rain-soaked farmland to fetch more supplies. He was stoical of the discomfort as he stumbled in the twilight and underestimated the depths of puddles. Still it rained.

He was inspired by Elyda. He had assumed that he was as intimately acquainted with her character as with the scars on her body. Ages ago, he had learnt that her crisp, sometimes rude, manner masked shyness and unhappiness. In Nadonnu, he had discovered her persistence. In the Nilenish village, she had transformed again. He did not want to believe that she had lived a previous life there, yet he could find no other explanation for her familiarity and ease in surroundings that were alien to him. Madame Filowet would have been ashamed to consort with whores, whereas Elyda had laughed and had visited the brothel to thank Maryna personally. This evening Elyda had surprised him again, by treating the construction of the makeshift camp on top of the escarpment as a game that she played wholeheartedly for the sake of the children.

If they survived the floods and the end of the war, Nallikino longed to be able to give her the life she deserved, although he could not imagine how to make it possible. He shouldered that load along with the pack full of food.

During the night, Elyda ran out of laughter and courage. Perched on a folded coat, under a temporary roof of sailcloth, she was damp and cold. Cuddled on her lap, Mhailo complained. Elyda snapped at him before she burst into tears. Nallikino the stoic took their son on to his lap and embraced them both, while they watched the guttering torches that signalled the movement of settlers from Nadonnu to the refuge of higher ground.

It rained as hard as ever.

To mark the arrival of morning, the clouds turned a lighter shade of grey. The rain continued. The men aboard the barge were able to see more clearly what lay ahead. Sinews stretched, muscles aching, Zharalov took another shift at the tiller. He feared that the current would sweep the barge past Nadonnu and on to the shoals of the Don delta, maybe even out to sea. To the barge-master with whom he shared the tiller he said, "The second half of your fee will be forfeit unless you deliver us to Nadonnu."

"Blast the fee!" the ruffian growled. "I jus' want to get my mate, my boat and me through this alive."

"You will," roared Filowet, as he emerged from below decks. The hair on the nape of Zharalov's neck prickled. The accent was Heartland, and the certainty Chrezdonow's.

Chrezdonow directed every subsequent movement on the tiller, anticipating what had to be done better than the barge-master who had worked the river most of his life. It seemed to Zharalov that the force which appeared to be the enemy was actually in eerie alliance with Chrezdonow. It was too much. Zharalov clung to the tiller because it was real.

The light of morning filtered through the thin curtains of Tenja's bedroom. Her mother was beside her. "You've had a rough night."

Rough? Tenja could not find an alternative because words were inadequate. "I'm with the guardians," she said.

"I'd guessed," Fahra replied. She had lain awake most of the night, aware of her daughter's turbulence, aware also that mother love could not protect her beloved child. She could try to reassure, "Better this than the alternative. This is unpleasant but it will soon be over, whereas the war could have dragged on for years... You will come through this. It's like labour."

"I'm not giving birth. I'm bringing death," Tenja said. "They're a million miles apart."

"They're closer than you think," Fahra responded.

Tenja did not argue. She was too far away. The tide, which had hurled itself against every obstacle until it broke through, was now concentrated on some massive blocks of granite that had withstood the power of the flood throughout the night. The serpents battered them with deadly intent, and still the stones stood in place. Tenja could not think where they were or why they had to give, but she lent her will, such as it was, and her prayers, to the serpents' endeavours.

The chimneys of the town came into view. Not even Chrezdonow had the skill to bring the barge safely into harbour. He ordered the barge-master where to angle the boat, so that it nosed into the bank upstream of the town. Marshal Filowet added a bonus of ten crowns to the barge-master's fee.

The six soldiers walked towards Nadonnu, unaware that the river washed through the streets until they started to meet refugees. Filowet permitted his weary men to follow the townsfolk up the scarp to find food and shelter while he went to help in the rescue of those who remained trapped in the flooded town. He was a hero.

Nallikino rowed Alsim's skiff along a short street already emptied of its inhabitants. Everyone who lived on the edges of the town had managed to wade to safety, but the Don had risen so rapidly during the night that hundreds of people had been marooned in the districts closest to the river. After most Settler boats had been pounded to bits against the harbour walls, the Nilenish offer of their skiffs had been welcomed although each craft could only carry three adult passengers or the equivalent weight of children. Nallikino had already ferried twenty-nine individuals to higher ground. It was dangerous work.

Though the floodwater in the streets seemed tame compared to the rushing thunderous river, conditions were more hazardous than they appeared. Debris, such as household items, industrial rubbish, a dead pig, floated on the surface, and unpleasant as these objects were, nastier things lurked submerged, sharp and heavy things that could pierce the skiff's thin planking. Yet more dangerous were the eddies and undercurrents where the muddy water draining off the land met the incoming river.

Nallikino's palms were raw, his arms, back and legs protested. He tried to forget the pain. He rowed towards a crossroads. A half-glance over his shoulder showed him the approach of another boat. It took almost a second to register through his tiredness that the rower was familiar. He turned again to check that he was indeed about to confront Erwan Filowet.

Above the thunder of the Don, Nallikino heard Filowet's challenge, and instinctively he dragged on his oars to slew the boat round to face his enemy. Filowet tried and failed to grab the bow, then the side of Nallikino's boat, and in overreaching lost his balance. With a shout and a splash, the marshal sprawled full-length in foul water. Arms flailed, legs kicked, and his head emerged, water streaming from his hair. He gasped for air, inhaled water, coughed, and as he struggled to breathe, he glared up at Nallikino with murder in his eyes.

Nallikino raised one of the wooden oars in a reflexive movement of defence in case Filowet snatched at it, or as an act of aggression.

The massive granite blocks that formed Nadonnu's harbour wall could no longer stand against the battering. They tumbled into the Don. Tenja and the Nilenish mages felt the abruptness with which the Rushing Serpent and the Winding Serpent quit this world. The rain stopped.

The collapse of the harbour wall released a great wave of water across the town. Dissipating as it rolled over Nadonnu, the wave was about a foot high when Nallikino saw it behind Filowet. Aleksandr opened his mouth to say something, a warning, a cry of horror, but nothing came out.

"Please," Filowet begged, eyes on the uplifted oar, unaware of what hurried towards his back.

The wave flung Nallikino's skiff forward. The rope fenders slammed into the corner of a house. The collision pitched him forwards. The stock of the oar raked his ribcage, hit his chin. He was lucky not to bite through his tongue. He heard the sickening thud of blade on bone.

"Please," Filowet had begged. Please, kill me or please, do not. Which? Whichever, the deed was done.

Doubled over the oar, Nallikino was too jarred to move for a time that was long enough for another man to drown.

Much as he longed to hold Elyda, Nallikino had to speak to Alsim first. The mage was waiting for him at the foot of the scarp.

"Filowet is dead," Nallikino announced. "At least I think he is. I... he was hit on the head. I heard his skull break. He must have drowned. I couldn't find his body... Did I kill him or was it an accident?"

Alsim said, "I cannot possibly tell you because I wasn't there. Were I in your shoes, I'd say the Rushing Serpent meant him to die, but you'd probably reject that idea. Whether you choose to carry guilt or not, the fact remains that Filowet's death sets Elyda free... I urge you my friend to look forward. This," Alsim indicated the flooded land and meant much more, "will pass. You and she may, if you wish it, live long and happily together."

"I wish for that more than anything, but there is still Shennikov... unless the Rushing Serpent finished him off too."

"Shennikov lives. He is in Nilens and I don't suppose the Nilentins are as pleased with him today as they were last week. Forget him and Filowet both. Go to Elyda and be as free as she is."

9.

The rationalists produced a century's worth of meteorological records to prove that dry summers in the Don basin always ended in storms and floods, and they dismissed as odd cloud formations the appearance of dragons in the skies above Donsgrat. The emperor did not agree. He had seen real dragons, he was certain of it, and he blamed Tenja.

Mishka Sillin murmured to Bogan, "I'm sorry, I can't help her, or you, with this one. His Imperial Majesty is furious."

"She prevented war with Nilens, she saved the lives of the Most Holy knows how many soldiers, and millions of crowns, and Nikolka is angry?" Bogan protested.

"I gather it's how she did what she did that upsets him, that and the number of innocents who drowned. He's waiting for more precise reports of the loss of life and of the damage done to property before he decides on a suitable punishment."

Of course, Tenja blamed herself so profoundly that she accepted Nikolka's judgement as better than she deserved. Her father was not so meek. For the third time in his life he dared to argue with an emperor and for the second time he was severely punished.

10.

"It's midnight," Fyedora announced. "I think this is a good place to stop."

"But what happened?" asked Inika. "How did the emperor punish them?"

"He gave the Sillin-Vrekov estates and this house to a dreadful little man called Tereshkov." Fyedora folded down one finger. "He put Bogan's businesses under the control of the council of ministers." She folded down a second finger. "He banished Bogan and Fahra to Nadonnu and forced them to pay for repairs and reparations out of their own wealth." She folded down a third finger and fell silent.

Inika prompted, "Tenja."

"How could I have forgotten? I suppose because she hated to be reminded of the wasted years, as she called them. I expect they improved her character. Adversity often does improve people. Van could do with some." She smiled at her grandson not altogether affectionately.

Van deflected her. "Tell Inika about Tenja."

"Ah yes. Nikolka forced her to marry Antoni Marmasy."

"At least he was better than Shennikov," Inika said.

Fyedora drew herself up to her full height and said stiffly, "With all his faults and wickedness, Voldimir Shennikov was more of a man than that prig Antoni Marmasy. Now if you will excuse me, it is past my bedtime." She sailed out of the room.

"Ouch!" said Inika.

"Gran loathed Father Antoni, and when you hear what he did you probably won't like him much either," Van added.

"I wonder when that will be. I'll try to come back soon."

On the way to the station with Pavl and Van the next morning, Inika asked, "Who was my grandfather?"

"Our grandfather," Pavl corrected.

"Well, who was he?" Inika demanded, after Pavl's silence had lasted too long. "Shennikov the traitor or Marmasy the prig?"

"Why assume he was one of them?"

"Because Fahra predicted that Tenja would have a lifelong relationship with Shennikov and because Tenja was forced to marry Father Antoni."

"I have heard that in England some women marry more than once, and some have children outside marriage," Pavl said with a grin. "It is the same here."

"Let me ask it another way round. What's your surname?"

"Suppose I told you it's Chrezdonow," Van interrupted before Pavl could reply.

Inika sighed, "I'd say he thought he was the next incarnation of Woldymer."

It was her last attempt at humour. Parting was more emotional than she had expected, although she did not actually shed a tear until after the train had pulled out of the station. She watched the cityscape and then the countryside roll past the carriage window, wishing that she did not have to leave, calculating when she might be able to return.

According to the itinerary attached to her travel documents she was supposed to change trains at a place called Derzhnez where she had a wait of two and a half hours for the express to Huldenfort. No sooner had she hauled her suitcase on to the platform than an Australian woman came up to her, "Are you Inika by any chance? I'm a friend of Sandro's. He's planned one last surprise for you."

With Inika's luggage into the boot of her electric car, Cass drove the mile or so from the station to the embankment that ran high above the river from which the town took its name. Indicating a huge and rather ugly red sandstone building that broke the terrace of town houses, Cass said, "That's the Imperial Memorial for the Dead of the Western War. Derzhnez is where the Katorians' advance ground to a standstill. They reduced the town to rubble but they couldn't cross the river or climb the cliffs. The museum's fairly horrible, graphic pictures and gruesome relics like the mock up of a field surgery, but there's one room dedicated to the work of the sculptor that Sandro wants me to show you."

"The sculptor?" Inika queried.

"Tenja's closest friend. You must have heard of him. He never signed his actual name or allowed it to be associated with his work. He's known simply as The Sculptor."

As if they were an embarrassment to the memorial's curators, four bronzes - a bust of Bogan Sillin-Vrekov, a red-stained bird of prey, a life-sized figure called *The Last Shoshanu*, and a man whose outstretched arms were in the process of turning into wings - had been consigned to a small room on the top floor of the museum. Both Cass and Inika were out of breath after climbing five flights of stairs, but only Inika experienced a jolt from the birdman like an electric shock. She gasped and pressed her hands against her heart. Her pulse raced. Tentatively, she touched the statue with the tips of her fingers. The metal was inert.

Cass said, "That's the piece that Sandro particularly wanted you to see. It's called *Shapeshifter."*

"It's... extraordinary," Inika said slowly. "Alive almost."

"No almost," Cass said.

In the car on the way back to the station, Inika said, "I know it's an odd question, I should already know the answer but please can you tell me Sandro's surname?"

Cass replied quietly, "Chrezdonow."

Twenty-eight hours later, Inika arrived home to an empty house. Evidence of Van's existence, and that of his mates, littered the lounge in the form of beer bottles, dirty plates and foil containers from the local takeaway, but the man himself was out. Before Inika could begin to tidy up, the phone rang.

With forced cheerfulness Inika's mother said, "Oh, hello darling, you're back. Did you have a good trip?"

Inika's irritation burst into cold fury. "Why didn't you tell me?"

AFTERWORD

The stories that make up **The Web between the Worlds** began in 1991 before the word web gained quite the meaning it has now. In the original beginning, the Heartland wise woman Maria toiled uphill on a hot humid afternoon, whilst at the crossroads above her village the shaman Kolli looked for meaning in the flames of a fire. Both characters have been demoted to minor parts in **The Power of Water**, but they reappear in later stories.

In writing Tenja's story and Nikolas's (and Fyedor the First and Great's) there have been all manner of coincidences and synchronicities, not least the chime of Woldymer, Voldimir and Voldemort, which I have allowed to stand.

As recently as January 2006, I discovered something called the solfeggio that caused the tiny hairs on the nape of my neck to prickle. This scale of six notes used in some Native American chants and European music up to the 16thC is alleged to have healing powers. Is it coincidence that Tenja's song contains six notes or did I draw the concept out of the collective consciousness?

I do believe that the collective consciousness is the source of all stories but I will not write more about that, except to use it to absolve myself of complete responsibility for what my characters say. They, not I, have used England and English when they mean Britain and British, and I have chosen not to correct them because they have not yet crossed the border to discover that Scotland is a different country. I can only hope that Van Nallikino's film will be shown at the Edinburgh Film Festival!

The first time I wrote the end of this story, the farmland around my then home was inundated by 'once in a century' floods, which have afflicted that area twice more since 1997. The next revision was completed on December 21st 2004. On January 9th 2005, the river that runs through the town in which I now live, burst its banks, and the sight and sound of it brought home the immensity of the tsunami of December 26th.

Since then, I have seen the river too low and too high, I have pondered on the use and non-use of its energy and on the unequal distribution of rainfall across the globe. I have listened to and read (rather than watched) news about the severity of the 2005 hurricane season and I have counted myself fortunate that water has never poured through my home. Such thoughts have led to the dedication at the front of this book.

The Web between the Worlds has its origins in the fascination with Russia that began during my teens. In my twenties and early thirties, I was engaged in a sort of historical research which has filtered through into the background of my writings. From Russia I have borrowed elements of topography, including in exaggerated form the more than physical barrier of the Ural Mountains, and of history, and of nomenclature. In the descriptions of train journeys and the wild barge ride down the Don I have come as close as anywhere else in this story to autobiography, and I acknowledge with respect the struggles that the peoples of the Russian Empire, the Soviet Union and the Russian Federation have faced over the centuries.

Amongst my borrowings is the word KAM which was used by a now extinct tribe from the Yenisei basin in central Siberia for a world walker or SHAMAN. I have preferred KAM to SHAMAN in order to have an exact meaning.

I have chosen to go the POD (print on demand) route to publishing **The Power of Water** because it saves trees. Also, rightly or wrongly, I have an idea that it is the kind of book that passes from hand to hand, which is a process that takes more time than I fear mainstream publishers are willing to devote to a first time novelist who does not quite conform to a recognisable genre. If you have enjoyed this book please help me network it. Pass your copy to a friend or better still suggest to all your friends that they order their own copy from your local independent book seller.

For further information on **The Web between the Worlds**, Fyedor the Great's biography **The Book of Tanis** and what happens next to Tenja Sillin-Vrekov, Voldimir Shennikov et al. please go to my website, **www.ShapeyBeings.com** and click first on writings, then on **The Power of Water**.

FMGP
June 2006